W9-BZF-131

FRIENDS *of the*
Livingston Public Library

Gratefully Acknowledges
the Contribution of

Joan Scher

For the 2016-2017 Membership Year

LIVINGSTON PUBLIC LIBRARY
10 Robert H. Harp Drive
Livingston, NJ 07039

This House Is Mine

This House Is Mine

Dörte Hansen

Translated from the German by Anne Stokes

St. Martin's Press

New York

This is a work of fiction. All of the characters, organizations, and events portrayed in this novel are either products of the author's imagination or are used fictitiously.

THIS HOUSE IS MINE. Copyright © 2015 by Dörte Hansen. Translation copyright © 2016 by Anne Stokes. All rights reserved. Printed in the United States of America. For information, address St. Martin's Press, 175 Fifth Avenue, New York, N.Y. 10010.

www.stmartins.com

The translation of this work was supported by a grant from the Goethe-Institut, which is funded by the German Ministry of Foreign Affairs.

Library of Congress Cataloging-in-Publication Data

Names: Hansen, Dörte, 1964– author. | Stokes, Anne Marie, translator.
Title: This house is mine / Dörte Hansen ; translated by Anne Stokes.
Other titles: Altes Land. English
Description: First U.S. edition. | New York : St. Martin's Press, 2016. | "Originally published in Germany under the title Altes Land by Albrecht Knaus Verlag"—Verso title page.
Identifiers: LCCN 2016021591| ISBN 9781250100856 (hardcover) | ISBN 9781250106469 (e-book)
Subjects: LCSH: Aunts—Fiction. | Nieces—Fiction. | Women—Family relationships—Fiction. | Belonging (Social psychology)—Fiction. | Hamburg Region (Germany)—Fiction. | Domestic fiction. | Psychological fiction. | BISAC: FICTION / Contemporary Women.
Classification: LCC PT2708.A655 A4813 2016 | DDC 833/.92—dc23
LC record available at https://lccn.loc.gov/2016021591

Our books may be purchased in bulk for promotional, educational, or business use. Please contact your local bookseller or the Macmillan Corporate and Premium Sales Department at 1-800-221-7945, extension 5442, or by e-mail at MacmillanSpecialMarkets@macmillan.com.

Originally published in Germany under the title *Altes Land* by Albrecht Knaus Verlag

First U.S. Edition: November 2016

10 9 8 7 6 5 4 3 2 1

11.11.1.6
12

For my apple house folks

This House Is Mine

1

Cherry Trees

SOME NIGHTS, WHEN THE STORM came in from the west, the house groaned like a boat tossed back and forth on a heavy sea. Gusts of wind squealed before being deadened by the old walls.

That's what witches sound like when they're burning, Vera thought, or children when they get their fingers caught.

The house groaned but wouldn't sink. The ragged roof held fast to its timbers. There were masses of green moss nests in the thatch; it was only sagging at the top.

The paint had peeled off the timber frame facade, and the exposed oak posts were embedded in the walls like gray bones. The inscription on the gable was weather-beaten, but Vera knew what it said: *This hoose is mine ain and yet no mine ain, he that follows will caw it his.*

It was the first Low German* sentence she had learned upon entering this farm in the Altland in northern Germany, holding her mother's hand.

The second sentence came from Ida Eckhoff herself, and set the tone for the years they would spend together: *How many more of yez Polacks are comin' here anyhow?* Her entire house was full of refugees. It was enough already.

Hildegard von Kamcke had no talent whatsoever for victimhood. She moved into the ice-cold servants' quarters off the hallway that Ida Eckhoff assigned them with her lice-ridden head held high and three hundred years of East Prussian pedigree behind her.

She placed the child on the straw mattress, put down her

---

* Translator's note: Low German (*Plattdeutsch*) is the West Germanic language spoken in the Hamburg area, where most of the novel is set. There are a number of variants of Plattdeutsch in northern Germany and the eastern part of the Netherlands. It is descended from Old Saxon, so has affinities with English in terms of grammar and pronunciation. In the novel, the dialect is used by locals of the Altland, representing not only regional belonging but also the warmth and earthiness of the people living there. I have thus rendered their Low German speech in colloquial English, while I've rendered the old inscriptions in Old Scots.

backpack and, in a quiet voice and with the precise articulation of an opera singer, declared war on Ida: "My daughter needs something to eat, please." And Ida Eckhoff, a sixth-generation farmwoman from the Altland, a widow and the mother of a soldier who had been wounded at the front, immediately fired back: "You're not gettin' anything from me."

Vera had just turned five. She sat shivering on the narrow bed, with her damp woolen socks scratching her legs and the sleeves of her coat soaked with snot, which ran incessantly from her nose. She watched as her mother planted herself right next to Ida Eckhoff and started to sing in a fine vibrato and with a sneer: *For reading and for writing I did not give a damn, The only thing I care about is pork and lots of sauerkraut. . . .*

Ida was so taken aback that she stayed rooted to the spot until the chorus. *My pigs are my obsession, My life and my profession,* Hildegard von Kamcke sang, raising her hands in a grand operatic gesture in her small refugee room, and she was still singing when Ida, frosty with rage, was seated at her kitchen table.

When darkness fell and the house was still, Hildegard crept through the hallway and went outside. She returned with an apple in each coat pocket and a cup of milk straight from the cow. After Vera had emptied it, Hildegard wiped it out with the hem of her coat and returned it quietly to the hallway before lying down next to her daughter on the straw mattress.

Two years later, Karl Eckhoff returned from a Russian prisoner-of-war camp. His left leg was as stiff as a splint, his cheeks were so hollow it looked as if he was sucking them in, and Hildegard von Kamcke was still having to steal her milk.

You're not gettin' anything from me. Ida Eckhoff was a woman of her word, but she was aware that the *individual in question* made nightly visits to her barn, and at some point she placed a jug next to the old cup in the hallway. She didn't want half the milk going to waste during the nightly milking. And in the evening, she no longer removed the key for the pantry where the fruit was stored, and sometimes she gave Vera an egg, if the child swept the hallway with the broom that was much too large for her or sang her the East Prussian anthem, "The Land of the Dark Forests," while she was trimming green beans.

When the cherries ripened in July, and the children were required to drive off the starlings from the orchards—the birds swooped down onto the cherry trees in large swarms—Vera stomped through the rows of trees like a windup toy monkey, drumming an old pot steadily with a wooden spoon and bawling out all the songs her mother had taught her over and over again, with the exception of the one about the pork.

Ida Eckhoff observed the child marching through the cherry orchard for hours on end, until her dark hair stuck to her head in damp curls. By midday, the child's face had turned bright red. Vera then slowed down and began to stumble, but she carried on drumming and singing, and marched on, staggering like an exhausted soldier until she tumbled head over heels into the mowed grass next to the cherry trees.

The sudden silence made Ida sit up and take notice. She ran to the front door and saw the girl lying unconscious in the cherry orchard. She shook her head in exasperation and ran over to the trees, hoisted the child onto her shoulders like a sack of potatoes, and lugged her over to the white wooden bench that stood next to the house in the shade of a large linden tree.

This bench was usually off-limits to riffraff and refugees. It had been Ida Eckhoff's wedding bench and was now her widow's bench. No one apart from Karl and herself was allowed to sit on it, but now the Polack kid was lying on the bench with sunstroke and would have to stay there until she came to.

Karl came hobbling out of the shed but Ida was already at the pump, filling a bucket with cold water. She took the dish towel that was always draped over her shoulder, dipped it in the water, made a cold compress, and pressed it against the child's forehead. Karl then lifted Vera's bare feet and placed her legs over the white armrest.

The distant clatter of wooden rattles and pot lids could still be heard from the cherry orchard. Here, close to the house, where it was now eerily quiet, the first starlings were venturing back into the trees. You could hear them swooshing and eating noisily in the branches.

In the past, Karl and his father had shot at them to scare them off. They had moved through the arbor with their shotguns and blasted into the black swarms as though they were intoxicated. Afterward, gathering up the broken little birds was sobering. The huge rage and then the puny bunches of feathers in its wake.

Vera came to, retched, turned her head sideways, and threw up on the white wedding bench under Ida Eckhoff's grand linden. When she realized what she had done, she started violently and tried to get up, but the linden was spinning above her head, the high crown with the heart-shaped leaves appeared to be dancing, and Ida's broad hand was pressing her back down onto the bench.

Karl fetched a cup of milk and a slice of buttered bread from the house and sat down on the bench next to Vera. Ida grabbed the wooden spoon and the battered pot to drive off the impudent birds that were making themselves at home in her orchard and eating what didn't belong to them.

Karl wiped the child's face with the white dish towel. When Vera noticed that Ida wasn't there, she gulped the cold milk down and snatched up the bread. Then she got up and gave a wobbly curtsy before scurrying across the hot cobbles holding her hands out at her sides like a tightrope dancer.

Karl watched her head back to the cherry trees.

He stuck a cigarette in his mouth, wiped down the bench, and threw the towel into the grass. Then he tilted his head back, took a long draw, and produced beautiful round smoke rings, which hovered high in the crown of the linden tree.

His mother was still raging through the rows of cherry trees with the old cooking pot.

Soon you'll be lying here with sunstroke too, Karl said to himself, just carry on drumming.

Ida then ran into the house, fetched the shotgun, and fired into the swarms of birds, blasted into the sky until she had driven every last glutton from the trees, or had scared them off for a while at least. And her son, who had two good arms and one good leg, sat on the bench and watched her.

* * *

All in one piece, thank God, Ida Eckhoff had thought when he'd come limping along the platform toward her eight weeks earlier. He had always been thin but now looked exhausted as well, and he was dragging his leg. But it could have been a whole lot worse. Friedrich Mohr had gotten his son back without any arms. . . . He'd now have to see what became of his farm. And Buhrfeindt's Paul and Heinrich had both been killed in action. Ida could consider herself lucky that she got her only son back in such good shape.

And that other thing, the screaming in the night and the wet bed some mornings, that was nothing to worry about. Just nerves, Dr. Hauschildt said, it would soon sort itself out.

When the apples ripened in September, Karl was still sitting smoking on Ida's white bench. He blew beautiful round rings into the linden's golden crown. A crew of pickers was working its way basket by basket through the rows of trees, and at its head was Hildegard von Kamcke. Being from East Prussia, she was used to farming on an entirely different scale, she had declared, and Ida had once again felt like chasing the haughty dame off the farm. But she couldn't get by without her. She had a tough time of it with this thin woman, who mounted her bike early in the morning as though it were a horse, then rode off to milk with impeccable posture, who toiled away in the orchard until every last apple was down, and swung her pitchfork like a man in the barn as she sang Mozart arias, which didn't impress the cows.

But Karl on his bench liked it a lot.

And Ida, who hadn't wept since her Friedrich had floated as lifeless as a cross down the drainage ditch eight years earlier, stood at the kitchen window and sobbed when she saw Karl sitting listening beneath the linden tree.

If you don't feel the longing of love . . . , Hildegard von Kamcke sang, thinking of course of someone else who was now dead. And she knew as well as Ida that the man sitting on the bench was no longer the Karl that the mother had longed to see for years.

The heir to Ida's farm, Karl Eckhoff, so strong and full of promise, had been left behind in the war. They had brought her back a cardboard cutout. As pleasant and unfamiliar as a traveler, her son sat on her wedding bench blowing smoke rings up into the sky. And at night he screamed.

When winter came, Karl, whistling softly, built a doll's baby carriage for little Vera von Kamcke, and at Christmas, the countess of dubious origin and her constantly hungry child sat at Ida Eckhoff's large dining table in the parlor for the first time.

In spring, when the cherry blossoms fell like snow, Karl played accordion on the bench and Vera sat beside him.

And in October, after the apple harvest, Ida Eckhoff retired and had a daughter-in-law she could respect but couldn't help detesting.

This hoose is mine ain and yet no mine ain . . .

The old inscription applied to both of them. They were equals who battled hard in this house, which Ida didn't want to give up and Hildegard no longer wanted to leave.

The screaming that lasted for years, the swearing, the banging of doors, the breaking of crystal vases and gold-rimmed cups entered into the crevices of the walls and settled like dust on the floorboards and ceiling beams. On quiet nights, Vera could still hear them, and when a storm was rising she wondered whether it really was the wind that was howling so fiercely.

Your house isn't anything to write home about anymore, Ida Eckhoff, she thought.

The linden stood in front of the window and shook the storm out of its branches.

2

The Magic Flute

THE OPEN HOUSE WAS THE worst. Once every six months, the three- to five-year-olds streamed into the big rehearsal room with their parents and Bernd wore his blue denim shirt and baby-blue hair tie to match.

Bernd wasn't the type of guy to leave anything to chance, he just liked to give that impression. The round glasses, full beard, and graying hair pulled back in a ponytail were all designed to inspire confidence. Early music education was a business that required a great deal of sensitivity.

When the parents from the Ottensen neighborhood of

Hamburg brought their children along to the open house, they
didn't expect to see a run-of-the-mill music teacher in a bow
tie. Bernd gave them the creative forty-something they were
after: approachable, dynamic, laid-back—but professional. This
wasn't a community college, after all.

Musical Mouse represented a sophisticated concept of head
start music education, and when Bernd gave his short welcome
speech, he carefully incorporated all the appropriate keywords.
Playful was always the first.

Anne sat in the big circle on the wooden floor of the rehearsal
room with the corners of her mouth and her eyebrows turned
upward and her flute on her lap. It was her eighth open house
and she closed her eyes for a moment when Bernd said the
word *gently*. Now all that remained were *talent* and *potential*
and *cognitive abilities*.

The girl sitting on her mother's lap next to Anne was three
at most. She was chomping on a rice cracker and drumming
her feet out of boredom. She stared at Anne for a while, then
leaned across and reached for the flute with her sticky fingers.
Her mother looked on, smiling. "Would you like to try blowing into that, darling?"

Anne looked at the kid's wet mouth, which still had bits

of rice sticking to it, gripped her instrument tightly in both hands, and took a series of deep breaths. She could feel a wall of rage slowly rising up inside her and wanted to hit the kid on the head with her soprano flute, which was made of sterling silver—or, better still, strike the mother, who was wearing striped tights and had a flowery scarf in her hair. Mommy was now frowning in disbelief because her three-year-old, who was covered in slobber, wasn't allowed to blow into a professional instrument worth six thousand euros.

Calm down, Anne said to herself, the kid can't help it.

She heard Bernd draw to the end of his short speech: ". . . just JOY in music!" His keyword, her cue. She stood up, turned her stage smile up a notch, and walked across the circle to him. Anne on her magic flute, Bernd on guitar. Each time, she played Papageno's theme three times on the flute. Then Bernd gave a short intro on guitar before announcing, "And now all the children can fetch a triangle or wood block from the center and the parents can sing along. You'll know the song for sure, all together now . . . three, four: *It rings out so joyful, it rings out so nice.*"

While the kids pounded away on their instruments, and the parents sang along more or less joyfully, Anne danced through the room with her flute and Bernd strolled behind her with his guitar, singing and smiling away.

He managed to rock his head back and forth enthusiastically the whole time. Bernd was a pro.

He had choreographed the open house perfectly and it was paying off. The Musical Mouse courses were more sought after by parents in this affluent neighborhood than a community garden with utility hookups. The waiting lists were very long.

Anne should consider herself lucky that she got the job. Bernd usually hired fully qualified music tutors or graduates from the music school. Having dropped out of school, she shouldn't have stood a chance, but Bernd noticed, first of all, that Anne easily outshone his tutors with music diplomas, and, secondly, she'd fit into his *overall concept*.

What this meant in practice was that she looked good prancing through the room with her flute and dark curls, in a dress that was *not too long,* which was Bernd's dress code for the open house.

"Always remember, it's the daddies who pay for the lessons!" But the dress couldn't be too short either. "We don't want to upset the mommies!"

Bernd would grin broadly and wink whenever he said that, but Anne had known him for nearly five years. He was dead serious.

She hated his bright-blue denim shirt and the ponytail, and she also hated herself as she performed her Pied Piper routine while the prospective Musical Mouse pupils mercilessly beat the Orff percussion instruments in the big rehearsal room.

She felt like the hostess on *The Love Boat* who had to carry in the ice cream cake with the sparklers on top during the captain's dinner.

But at least cruise ship passengers clapped in time.

"Isn't that a little beneath you, Anne?"

Why had she answered the phone last night? She had seen her mother's number on the caller ID and picked up nonetheless. A mistake, time and time again.

Marlene had spoken with Leon for a few minutes at first, but he wasn't very good on the phone yet. He just nodded at the receiver or shook his head whenever his grandmother asked him a question. Anne had to put her on speakerphone and translate Leon's silent responses.

"What would you like Grandma to get you for Christmas, darling?"

Leon looked helplessly at Anne. They had only just started making jack-o'-lanterns at his day care center.

"I think Leon will have to think about it, Mama." Mama with the stress on the second syllable. That mattered to Marlene.

When Leon disappeared into his room, Anne turned off

the speakerphone and got up from the sofa. She still snapped to attention whenever she spoke with her mother. She caught herself doing it and sat back down.

"Anne, how are you? I rarely hear from you."

"Everything's fine, Mama. I'm good."

"That's nice." Marlene was a master of the pause. "I'm also fine, incidentally."

"I would have asked you, Mama."

Anne had inadvertently stood up again. She picked up a cushion, dropped it on the floor, and kicked it across the living room.

"And what do you mean by everything's good?" Marlene asked. "Does it mean you've finally quit that stupid job?"

Anne took the second cushion from the sofa and kicked it against the wall.

"No, Mama, that's not what it means."

She closed her eyes and slowly counted to three. There was a brief pause for effect on the other end of the line, then a deep intake of breath, followed by an exasperated sigh. Then, wearily, and almost in a whisper: "Isn't that a little beneath you, Anne?"

She should've hung up at that point, normally she did, but yesterday obviously wasn't her day.

"Mama, cut the crap!"

"Watch your language, Anne. . . ."

"It's not my fault my life's an embarrassment to you."

A moment or two lapsed before Marlene was able to speak again. "You had it all, Anne."

The other girls were always really nervous before the recitals. Pale with fear, they'd sit next to their piano teachers, awaiting their turns. Then, with their heads hanging low, they'd drag themselves up the few steps onto the stage, as if ascending the scaffold.

Anne had loved it, though. The churning in her stomach when her name was called, then mounting the stairs onto the stage with her curls bouncing, swinging herself onto the piano stool, tilting her head back briefly—and off she'd go.

"Of course you think it's great, you always win," her best friend Catherine had said without a trace of envy. She was simply stating a fact. Anne's first place at Young Musicians was more or less routine. In regional, state, and national competitions, it was a pretty bad day if she got second or third place, and then she'd be so annoyed with herself that she'd torment herself even more when practicing afterward.

In the first three years, Marlene had taught Anne herself, and after that she went along to all of her competitions. There were large ice cream sundaes after her concerts, and as Anne got older, big shopping trips, arm in arm. They were so very happy.

It still hurt to think about it. And about her father as well, his smile, his hands on her shoulders when she came home with a first prize, large hands that betrayed his origins as a farmer's son. "Potato-digger hands," Marlene used to say, and on good days it sounded affectionate.

It seemed then that it didn't matter to her that her husband had climbed the social ladder. He was a country boy who may have lost his farmyard smell in libraries and lecture halls, but whose *r* occasionally slipped to the front of his mouth, where he rolled it as they do in Low German. Marlene winced every time she heard it. *Like a farmhand.*

But Anne loved it because at those moments Enno Hove the physics professor was approachable as he seldom was otherwise. Papa with the stress on the first syllable.

"She gets her talent from me!"

Marlene had renounced her music career when she'd gotten pregnant at twenty-one. Or that was her version of events at least.

But it wasn't a great sacrifice, Grandma Hildegard always added. "Let's just say it was a small sacrifice. Marlene and a career, good Lord!"

But Anne seemed to have what it takes. Not even Hildegard von Kamcke doubted that. So, a magnet school with a focus on music, naturally, her first concerts in schools and at cultural centers, and then for her fourteenth birthday, her own grand piano.

It was almost too large for the living room, a Bechstein, secondhand, but her parents still had to take out a loan. They stood listening arm in arm as Anne played her expensive instrument for the first time, the black varnish as serious and solemn as a promise.

Thomas, her younger brother, was seven at the time. He was just about to enter second grade and had four loose teeth. Oddly enough she still remembered that.

Anne had shown him his first pieces on the piano very early on. Thomas on her lap, his fat little fingers on the keys. He learned fast. Soon they were playing duets.

By eight he had caught up with her.

At nine he overtook her.

At his audition at the conservatory, the assessor had a hard time remaining composed. Their mother was blissfully happy, their father almost timid in his reverence. A child prodigy!

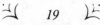

The whole world was lit up by the radiance of this child.
You had it all, Anne.

First she had it all and then nothing at all. Lights out. A total eclipse of the sun at sixteen. No one noticed a talented child when a gifted one entered the room.

After the Pied Piper routine, she ran to get Leon from day care, but she still got there much too late.

Red-faced, she crept along to the room where Leon was playing on his own in the Lego corner, his coat already on, while the preschool teacher swept under the lunch table. She greeted Anne with raised eyebrows.

Anne had gotten used to simply shouting *Have a nice evening!* into the room instead of apologizing. She grabbed Leon and carried him out quickly, like a ticking time bomb that could go off at any moment.

She bought a roll for him and a cappuccino to go for herself, then pushed his stroller in the direction of Fischers Park, joining the trek of Ottensen's Organic Moms, who streamed out of their town houses every day to air out their offspring. Cappuccinos in hand, they carried their shopping from the organic supermarket in the nets of their premium strollers, whose pure-wool foot muffs each contained a small child holding something soggy made from whole grain.

Like everything else in her life, this also seemed to have simply befallen her somehow: being a mom in a hip urban neighborhood.

It was a cold afternoon with a sky as gray as stone. They wouldn't be able to hold out much longer in Fischers Park, or the Fischi as all the mothers called it. But Leon needed some fresh air after spending the morning cooped up in the day care center.

His "Beetle" group didn't get outside often enough. The topic would be raised yet again at the parents' evening she had no intention of attending.

Anne lifted Leon out of the stroller and gave him his Playmobil digger, sat down on a bench, and watched him march over to the sandbox, where a small boy was sitting with a turtle sand mold. He had already produced a considerable number of reptiles and intended to populate the rest of the sandbox with even more turtles, it seemed.

Leon stood at the edge of the sandbox with his digger and was clearly anxious about going in. Anne looked away. It was better not to interfere.

Two benches over, a woman was coaxing her daughter up

the steps of the slide, rung by rung. The mother was wearing a parka with a number of drawstrings and zips and a pair of Campers.

Most of the mothers at the playground wore these shoes. They left long, curling oval patterns in the sandy surface of the playground whenever the women, like good-natured family dogs, retrieved the pacifiers and drinking bottles that their small children threw out of their strollers.

Leon was still standing at the edge of the sandbox. He had swung one leg over but hadn't gotten any farther because Turtle Boy was defending his territory loudly.

"You can't come in here! It's only for turtles!"

Leon glanced briefly at Anne, and when she nodded, he placed his other foot in the sandbox and put down his digger. Turtle Boy started to scream and tried to push Leon away.

Anne saw a pregnant woman struggle up from one of the benches and walk over to the sandpit, smiling. She bent down to Leon and cocked her head slightly to one side: "Hey, listen, could you maybe dig someplace else? Is that okay? Look, Alexander was here first, and he's making such lovely turtles right now."

Anne leapt to her feet and headed over to the sandbox.

She knew herself well enough to realize that she wouldn't win a war of words with one of Hamburg-Ottensen's supermoms, so, without saying a word, she joined Leon in the sand-box, flattening a few turtles in the process, sadly, and destroying a few more as she knelt down in the sand to kiss her son.

"Right, Leon, get digging. Or shall I do it?" She pretended she was going to take the digger from him. Leon laughed, yanked his toy away from her, and started to dig.

Anne sat down at the edge of the sandpit and watched him.

Turtle Boy's mother stared at her with disgust. Her son's bawling, meanwhile, was drowning out all other sounds in the playground, so Anne couldn't make out what she was saying. She just saw the woman yank her screaming child out of the sandbox, console him as she put him into his stroller, then take off.

They had spoiled the day for poor little Alexander, his pregnant mommy, and—very likely—the unborn child in her tummy too.

Anne hoped they wouldn't turn up at the next Musical Mouse open house.

3

Staying Put

Two women and only one stove never bodes well.

Ida and Hildegard had known that, and in a rare show of unity, they'd insisted on a kitchen with a double hot plate for Ida Eckhoff's mother-in-law apartment.

But things got pretty bad regardless.

They turned the house into a battlefield.

Every morning, Hildegard drank her tea out of Ida's Hutschenreuther fine china collectible cups that were too expensive for everyday use. One by one they lost their handles,

their gold rims faded due to thoughtless washing up—or they shattered on the kitchen's terrazzo floor.

When Ida pulled up weeds from *her* flower bed, in front of *her* window, the stock plants beneath her daughter-in-law's window also disappeared, and when Hildegard scrubbed the white wooden fence in front of the house and repainted it, the following day Ida stood on the street with a pail and brush and painted it all over again.

Hildegard invited the neighboring women over for afternoon coffee, set the big table with Ida's silverware, and *forgot* to set a place for her mother-in-law. And without saying a word, she took down Ida's rose-patterned curtains, cut them up into dust rags, and hung up new ones.

And Ida, who hadn't yet signed the farm over to Karl, who still had the say and the money, would fire the seasonal workers Hildegard hired at harvesttime and take on new ones. And, on her double burner, she cooked *proper Altland lunches* so the pickers didn't have to eat the *miserable* blintzes, pierogies, or potato dumplings that her Prussian daughter-in-law *cobbled together.*

Karl, who was caught between the fronts and constantly had to dodge bullets from both sides, seemed to be impervious. He whistled quietly to himself and remained in his own world, which was peaceful.

In the winter, he sat outside on the bench without a jacket or a cap, watching the snow fall. He'd stretch out his hand, let the snowflakes land on it, and examine them through a magnifying glass until they melted away. Vera sometimes watched him from the window. His lips would move, but she couldn't make out whether he was talking to the snowflakes or himself.

In the summer, he hung a swing from a branch of the linden tree for Vera, but most of the time he sat on it himself, smoking and rocking gently back and forth, looking down at the grass, which was teeming with ants. When Vera arrived, he would push her high into the air until her feet touched the leaves at the top of the tree, and he'd only stop when she'd had enough.

Karl also made her a pair of stilts in the shed, and he made another pair for Hildegard, who found them childish at first and didn't want to try them out. But then she practiced to the point where she almost always beat Vera whenever they raced.

Hildegard laughing—that rarely happened.

Vera learned to make herself invisible. She'd vanish in the barn or play with the cats in the hayloft whenever the grenades started flying around the house. Sometimes she went over to Heinrich Luehrs's place and helped him pick dandelions for his rabbits, German Giants that earned him good money when they were ready for slaughter.

"Stalingrad over at yours again, huh?" Hinni would ask. Word had gotten around that the walls shook fairly often at the Eckhoffs', but it wasn't any different at the Luehrses' place either.

Hinni's father was on the bottle. They never knew what state he'd come home in. It was best when he was just slightly tipsy and wanted to embrace the world and kiss his wife. But two more schnapps and the Luehrses' place was Stalingrad too.

Vera didn't say any more than she had to at home. You could make too many mistakes when speaking. Ida spoke only Low German with Vera and Karl, and Vera knew how much Hildegard hated that. When Vera answered in Low German, her mother had to be out of earshot. And if she answered in standard German, Ida would turn away. So, for the most part, Vera tried to get by with nodding, shaking her head, or shrugging her shoulders. That was the safest bet.

When Hildegard wasn't around, Vera often went across the hall to Ida's apartment. They'd sit in her small kitchen playing cards and eating rock-hard cookies, which Vera dunked in her milk.

Sometimes Ida would show Vera her treasures, the traditional Altland costume with all the silver chains and filigree button balls, and Vera was allowed to try the black bonnet on carefully and admire herself in the mirror.

But you needed light-colored eyes for the traditional costume, Ida Eckhoff thought, so she'd take the bonnet off the child again quickly.

She showed Vera how to do embroidery, cross-stitch and flat stitch, and for her ninth birthday she gave her a silver bracelet that Vera wasn't allowed to show her mother.

Vera hid it in an old can up in the hayloft, where she also kept the small amber necklace that belonged to her grandmother in Königsberg.

And she made certain that her mother never heard her say *Grandma Ida*.

On a cold morning shortly after Vera's ninth birthday, Hildegard got six farmhands to drag out the massive carved-oak armoire that had stood in one place for two hundred years, to make space for a piano.

That morning, Ida Eckhoff lost what remained of her self-control and gave her daughter-in-law two hard slaps across the face.

Hildegard struck back immediately, then packed suitcases for her child and herself, put on her coat, and went and got Karl. "It's your mother or me."

And stiff-legged Karl limped into the kitchen to Ida, sat down at the table next to his mother, took her hand, and looked out through the window at the orchard. He stroked the back of her hand with his thumb over and over, as though trying to smooth out her wrinkled skin, and didn't look at her, just stared out the window, and when he finally spoke, he was hoarse.

Then he started to cry.

Ida Eckhoff sat next to her son and didn't know what to do. He had placed his arms on the table and was wailing like a child. She didn't recognize him, now that he'd started talking to snowflakes and trying to escape from the Russians in the night. He was just a cardboard cutout of himself. He hadn't gotten a leg or an arm shot off, but pretty much everything else.

This hoose is mine ain, but what did she want in this house any longer?

That evening, Hildegard played piano. Mozart's "Turkish March," over and over. She pounded the keys, floored the pedals, hammered her instrument as though she wanted to demolish it.

Hildegard played her new piano like a Katyusha rocket launcher, so no one heard Ida go out into the hallway and pick up the stool, fetch the clothesline from the closet, then climb up the stairs to the attic. Nor did they hear her throw the line over a beam and secure it tightly, then climb up onto the stool, check the knot, and jump.

Karl heard the stool fall over and thought the marten had gotten back into the house.

Vera heard the clatter and hoped it wasn't the two cats she'd hidden in the hayloft.

Hildegard was playing the piano, so she didn't hear Vera creep out of bed, walk barefoot through the hallway, and tiptoe up the stairs.

Grandma Ida was wearing her traditional costume and seemed to be dancing in the air.

Hildegard didn't calm down any after Ida Eckhoff was in the ground. Her anger simply changed direction, hurtling unchecked at Karl and Vera, both of whom became increasingly stooped in the gales of her perpetual storm.

Vera eventually walked tall again when she was fourteen

and her mother got pregnant and ran off with the father of her little girl, who was called Marlene.

But Karl never stood tall again. For the rest of his days, he walked around like someone who'd been beaten. His shoulders were constantly hunched over as though he expected to be struck again at any moment.

The little that had remained of Karl after the war eventually snapped completely in Hildegard's hurricane.

After Hildegard had cleared off to the Hamburg suburb of Blankenese with her new child and her architect, Ida Eckhoff's sister saw to it that the livestock was sold and the land was leased.

She put the money into a savings account and allocated her nephew and his refugee child what they needed to live on each month. She almost felt sorry for the girl, with her mother gone and a father who was like a child.

But Karl blew beautiful round smoke rings into the crown of the old linden, he got on well with snowflakes and with birds even when they devoured the cherries, and when Vera got out of school in the summer, she'd sit next to him on the bench and they'd peel potatoes together.

* * *

Karl gave Vera his old shotgun, his binoculars, and the backpack he'd used for hunting, and she very quickly learned how to shoot.

At school, the others had long since stopped teasing her. Not because she learned better than most, that didn't matter, but because they knew what would happen if they called Vera Eckhoff a *Polack brat*. Alfred Giese was the first to find out, and the last to try it. With his broken nose, he looked even more stupid than before.

For him school ended after the eighth grade, but Vera, the *Polack brat,* was a straight-A student at the girls' high school and Karl went to her graduation in the assembly hall when she got her high school diploma and he almost sat up straight in his suit that was much too baggy. She wore her silver bracelet and her amber necklace, and in the evening she celebrated with a few girlfriends from her class in Ida Eckhoff's hallway.

They drank strawberry punch and Karl played the accordion, which he could still do, and Hinni Luehrs and his brothers came over when they heard the music.

Old man Luehrs also stopped by later, much later, on his way back from the bar. He stumbled through the new side door, which Ida's sister had just had installed, staggered through the hallway, danced a couple of faltering steps in time to the music, then drank the rest of the strawberry punch straight from the large glass bowl.

When it was empty, he looked Karl angrily and drunkenly in the eye and dropped the bowl on the floor. "What you up to now, you wimp?"

Karl didn't react. He just stared at the keys of his instrument and gradually began to play again.

Heinrich tried to push his father toward the side door and out of the house, but the old man shoved him to the ground without much effort. Heinrich screamed as the shards of glass from the bowl pierced his hands and knees, and Vera ran off quickly to the hunting cabinet, fetched her shotgun, and aimed it at Heinrich Luehrs Senior.

Hinni was still screaming. His father staggered out the door, cursing.

Karl stiffened when he saw all the blood. He got up quickly with his accordion strapped across his stomach, went into the kitchen, and closed the door.

Vera grabbed Hinni by the shoulders and pulled him out of the heap of broken glass. He was still screaming and was covered in blood. She guided him carefully to a chair and pulled the glass out of his hand, one splinter at a time, and then out of his knees. Her friends fetched some bandages and a bowl of water from the kitchen, where Karl was sitting at the table, smoking calmly, because none of this concerned him anymore.

Blood and screaming now had nothing to do with him.

Heinrich and his brothers didn't dare go home that night. They were allowed to stay in the old farmhands' rooms, but they didn't sleep well in the dusty beds because they didn't know whether their mother had locked the bedroom door in time.

The girls whispered long into the night in Hildegard's wide marital bed, which had been Vera's since Karl had moved into his mother's apartment.

And Vera sat with Karl at the kitchen table and smoked her first cigarettes until the blackbirds and seagulls woke up outside and Karl finally summoned the courage to go to bed.

Then she went out into the hallway and waited for Heinrich Luehrs the Younger, the best. And she swept up the glass when he didn't come.

That's what happened when you dared to lay a hand on this house. You tore an old, rotten side door out of it and then paid for it with blood and glass in the hallway.

She'd come within a hairsbreadth of shooting Luehrs the Elder.

And they'd gotten off lightly. Vera knew it could've been a whole lot worse.

You moved a heavy oak armoire that had stood at its post for two hundred years, and that evening someone hung dead from a beam in the attic.

Karl and Vera didn't lay a hand on the house after Hinni Luehrs sat with bleeding hands among the shards of glass. They left everything just as it was. They didn't move the furniture around, didn't rip out the transom windows, and didn't knock the old tiles off the walls.

They didn't lay tiles over the terrazzo floors, installed no more new doors, and didn't remove old thatch from the roof.

And they never went up to drive off the marten in the hayloft.

They weren't crazy, after all.

Vera went off to Hamburg to study. *The fine lady,* Ida's sister said, but that was what Karl wanted. He was still able to make his own decisions, and even if he wasn't, what difference would it have made?

The adopted refugee child would still inherit the farm. Perhaps a farmer's son would turn up yet and marry into the Eckhoffs.

But what local man who wasn't out of his mind would want to marry Vera Eckhoff? Early in the mornings, she would stalk through the orchards in Karl's heavy old hunting jacket, picking off hares and deer. She only said hi when it suited her, let her mentally ill stepfather clean the windows while she pored over her books, and, if Dora Voelkers was to be believed, had bathed buck naked in the Elbe the previous year, near Bassenfleth.

A girl of eighteen!

And afterward she'd sat in the sand and smoked. *Smoking like a steamboat. Naked.*

Dora Voelkers's sons hadn't been able to contain themselves, but no girl was so pretty she could afford to take such liberties, Dora Voelkers said.

And a refugee to boot.

She won't get anyone to take her, that was certain.

But Vera couldn't leave Karl on his own at the farm for very long. One hot summer's day, as she was nearing the end of her third semester, Karl dropped one of his many cigarette butts and torched the old shed, which contained Vera's stilts and her doll carriage.

The fire department got there fast, so the flames didn't get a chance to leap up to the thatched roof. Karl Eckhoff had been lucky. *He had more luck than sense.*

* * *

When Vera finished studying and finally returned home to Karl and her farm as a Doctor of Dental Surgery, there was a stroller in the Luehrses' front yard, out in the sun. Heinrich Junior, the best, was an exemplary son for his boozer of a father; he'd also called his eldest Heinrich.

Hinni did the right thing. He married land and money and a woman who was like a tame bird: Elisabeth Buhrfeindt, of old marsh farming gentry, slim, quiet, and blond. What were you thinking, Vera Eckhoff? That someone would wait for you?

Elisabeth also did what was expected. She planted flowers, picked cherries, raked the yellow sand in front of their house day in, day out. She painted the white fence, and when the time came for a child, she gave birth to a son. Three times over, like Heinrich's mother before her.

Hinni seemed to be living his parents' life all over again, but properly this time, without schnapps or blows, as though he could paint over the stain that Heinrich Luehrs the drunkard had left behind.

Luehrs Sr. didn't grow old—at least he did his kids that favor—and Minna Luehrs had her best years after she buried her husband.

Vera watched her walk through the garden on her

daughter-in-law's arm, examining bed upon bed, shrub after shrub, rose upon rose. She saw them stop in front of each plant, nodding and talking quietly to one another. It reminded her of hospital visits, Sisters of Mercy, and Vera sometimes wished that she could join them, be a sister too—perhaps a daughter even.

For just as long as it took to do one round of the garden, she longed not to be the other, the foreigner. To join arms with Minna and Elisabeth, as though she were one of them.

Karl hadn't managed without Vera. He now rarely washed and forgot to eat. And at night, the Russians still came, so he was afraid of his dreams and no longer went to bed.

At night, Vera would find him in a kitchen chair, half asleep, exhausted, but still awake with a fat book about farm machinery or dike construction in front of him, his head almost touching the pages, and the cigarette in his right hand turned to ash.

When she opened her practice in the center of the village, she took Karl in to work with her. He sat in the waiting room, flipping through old magazines and doing crossword puzzles. He nodded at the patients, who all knew him and were aware that Karl Eckhoff had gotten weird and left him in peace.

At ten o'clock Vera's dental assistant would make him a sandwich and a cup of tea, and then he'd lie down on the sofa that Vera had pushed into the little room at the back for him.

They kept the door slightly open so Karl could hear her talking to her patients. He could hear the drill whining and sometimes a child as well. He could hear the assistant's quick steps on the linoleum floor, and also the doorbell and was able to sleep on this bed of peaceful noises.

At noon he'd limp back to the farm, boil potatoes, make fried eggs or fish for Vera and himself, and after lunch Vera would lie down before driving back to the practice.

For Karl wasn't the only one who slept badly in this house at night. Vera left the radio on in the evenings when she went to bed. She tried to get to sleep before the end of the broadcast day, but she didn't manage it most of the time. She was still lying awake when there was nothing but white noise.

Then she'd get up again, join Karl in the kitchen, and smoke with him until she was so tired that she could no longer hear the whispering coming from the old walls.

She still didn't trust this house, but she wasn't going to let it throw or spit her out. She wouldn't let herself be rejected like a foreign organ. She refused to be like the majority of refugees, who'd gotten out of the large farmhouses as fast as they possibly could and moved into small houses in developments, grateful and scrupulously intent on avoiding becoming a burden to anyone else for the rest of their lives.

If Hildegard von Kamcke had bequeathed anything to her daughter, it was her lack of humility.

Her mother had refused to act the part of a have-not. She'd been driven out of her homeland, lost everything, and that was already bad enough! For that reason, a farmwoman like Ida Eckhoff just had to share what she had—her farm, her house—and if that didn't suit her, she simply had to give way.

Chin up! is what Vera had learned.

But it wasn't only Hildegard von Kamcke's lessons in composure that had kept Vera here in this village, in this old timber-frame house.

She'd been washed up on Ida Eckhoff's farm like a drowning man on an island. The sea still surrounded her and Vera was afraid of that water. She had to remain on her island, on this farm, where she couldn't put down roots, to be sure, but could grow firmly on the stones, like lichen or moss.

Not flourishing or blooming, just staying put.

And she left no one in any doubt that she intended to stay. Karl had sold some land and given her money for the practice. Dr. Vera Eckhoff treated her patients in the center of the village, and like all dentists, she was feared, not loved.

And there was no reason either not to laugh to herself when leaning over the septic molar of an Altland farmer, who was sitting in her chair with sweating hands and had long since forgotten that he'd always walked past refugees without saying hi, that he'd thrown a rotten apple from his garden at a refugee child—"Ya wan' an apple?"—and then laughed.

She treated her former classmates' offspring, filled the holes in their milk teeth, and rewarded them with a marble or a balloon from her drawer if they didn't cry.

She pulled black stumps from the mouths of the elderly she had known when they were still strong back in their mid-forties, and fitted them for dentures, which made them look strange and serious and rendered their speech more hissing and sharp.

After every shooting club festival, one or two young men who had knocked each other's teeth crooked and loose would sit in her waiting room, and when their turn came, they'd stare at the ceiling while sitting in the dentist's chair because they were embarrassed to be lying with their mouths wide open so close to a young woman with beautiful brown eyes, vulnerable and at her mercy—that's how Vera Eckhoff liked them.

But she was much fonder of another man who didn't come to her practice, who wasn't looking for a dentist but for a woman with black curls.

When her friend came from Hamburg in his dark-blue car, Karl would leave the kitchen, whistling very softly. He knew that he needn't worry. She wouldn't leave him for anyone.

There was no Mr. Right for Vera. She wasn't looking for one and she didn't want to be found by a man who would drag her away from this big cold house that she clung to like moss.

Every now and then she had nice days and nights with someone who had a wife and kids and wanted nothing more from her than she wanted from him.

When she headed off toward the Elbe with this stranger of hers, Hinni Luehrs craned his neck from his longest ladder and Elisabeth sank down into her flower beds.

Vera and her stranger walked hand in hand, strolled along the river, sat shoulder to shoulder in the sand wearing sunglasses, smoking, and laughing. Vera knew you were never alone along the Elbe, but it didn't bother her if anyone saw Dr. Vera Eckhoff kissing some stranger. She was a free person and paid a high enough price for it.

She left the man to suffer the guilt pangs. She herself had no compunction. She wasn't taking anything away from the other woman. She wouldn't want her husband even if he became available. She was simply borrowing him and would return him hale and hearty.

He wasn't the only one either. Other strangers turned up and then disappeared again. Vera Eckhoff had done more in Hamburg than just study.

But she took care not to invite a man with serious intentions. Her life was already serious enough with Karl, who relied on her like a child, and the house, which held her in its thick walls.

In the evening, after work, Vera did her rounds along the Elbe, through the orchards, and across the farm tracks. She took large steps, as though surveying the land, as if she were measuring the yards and miles of her world. She marched over the fields, along the riverbank like a guard, *Frau Doktor on patrol*. She made an even greater impression with her large dogs at her side, which she'd bought when she started hunting again.

Later still, she rode her horses, whose shoes rang out like hammer blows on the village street. If you couldn't see that Vera Eckhoff was still here, you would hear it in all the houses. On her daily long march in the evening or early in the morning, she sized up the world around her like an animal trainer who lets his eyes roam around the circus ring and can't turn his back on any animal in his troop for long.

She saw the gentle river in its bed, the houses on the dike, the trees in the fields. She could identify the birds, all of them, knew where they nested, when they migrated and returned. She often saw hares and deer in the orchards, and she recognized them before she shot them. In the spring, she counted the lambs that had been born overnight on the dike. She passed the brick pump houses on the banks of the drainage ditches and knew how high the water was and how many colonies of bees Heinrich Luehrs had in his rows of cherry trees.

It couldn't ever slip away from Vera, this landscape in which she wasn't rooted but to which she clung fast.

And people had better watch out that they didn't get in the way when Vera Eckhoff galloped along the Elbe on one of her unpredictable mares.

"Watch out, the cavalry!" Heinrich Luehrs would yell, and placing his left hand on the seam of his corduroy slacks, he'd stand at attention and salute when she rode past his farm early in the morning.

"Shove it, Hinni Luehrs!" Vera woud say, trotting toward the dike. And on her way back she'd ride across his finely raked yellow sand.

Still, it was never certain who would win the daily riding contest—Vera or her Prussian Trakehners. Sometimes they managed to catapult her out of the saddle somewhere in the reeds along the Elbe. They would then make their own way home without their rider, and Vera would have to stamp across the raked bed at Heinrich Luehrs's in her riding boots, and Hinni would still be smirking days later about the *battle-axe on foot*.

But that's what Vera wanted. She also wanted her big gray hunting dogs that frightened mailmen and paperboys to death. At some point the mailman had had enough of being run down like a wild boar every morning in her yard by two superbly trained Weimaraners. Vera had had to put her mailbox out on the street in front of her fence. And she stuck a sign on it that she'd found in Heinrich Luehrs's shed: a black skull set against a yellow background. DANGER! But men who ran away from dogs like little girls obviously couldn't take a joke. Paul Heinsohn, in any event, now barely acknowledged her when he passed by on his bike.

When Vera was nearby, her dogs were the epitome of calmness. They obeyed her every word, accepted her as pack leader, lay beneath her table, and let her stroke their fur. But she didn't make that widely known. Her dogs' bad reputation was worth a whole lot more to Vera than any alarm system. Those who weren't in the know stayed away from her farm, and that was good.

* * *

Vera Eckhoff also wanted this house, even though it only suffered her reluctantly within its walls. It was a patron of stone and oak, domineering and complacent.

She had no idea how many people had lived in these cold walls before her. It must have been nine or ten generations who'd celebrated weddings, raised children, or given birth to them, then lost them again, who'd laid out their dead in this drafty hallway. Young women had entered the house in their wedding gowns, through the *wedding door,* and had left it again in their coffins— through the same narrow door, which didn't have a handle on the outside and was opened only for weddings and funerals.

You had to have been raised in these houses not to be afraid in them at night when the walls started to whisper.

Some nights a rope rasped against the ceiling beams of the old hayloft as though it were bearing a heavy load. The old voices murmured their orders, which Vera couldn't understand. They bad-mouthed her and seemed to be laughing at her as well.

Vera had always been freezing cold in this house, and not just in the beginning when she lived with her mother in the servants' room next to the large front door, which was the coldest of all its cold rooms, the farthest away from Ida Eckhoff's warm stove.

But even after they had slowly fought their way up, room by room, Vera continued to freeze after they had taken over the kitchen and the warm rooms next to the stove. She had long since grown to like coldness. The cold kept her awake.

This house wasn't built for people who wanted warmth and comfort. It was the same as with horses and dogs: you couldn't show any weakness, couldn't let yourself be intimidated by this colossus, which had stood with its legs apart on the marshy soil for nearly three hundred years.

Vera wasn't fooled by its scarred facade and its disheveled thatched roof: the house might be under the weather, but it would still be standing long after she had departed through the wedding door, feetfirst.

In the evenings, when it got dark, Vera let her dogs into the kitchen and the three of them sat as though they were keeping vigil over a sick person.

4

Fine Woodworking

BERND ALWAYS OPENED HIS CHATS with his staff with the same question, and it was best not to respond: "Why are we sitting here?" He preferred to answer it himself. "We're sitting here, Anne, because I've received a pretty strongly worded e-mail complaint."

He had printed it out, and it was lying next to him on his desk, two and a half pages covered in exclamation marks, parentheses, and question marks.

The mother of Rice Cake Girl, of course, expressing *total disbelief* that her little Clara-Delphine wasn't allowed to blow into a flute with her mouth full during the open house.

Anne looked out the window. The large poplar at the entrance had caught a thin green plastic bag in its bare branches. The wind was tugging at it as if it were torturing an animal simply for the fun of it.

Bernd took off his glasses, placed his elbows on the desk, put his hands together, and pressed the tip of his nose to them. If there was one thing he couldn't stand, it was a bad atmosphere at the open house. Anne didn't look at him again until he posed another question:

"What is your problem?"

His verbal warnings were always carefully orchestrated. They started off quietly enough, but any minute now he would work himself into a lather for a bit, *molto vivace,* which was still bearable. The really bad part came after that.

It all really got to Bernd. No one ever realized the strength required day in, day out for this kind of work and now this crap here—the aggro, the negativity, all the bad vibes. It was making him ill, burning him out. He was going to start crying again. He looked up slightly, closed his eyes, and shook his head in slow motion. *Grave.*

The flood of tears was as integral to his conflict management discussion as the denim shirt was to the open house.

* * *

The problem was her temper. Foaming rogue waves, enormous breakers, great whoppers. An ocean of rage and a leak in her ship.

The children who came to her classes couldn't help the fact that they were called Clara-Delphine or Nepomuk, or that their parents carried them like trophies through the streets of Ottensen and dragged them from one early learning program to the next.

When they were brought to Musical Mouse at the age of three, they sucked their recorders quite happily and thrashed about on the xylophone and keyboards with aimless enthusiasm. But, after eight weeks at most, their parents would come and ask to *chat about their prospects.*

They always turned up with nice, self-deprecating smiles, but ambition protruded from their smiles like a cold foot from a blanket that's much too short.

Of course, the music school was supposed to be fun above all else, absolutely, but perhaps the keyboard wasn't quite right for Clara-Delphine?

Anne never contradicted them at this point. She would immediately suggest a complicated exotic instrument—the harp or flugelhorn, *so as not to underchallenge your child*—and the parents would go off quite happy.

This was also sanctioned by Bernd, who valued the fact

that the tutors of the unusual instruments were kept busy as well.

Musical Mouse was a dream factory. The school kids came in as normally gifted little children and left as amazing musical talents. It was all a matter of labeling. Bernd earned a ton of money with his mumbo jumbo, and any qualms he may have had were held in check. Anne sometimes asked herself how the little girls on harps or the little boys on flugelhorns would fare later.

At some point they would meet another child their own age who really could play, and the realization would be painful.

In the beginning, she had dreams that were as bad as actual crimes: an incurable cancer for Thomas, an accident, a coma, murder. In these dreams her brother would disintegrate, disappear, pass away, and then everything would be good again until she woke up and was dismayed to find he was still there and was still outshining her. And then she'd be alarmed again because she had been so happy in the dream.

When she was awake, it was impossible to hate him. Not even Anne could bring herself to that. He was a boy who never demanded anything because he already had everything: his inner life was bright and cheerful; there were no dust bunnies lurking in the corners, no spiders in his cellar. And he knew nothing of the spiritual abysses of others.

Anne could play the grand piano only when she was alone in the house, and even then she would break off in the middle of pieces. She could hear herself, after all, and could feel her fingers catching at the difficult spots, which Thomas managed with ease—indeed, seemed to dream his way through.

And even if she made it all the way to the end of a difficult Beethoven sonata without making any mistakes, when she played well and with confidence and *with feeling!*, as her piano teacher requested, it sounded different from when Thomas played it, no matter how much she practiced, no matter how much she loved the piece. It was as if the music didn't love her back.

When Thomas sat at the grand piano, the notes seemed to fly to him; he attracted them as some people attract kids or cats. "You know how that feels, don't you, Annie, when you're not playing the music but the music's playing you?"

He wasn't an enemy, he was her brother, and he understood nothing.

Oh, to smash the lid of the piano down on his hands and to hear his fingers snap! Some dreams were very difficult to shake off.

The black grand piano was no longer hers. They never spoke

about this, but Anne could sense it and she handed it over, just as people might hand over a foster child when the real parents turned up.

She tried not to notice Marlene's expression as she crept up to her room while Thomas was playing, or her father's false cheerfulness when they were sitting at the dining table in the evening—there were always flowers, always candles—and he realized at some point or other that everything had revolved around Thomas yet again, around some concert, a recital, a rehearsal.

Then he'd clear his throat, fold his napkin, rest his elbows on the table, and smile at her. "And what about my big girl, how was your day?"

And she would just make something up—it was never true, but no one ever noticed.

No one noticed either that her house lay in ruins and that she had to climb over ashes every day.

At sixteen, too late in fact, she went up to the attic to get her flute, her first instrument, which had long been forgotten, and Marlene immediately found her a teacher, *the best, Anne!*, who worked with her three times a week. She practiced until she could no longer sleep due to the pain in her elbows.

Two years later she could play Bach's Partita in A Minor for solo flute perfectly, and she passed the music school audition with flute as her main instrument and piano as her second.

Thomas picked flowers from the garden for her; her father wanted to celebrate as though he was proud of her, and he really seemed to believe it. As if it were some kind of a success. As if her little brother hadn't just made his first big appearance at the Hamburg Symphony Orchestra's Laeiszhalle.

Marlene smiled and embraced her, but she didn't look her in the eye.

After five semesters, Anne returned the flute to the attic and put her sheet music in the recycling. She lay down on the shiny, herringbone-patterned parquet floor in front of the piano and listened to Thomas play Schumann.

She suffered from incurable homesickness for a home that no longer existed. She was a displaced person who didn't know where she belonged.

She didn't tell them about the carpentry apprenticeship until she had already signed up, a few days after her twenty-first birthday. Her father, who rarely raised his voice, gave a loud lecture off the top of his head about accidents with veneer presses and mortise chisels, about fingers severed in circular saws, eyeballs pierced by splinters, crushed toes, irreparable hearing damage, and slipped disks; one of his brothers was a carpenter and had had his share of injuries over the years.

By this point, Marlene was worn down and simply shook her head wearily.

Carsten Drewe, master carpenter in Hamburg Barmbek, preferred to take on female trainees. He didn't fare so well with males and his general problem with men applied specifically to his father, a robust eighty-year-old who fired up the circular saw at seven on the dot every morning. When Carsten went into the workshop around seven thirty and saw the old man cutting particleboards to size for him, he'd already had it.

Carsten dreamed of solid wood, of fitted kitchens made of native sycamore, of curved oak staircases and oiled cherry chests of drawers, but he made his living from veneer and vinyl window frames. It wore him down when his customers, who didn't have the foggiest idea, wanted to have their old pine floorboards replaced with laminate; he didn't always manage to remain objective because this whole goddamned flat-pack business totally sickened him.

Above the workshop was a dusty room where the trainees could live rent-free. It smelled of sawdust and wood oil and had as much stuff piled up in it as a furniture warehouse because this was where Carsten stored the chairs, bedside cabinets, and bureaus that he made. Most of the space was taken up by a massive four-poster bed made of wild oak, his masterpiece—*No glue! It could be dismantled! Not a single screw!*—with an inlaid rosette on the headboard and heavy red velvet curtains that his mother had made for him. The bed looked as though the heir to some throne was to be born in it.

"You can make the place quite cozy," Carsten told her, but she'd have to go out into the yard if she wanted to smoke. His parents lived right next to the workshop, and though Karl-Heinz Drewe was a kindhearted soul, the fun stopped if the fire regulations were broken.

"Look after yourself. Keep in touch." Marlene didn't want to hear any more about Anne's childish plans. She wouldn't even go look at the dive in Barmbek in which her daughter had decided to live.

She helped her with her backpack, slammed the car trunk shut, then turned around and went back into the house. There was nothing to be done. The collateral damage of a prodigy, surely. That was how she saw it anyhow, and the prodigy was standing in the hallway, crying inconsolably.

Professor Hove drove his daughter to the Drewe firm himself. He had at least taken off his tie. He shook hands with Carsten and his parents, and while Drewe Senior showed him round the workshop, he inconspicuously checked out the safety arrangements for the circular table saw. The blade guard, the crosscut fence, the push stick, everything was there, and all the Drewes seemed to be physically intact as well. That was something at least. Even the room above the workshop wasn't as bad as he'd feared, and that was just for the time being, Hertha Drewe had said. Carsten was going to move out of his parents' apartment soon, "and then the kid can move in there." She'd baked bee sting cake and they broke for coffee at three as usual.

Anne's father sat in his white shirt on the corner bench between Karl-Heinz and Carsten, and it slowly dawned on him that an apprenticeship with the Drewe firm was also an adoption of sorts. Quite absurd perhaps, but no cause for alarm.

Hertha put one piece of cake after another on his plate but he didn't seem to notice. Nor did he see his coffee cup being filled over and over again, and he didn't hear that at this kitchen table with the checkered wax tablecloth his *r*'s skept slipping to the front. The *r* was rolling freely and no one paid any attention to it but Anne, who was sitting perfectly still, dabbing at the crumbs on her plate with her finger, focusing her eyes on the onion pattern and trying not to cry.

Before he got into his car, Enno Hove gripped his daughter's shoulders with his potato-picker hands and shook her a little awkwardly. "You're not on the other side of the world, Anne."

But of course she was. The Drewe family scattered when Anne started to cry.

The training at the Drewe firm was an apprenticeship for life. There were family therapy sessions on a daily basis. Father and son could go three days without talking to one another if Carsten lost his cool at the sight of a laminate wall unit.

"I wouldn't build a crap storage rack like that even if I was stoned." That wasn't exactly what the Drewe firm's regular customers wanted to hear when they came to have their living room furniture refurbished.

Karl-Heinz also regularly went ballistic when he got a delivery note from Nature Depot, where Carsten ordered ecological wood glazes and furniture oils *for a small fortune*! There'd be a big blowup in the workshop, followed by a few days of deathly silence, then peaceful sawing, planing, and sanding until the yelling started up again. This had been the pattern for two and a half decades.

Fifteen years ago, on Carsten's thirtieth birthday, Karl-

Heinz Drewe had signed the company over to his son. He still found it difficult to take orders from Junior.

When they were screaming and shouting at one another, Carsten would toss two-by-fours and folding rulers around; then he'd turn white and start shaking at some point, and clear off to his girlfriend Urte's, who would help him relax with aromatic oil massages and a couple of Ignatia globules. Urte was a teacher in a Waldorf school and lived with two other women in a shared apartment characterized by mutual appreciation and mindfulness, and she had a complicated on-off relationship with Carsten. It was basically a matter of whether they could tolerate their contradictions, or whether these had to be resolved.

All the contradictions in Carsten's life were sometimes overwhelming. Solid wood and factory-made wood parquet, stuffed cabbage leaves at noon and detox in the evening, Urte's hard futon and Hertha's fabric-softened flannel sheets, the terror with the old man and the beautiful cold Astra beer that they drank shoulder to shoulder on the bench in front of the workshop once things were running smoothly again.

Pentatonic concerts in the assembly hall of Urte's Rudolf Steiner School and jigsaw puzzle evenings with his parents. Five thousand pieces, the great coral reef. The three of them got them done in no time at all.

When father and son were going at it full tilt, Hertha kept out of it. "I'm not saying a word! Not one word!" It certainly riled her up when Carsten ran off to Urte in a rage, but she didn't comment on that either. "Not a word!"

Urte had voiced her opinion on the generational conflict and the Drewe family's problem with cutting the umbilical cord more than once, but her psychobabble always got Hertha's hackles up because every sentence that Urte said began with "I think. . . ." And anyhow, it was none of her business. Those were family matters, "and over and out."

Hertha no longer said anything on the subject of grandchildren either. Urte was past that now and that was no bad thing, as any kids would have gone bonkers with a mother like that. But Carsten wasn't too old yet. He just needed to find the right woman and Hertha was constantly on the lookout. But where on earth was she going to find one?

Carsten Drewe was a very patient teacher. He never got annoyed when Anne made a mistake, and as a matter of principle, he never let his apprentices sweep out the workshop or tidy up the storehouse because that reactionary master-apprentice stuff got on his nerves. The whole sweeping-up nonsense in the business bordered on sadomasochism. *Yes, master. Right away, master.* That's how subordinates were made, grovelers and brownnosers. But not on his watch! Carsten found that in general there was too much sweeping up but Karl-Heinz saw it a little differently—"There you go, the broom's over there, Father!"

Anne couldn't just stand by and watch Drewe Senior sweeping the floor at the end of the day, all stooped over; she would pick up the broom herself when Carsten was driving to the wholesaler's or sitting in the office with Hertha, preparing invoices. She just had to make sure he didn't catch her, since that would get him all hot and bothered. "And you a woman! Do you want to iron my boxers when you're done? Should I call you 'sweetie pie'? I can't have this sort of thing going on around here!"

After a one-and-a-half-year apprenticeship, Anne was able to handle difficult customers without Carsten's help. And while she showed customers laminate samples or measured up for vinyl window frames, he would sit in the company car and read his trade journals, *Fine Woodworking* or *Working with Wood,* smoke a couple of hand-rolled cigarettes, and become engrossed in long articles about turned walnut chairs or the gluing of drawers. He didn't mind Anne teasing him about his "solid wood porn." He was glad she volunteered anything at all. Her voice was already sounding like a rusty hinge.

"It's always sounded like that!"

All right, he wouldn't bring the matter up again. He was her boss, not her shrink.

Even Hertha couldn't figure out what Anne got up to all alone in her room.

Sometimes she stayed after supper and did puzzles with them for a bit, and Hertha would put a fourth small bowl of chips on the table.

The final piece of work that Anne produced at the end of her apprenticeship was a swivel piano stool made of cherrywood, which really pleased Carsten. As long as his apprentices turned out things like this, he hadn't yet lost the battle against all the mass-produced particleboard crap. He took photos, including one of Anne, and wrote his first workshop report for *Fine Woodworking* magazine, a two-page spread. It took him longer than it had taken Anne to design and build her stool, but he never did things halfway.

Karl-Heinz cut the article out when it appeared in the magazine and taped it to the glass panel of the door to the workshop. "You didn't have to go and do that, Father." But it stayed up and Hertha simply peeled it back briefly when she cleaned the glass.

Anne had noticed the somewhat yellowed piece of paper immediately when she'd returned after three and a half years of traveling as a journeyman carpenter, and had stood in front of Carsten Drewe's workshop in her black journeyman outfit.

Bernd took a Kleenex out of his desk drawer, wiped his glasses, which were a bit misted up from crying, dabbed his eyes, and took a deep breath. "You know, Anne . . ."

He was sticking to his script. Now came the history, twenty-four years of Musical Mouse in Hamburg-Ottensen, a man living his dream.

Bernd's monologue was very emotional and lasted for a good ten minutes, even if he omitted the bit about his childhood. Anne looked at the clock. Leon's day care closed in five.

She got up slowly, placed her hand briefly on his arm, and left.

As she was closing the door, she heard Bernd fall silent and then continue talking in a low voice.

5

Silent Movie

THE SEAGULLS WERE BACK. NOT that he cared for them particularly. In the summer, flocks of them would attack Vera's cherry tree again and then they'd fly over his farm, back toward the Elbe, and their crap would land in his garden.

The tree would have to go anyhow, that old piece of junk in her front yard. The trunk was overgrown with ivy, and the branches were growing every which way without rhyme or reason. Because Vera never thought of cutting them back. It was so tall now that you could no longer throw a net over it in summer.

She hadn't gotten a single cherry from it last summer. She simply let the birds do as they pleased. "Just don't look, Hinni."

And that was the best that you could do if you were unfortunate enough to be Vera Eckhoff's next-door neighbor: just not look.

Heinrich Luehrs tried very hard not to see her mossy, unkempt lawn that was littered with molehills, the weed-infested, lopsided flower beds, and the tattered hedge. He couldn't comprehend how anyone could simply leave everything in a state like that.

Just don't look was much easier said than done.

Whenever Vera drove off in her car, Heinrich would rush over to her garden and prune a couple of rosebushes, or stake up the gooseberry bush, which was drooping. In the mornings, he would sometimes wait until she'd trotted off on her wayward horse in the direction of the Elbe before popping over to plant a few traps in her molehills and go once around the bottom of her hedge with his Roundup spray. Vera never noticed and that was how it had to be. Her goutweed would otherwise get out of control and spread over to his place again—and the mole didn't respect property boundaries either. If Vera wanted to live in her wilderness she could, but he wanted none of it.

The seagulls were back. The first ones had just perched on the little island in the Elbe where they spent the summer nesting and teaching their ugly fledglings how to fly. Heinrich Luehrs could hear them at half past six in the morning, when he fetched the paper from his mailbox.

When the seagulls arrived, the winter was over. Yet another one.

He always prepared his two slices of bread with liverwurst and honey, then covered the plate with plastic wrap and placed it in the fridge before going to bed. He put water and three spoonfuls of coffee into the machine and placed a cup and saucer and the sugar on the table, so that he only had to turn the machine on in the morning on his way to the bathroom.

Elisabeth had always done it that way because everything had to go chop-chop in the mornings.

But since Heinrich Luehrs had leased the fruit trees to Dirk zum Felde, he now had time to read the paper in the morning, and he turned the radio on as well so that it wasn't so quiet in the kitchen.

There was no need to go chop-chop anymore, and the winters were getting longer and longer.

But now there were snowdrops under the kitchen window, and he'd picked the first five and put them on the table in the small crystal vase that was no bigger than an egg cup. Elisabeth had used it for the daisies and the pansies and the dan-

delions with short stems that the kids used to pluck out of the
dike for her when they were little. They weren't allowed to take
any flowers from her garden, she was quite strict about that,
but the first five snowdrops were always placed in the small
vase, one for each member of the family.

It was so quiet.

Not that they would have spoken much to each other. But
Elisabeth had always sung and hummed from the moment she
got up—in the kitchen, in the garden, among the fruit trees—
all day long. She didn't seem to be aware of it, but he could always tell where she was because of it.

And if she wasn't humming he knew that she was angry
with him for coming down too hard on the boys or tramping
through the house in his muddy boots. Once, she didn't hum
for two days because he had danced with Beke Matthes a few
times too many at the Blossom Festival. And yet there had
been nothing in it. He liked Beke Matthes, all right, but not
like *that*.

But Elisabeth no longer hummed because a painter and deco-
rator from the nearby town of Stade, who was doing twenty-
five miles an hour over the speed limit, had swept her off the

bike path at the big curve in the road, so now Heinrich Luehrs lived without a soundtrack. There'd been twenty years of silent movies since she died.

For He shall give his angels charge over you to keep you in all your ways, her friends in the women's church choir had sung at the funeral service. It had been her confirmation motto, and Heinrich knew then that he would never enter the church again. The graveyard, yes, he went there every Saturday. He kept the grave tidy, planted begonias in the spring, alternating red and white ones, as Elisabeth had done in her garden.

But his wife hadn't deserved to die at the age of fifty-three, run down like an animal at the side of the road.

And he hadn't deserved it either. Heinrich Luehrs had spent many a day and night turning over stone after stone of his life, looking for some mistake, the big crime he must have committed. And he wasn't able to find any. He had been good to his wife and his children. Strict, yes, even quick-tempered now and then, but never nasty. He didn't smoke, didn't drink any more than anyone else, and there hadn't been any womanizing either. Beke Matthes certainly didn't count. He hadn't disgraced his parents, had always kept his yard shipshape, 100 percent in order. He was hardworking and efficient, a helpful neighbor, and he never cheated on his taxes. In fact he didn't even cheat at cards.

* * *

The angels of God could buzz off. They had a strange idea of what it meant to watch over you *in all your ways* and *carry you on their hands*. "We can't always understand the ways of God," the lady pastor had said, but Heinrich Luehrs had understood very well what was meant: show a bit of brawn now and again, bend a straight back, force a man to his knees so he'd run to church and learn how to pray. That's what it was all about.

Not with him. This whole thing wasn't right and he wasn't of a mind to accept it. If he had paid as little attention to his farm as these angels had paid to his wife, then it would look like Vera Eckhoff's yard right now.

"Me neither, Father," Georg had said a couple of days before Elisabeth rode off on her bike. And he'd have been the best of the three. Heinrich Luehrs had three sons and no successor.

He didn't know if Elisabeth had hummed on her final morning.

6

Chain Stitches

IN THE BEETLES' CLASSROOM, THE chairs were up on the tables, the floor had been swept and mopped and had dried again, and Marion was now in the baby changing room folding towels, which was absolutely not her job. She wasn't the cleaning lady around here, she was the lead teacher of the Beetle group, and as she pulled a little harder than required at the blameless towels, she kept an eye on Leon, who was sitting in the play corner all by himself. It didn't seem to be bothering him though. He was concentrating on building a tower, which by this point was almost as tall as he was.

It was always the same parents who arrived panting, way

too late, then wanted to stage a big show of apology. But she'd gotten them out of that habit by now.

When Anne came rushing into the room, Leon gave his tower a kick and the building blocks scattered across the floor, which Marion didn't think was all that great, especially since it was eight minutes past five.

In fact, she even turned off the lights while Anne was still bustling around, gathering up the blocks. The keys were jangling in Marion's hand.

Anne grabbed hold of Leon, said, "Have a nice evening, Marion," then fished around in the hallway for his boots and stormed out. She had already stuffed his hat, scarf, and gloves into the hood of his snowsuit. Out in the vestibule, she stood Leon next to his stroller so she could finish getting him ready.

The mothers from Hamburg-Ottensen were invariably in a hurry. They pushed their strollers like luggage carts, as though they were travelers at an airport, needing to get to their gates urgently, so as not to miss their connecting flights.

Anne watched the other mothers march past her. For a while, she'd run along with them to baby massage appointments, Gymboree, and baby swimming lessons, but she felt as foreign and out of place as an atheist in a prayer group.

After once spending two torturous hours at baby swimming lessons, she had started sending Christoph instead. He didn't mind singing in a paddle pool and jumping up and down with a dozen parents and small children who held hands at all times. He did this just as uncomplainingly, in fact, as he made waffles during parties at the day care center or bought diapers at Budnikowsky's.

Christoph lived with them like a good-natured guest. He never seemed to grasp that he belonged to this family, that family life actually concerned him.

When the three of them walked through the town, a man and a woman with a small child in a stroller, Anne would sometimes catch their reflection in a store window and try to figure out what made them different from other families.

It wasn't their clothes or their hairstyles. Their reflections looked absolutely fine. Their kid was cute and Christoph placed his hand on Anne's shoulder whenever she was pushing the stroller.

But there was always a momentary hesitation if Leon spat his pacifier onto the sidewalk or began crying because he didn't want to sit in the stroller anymore. What they lacked was the spontaneity that she thought she saw in all other families. The bending down to retrieve the fallen pacifier, couples continuing to talk as the child was lifted out of the stroller, in passing almost. Breast-feeding scenes in the café, the mother drinking caffeine-free coffee, relaxed to the point where she lacked any will whatsoever, and beside her the father with his laptop in front of him, the dribble cloth over his shoulder, and his hand on her back, stroking it slowly and gently.

The family still lifes in the cafés and parks of Ottensen made it obvious to Anne what they were not: a tightly wrapped package, father-mother-child, woven into a stable family fabric.

They were two people with a child, loosely crocheted—three chain stitches.

Compared to all the couples walking casually through the neighborhood, she and Christoph always seemed to be walking on tiptoe.

These days she was no longer certain that Christoph had really buttoned his shirt incorrectly by accident on the day they met. Perhaps he had done it on purpose. A white shirt with the sleeves rolled up. Indeed, the fact that his shirt was buttoned the wrong way was the first thing she'd noticed about him. He sat with his laptop in front of him, one of the many wordsmiths in the café, at a table next to the big window. The entire man was a bit unironed. Two creases ran handsomely from his nose to his lips, his blond hair hadn't been combed, his fingers were quite fast on the keys, until the small collision when a kid ran into his table. The tables always got in the way when kids were romping around the café . "Whoa there, sweetie," said the mother, "be careful you don't hurt yourself."

The organic soft drink slopped out of his glass, his notebook started to foam, and Anne threw her cotton scarf over the pool of soda.

The laptop was shot nonetheless, but the evening turned out to be very nice.

And then the summer.

She got pregnant right away.

Christoph wrote his crime novels in the same way that engineers build bridges. The books were well conceived, sound, straightforward. He'd heard of but not experienced the anguish of writer's block and tuned out the bitchiness of his fellow authors, who could only dream of his sales figures. They suffered on account of their thin volumes, which they wrested from themselves in torment at night, and they despised Christoph's mainstream publisher, who always courteously turned down their complicated tales that were light on plot. They called him *our writer of the people* and smiled with tight lips when he was celebrated as a *local hero* at readings in local bars and cultural centers.

Christoph's readership was loyal and mainly female. Anne would watch the women's faces during his readings. They cocked their heads to one side and smiled, sipped their wine and saw what Anne had also seen: the beautiful, slightly disheveled man in the white shirt.

Absentminded as writers often are, he sometimes even buttoned his shirt the wrong way. They loved that about him—his boyishness, the fact that he was slightly chaotic—and Anne felt embarrassed that she had fallen into the same trap.

The zipper on Leon's snowsuit was catching again. She had zipped it up wrong and it got stuck halfway up. "I'll get that," said Marion, who had locked the door of the day care center and was heading home *at last*. She took her gloves off, yanked the zipper down a bit, then pulled it back up. "There you go, little man, see you tomorrow."

If it wasn't too wet and windy, Anne would walk through the green spaces along the Elbe with Leon, and they'd watch the dogs, the big long-haired ones that stumbled through the bushes like juveniles, and the worldly-wise dachshunds belonging to the Altona widows, lying under the park benches, waiting patiently while their mistresses smoked.

Sometimes she let Leon ride a blue rocking horse for fifty cents in front of the organic supermarket on the main street of

Ottensen, but it was broken half the time. Then he'd sit for a bit on the motionless plastic animal and jerk it back and forth until he realized that it was pointless.

Anne would stand next to it, aimless and weak willed. The days were too long and it seemed to be raining most of the time.

At night, though, everything was different. When Leon was asleep, she'd lie in his room in front of the crib and stroke his dreaming face, his narrow shoulders, his chubby little hands. He smelled of milk and warm sand and undeserved happiness.

Then the daytime would arrive again with all its diapers and bottles, with pacifier chains, gloves and hats, which she could never find, with pediatrician appointments, sand molds, muddy pants, and diaper bags, and suddenly the joy of motherhood as well as her gratitude were nowhere to be seen. They slipped deep beneath the packets of wet wipes, and drowned in the kiddie pool and the baby cereal.

Sometimes when she was sitting at the playground with all the strange women, she noticed the dark circles under their eyes and wondered whether there were others like her, night mothers, who wished another life for themselves by day. But if there were, she knew they wouldn't admit it even if you tortured them. It was all right to sit exhausted on a bench in Ottensen, stressed and unkempt, without any makeup on—all that was okay—but to lack the joy of motherhood was unacceptable.

It had been a little cold the past couple of days. The sandy path in Fischers Park was hard and free of mud—a perfect racetrack, in other words. Anne lifted Leon's balance bike from the carrier rack of the stroller, and he jumped on it. He rode off with the wild enthusiasm of a child who could finally outpace his parents and all other impediments. Leon was "Easy Rider" in a ladybug helmet. He didn't brake for mothers.

Not much could happen in the park, though. The pedestrians managed to get out of his way most of the time, and if he fell over, his snowsuit cushioned him against the worst scrapes and scratches. The problem was the road home, after they left the pedestrian zone and had to go through the dark, smelly Lessing tunnel—where pigeons met a miserable end—and Leon raced his balance bike between four lanes of traffic, slaloming rapidly around crushed soda cans and old hamburger boxes. Anne galloped after him, shouting for him to stop, as if she were on the heels of a purse snatcher. It was pointless, of course. No one could rein in a four-year-old boy's thrill of speed.

This afternoon it was clear and cold and much too bright for early February.

As she turned onto their street ten meters behind Leon and out of breath, Anne realized she'd forgotten all about their pediatrician appointment.

She noticed a white Fiat in front of their building, yet again, once too often, and then the penny finally dropped. She unlocked the door, left Leon just inside the entranceway, climbed the four flights of stairs, and stood like a burglar in her own hallway, where she saw a pair of black boots that weren't hers.

Christoph and Carola always sat in the kitchen whenever they were discussing a new book project. She was the best copy editor he'd ever had. Today they were sitting at the kitchen table drinking white wine and tea, and everything was the same as usual except that they were both naked. The first thing Anne noticed were the bare feet with red toenails. Carola dropped her cigarette into her wineglass when she caught sight of Anne.

Leon was shouting from the stairwell. His ego had become as big as a dictator's after his triumphant afternoon in the saddle of his balance bike, and he wanted to be carried up. "I'll get him," Anne said, and Christoph slumped back in his chair with his eyes closed, as though she'd just executed him.

Anne went downstairs and lifted Leon. He stopped

screaming instantly and then let himself be dragged upstairs reproachfully.

Carola's hair was black and reached all the way down to her hips. She was standing in the hallway and was having some difficulty zipping up her skirt. I'm no use with zippers either, Anne thought as she pushed away the hand that Carola was intending to place on her arm in a pseudosisterly way and went into the kitchen, where Christoph was standing only half-naked by this point, but still as pale as a ghost. Anne tore open the balcony door, threw Carola's cigarette butts, her half-full packet of cigarettes, and her silver lighter over the railing, then flopped down into a chair.

Leon, who was happy that Carola had come to visit again, wanted to look at a storybook with her. Occasionally they did that, but not today, so he marched off to his room, wound himself out of his snowsuit, turned on the CD player, and danced a bit to "I'm a Little Teapot," his favorite song.

Anne sat down at the kitchen table. She still had her coat on and was digging around with a large spoon in a jar of hazelnut cream from the organic supermarket. And she didn't stop when Christoph sat down next to her, she just kept shoveling the expensive full-cane-sugar goo into her mouth until he took the spoon out of her hand and screwed the lid back on the jar.

Then she lay her head on the table and closed her eyes, as though she were listening to the scarred wood and no longer needed to pay attention to him when he took her hand because she'd seen the toes with the red nails and the black hip-length hair.

Snow White in her white car, and here she sat: Anne, the little teapot.

7

Winter Moth

BY THE TIME SHE'D GOTTEN the boxes of clothes and books, her own bike, Leon's balance bike, the big crate full of toys, and their African linden into the rented van, it was already early afternoon.

A horn sounded from the street, twice briefly, and Christoph took off. He jumped up from the kitchen chair and almost sprinted along the hallway. Then he pulled the door shut gently so as not to wake Leon.

Anne had no idea what a Fiat horn sounded like, but she didn't go over to the window because she didn't want to see him getting into the car, and she definitely didn't want *to be seen*. The deserted wife at the window, what a pitiful sight.

Their last long days together had felt like rehearsals for a new play. The couple that had fallen out of love in their old apartment. The roles were cast, but they hadn't yet mastered the script. They performed the old classic of loving and leaving quite ineptly. The cheat, the betrayed woman, packing boxes, taking down pictures, screaming, whispering, crying, with red eyes and pale faces.

A drama of prefabricated parts, Anne thought, we're nothing more than that.

Christoph had followed her around all morning, even while she was packing, with his shoulders hunched over and his hands in his pockets. He had acted sheepish and guilty. "Anne, if you need anything..." His performance was awful, that of an amateur actor who had bitten off more than he could chew.

He had watched Leon sleep for a while and cried silently while doing so, shook his head, put his hands on her shoulders, and pressed his forehead against hers. "Jeez, Anne."

And she had searched a long time for the one powerful sentence that would torpedo and sink him and open his eyes. But Christoph was wide awake, and Anne knew it. He was in love. What could he do about it?

There was thus no reason to swear at him, throw his

laptop out the window, rip the CD rack off the wall, overturn the kitchen table, or, at the very least, pull the tablecloth off with the breakfast still on it, to hear the crashing and shattering, the noise of things breaking to pieces. There was no chance of riding the wave of a powerful rage through their final days together.

She was glad that it was over. Glad to be getting out of this apartment, out of the city, away from the filthy pigeon tunnel, and glad she'd never have to sit at the playground with the edgy mothers again, and wouldn't be seeing the man in the white shirt any longer. She would walk through fields, live in the country.

Leon woke up, and Anne lifted him out of his crib, feeling his warm sleeping face against her cheek. At the back of his neck, there were a couple of little curls that had become frizzy with sweat.

She stood like that for a while, with the soft, tired child in her arms. He smelled so good, like a perfect world.

Outside in front of the window, the buckeye tree extended its branches into a colorless sky. They thrashed about in the wind that blew through the courtyard like marauding gangs. Leon's pinwheel rattled in the hard soil.

* * *

Anne carried Leon into the kitchen to prepare a bottle for him. He was actually too old for bottles, but still loved having one in the afternoon. She tried to do it as casually as she usually did, without giving it a second thought, but it didn't work. She was watching herself doing things for the last time: switching on the blue electric kettle, taking the milk out of Christoph's impractical retro fridge, fetching the bottle with the fish pattern out of the dishwasher and the lid with the nipple from the tin next to the sink. Then she saw herself sitting with Leon on her lap sucking on his bottle, at the kitchen table, which was pitted and stained with red wine and oil—a veteran on wooden legs, who'd survived two apartment shares and now a nuclear family as well.

Anne traced its scars with her finger: burn marks from hot pots, nicks from slipped knives, the small hole from the corkscrew that Christoph—lost in thought at the time—had twisted into the tabletop just after they'd discovered that she was pregnant. The stabbings from Leon's toddler fork, the marks left by modeling clay and crayons.

A table like a family album, a notion of home. But she was so bad at staying put. She'd fled once and never arrived at a new destination.

A prodigy now ruled her home. He sat at her black grand piano like a sun king; she couldn't go back. She had turned into something adrift, a creature bobbing in the current, a floating animal, a piece of plankton in the sea.

Three years on the road, traveling for the most part on her own. It had been so easy, like an endless tour: every few days a new stage, turning in a couple of performances and moving on.

Arrive, sparkle, take off, as she had done before at Young Musicians. Child's play, even being with men—just a game, dead easy. The trick was to take off before things got complicated, before the varnish showed its first scratches.

She had gotten very good at that, become a champion at breaking up and moving on.

But it was a whole lot harder with a little boy in her arms.

Anne put Leon's snowsuit on him. Then they both carried the crate containing his pygmy rabbit out of the apartment. "Last one out turns off the light, Willy," she said before locking up and tossing the key through the mail slot. But the rabbit was in no mood for joking. He sat in his crate like a bad-tempered prince in his sedan chair.

When they were finally all settled in the white transit van, the traffic was so heavy it felt as if the city were being evacuated. It was late afternoon and the mass exodus from the offices was under way. The commuter cars were piling up on both sides of the Elbe tunnel, and Anne, who'd driven only rarely since getting her driver's license twenty years earlier, could feel her palms getting sweaty on the steering wheel.

Leon thought it was great to be riding in a *truck*. He sat contentedly in his car seat, swinging his rubber boots against the front seat and singing a song he had learned at day care to the anxious pygmy rabbit, whose crate was buckled in next to him. Willy's mood wasn't much improved by this. He was squatting in his crate with his ears turned down and would drum his hind quarters nervously every now and then.

Leon pushed a piece of carrot through the bars to him, and when Willy turned away, he ate it himself. After that, he tried the Vitakraft rabbit treats that they had bought during their farewell visit to the pet store. Anne wondered fleetingly whether she should stop Leon from eating the rabbit food. The supermoms wouldn't have allowed their kids to chew on pet snacks. They'd have cited many good reasons against it, but Anne couldn't think of any, so she let Leon eat the grain feed while she steered the van through the Elbe tunnel at a snail's pace. She tried to ignore the guy in the car next to her, who was cutting his fingernails and steering his Opel Astra with his knees. At the end of the tunnel, he threw the nail clippers onto the passenger seat and hit the gas.

When Leon saw the cranes at the port, he pressed his face against the window and forgot all about the rabbit food. The cranes stood on the wharf like enormous dinosaurs, their steel necks extending up into the gray sky, and they appeared to be waiting on prey. They were driving in the direction of Finkenwerder, and Anne was thinking of the trips she had taken with her parents, all those Sundays in the Altland during cherry season. They had never stopped off at any of the farm shops or little road stands.

"I'm certainly not buying cherries," Marlene would say, "we've got plenty of those ourselves." During cherry season, Anne's mother refused to concede that the Eckhoff trees weren't hers, that it was Vera who had inherited the farm, and that she was nothing more than a guest in the old farmhouse.

On Sundays in July they'd go rushing to the farm with empty buckets in the trunk of their car, "pretending to be farmhands for a bit," Vera would say with a sneer. But she'd still place ladders against the trees and lay out the old blue work jackets for them.

When her parents disappeared into the branches of the cherry trees and Thomas was over visiting the neighbor, who had enormous rabbits, Anne would propel herself up into the linden tree on Vera's old swing or gently stroke the two Trakehners that grazed in the paddock, sweeping the summer flies away from their bodies with their tails. They were beautiful, high-strung horses that no one besides her aunt dared to ride.

After picking cherries, they'd sit on Vera's bench next to the house and eat the cake that Anne's mother had brought from home—each piece meant as a silent reproach of the elder sister, but Vera had always been stone-deaf in that respect. The only things she ever offered her guests were apple juice from Heinrich Luehrs, which stood in a canister on the table, and coffee, which tasted as though it had come out of a cement mixer. It stood like tar in the cups, its surface shimmering like pools of gasoline. Anne's parents often tried to drink the stuff. They'd dilute it with water, dump milk into it, heap in sugar, and try to knock it back as hot as they could stand, because it tasted a heck of a lot worse when it cooled off. Vera was the only one who liked it—and the weird grandpa Karl, who always sat slumped over on the bench. After a while, Anne's mother had given in and, on those Sundays in July, in addition to the cake, she'd started bringing a thermos full of coffee too, but that reproach was lost on Vera as well.

* * *

On their journeys back to Hamburg, with the cherries in the trunk of the car and her father at the steering wheel, looking unusually laid-back in his sunglasses, her mother would smoke in the passenger seat and talk herself into a frenzy about the sister who was letting the house go to rack and ruin, about the weeds, the unpainted fence, the cherry trees that were running to seed, the rotten window frames, the burn marks and coffee stains on Ida Eckhoff's hand-embroidered tablecloths, and the scruffy old man who belonged in an insane asylum. Her mother's hands would wave about as though she were directing an atonal piece of music. Vera's eccentricity! Vera's arrogance! Vera's horrid mutts! Sometimes the ash from her cigarette would fly off toward the children in the backseat.

In Anne's memory, every visit to the Altland had ended like this: cherries in the trunk and tirades from the passenger seat. And her father, who found his idiosyncratic sister-in-law highly amusing and was used to his wife's temper tantrums, would light two new cigarettes with the electric lighter, roll down the window a little, and say with a smile: "Let it be, Marlene."

As Anne was driving with Leon toward Stade, she realized that she had only ever seen this landscape in the summer.

For the first time she was seeing the Altland in its cold

starkness, the fruit trees standing like soldiers in the heavy earth, bald regiments in endless rows and between them the marsh soil hard with frost. In the deep ruts left behind by the tractors, rainwater had turned to ice. Large birds of prey, whose names she didn't know, perched on the branches as though they were too heavy to fly. On the dikes and at the edges of the ditch, the grass lay ragged and pale—a landscape devoid of color except for the neon yellow of the safety vests worn by an orderly group of day care children who were saun-tering in pairs along the sidewalk with their teachers. Two little boys at the far end of the line were stamping through the ice on a puddle with their rubber boots, and Anne tried to imagine Leon on this day care excursion, holding another child's hand and carrying an apple from the farm they had just visited in his other hand.

She needed to find out where you could get one of those yellow vests.

Shortly before Lühe, Leon woke up and was hungry, but Willy had already eaten the carrots and rabbit treats. Anne turned off at the pier in Lühe and pulled in next to a food truck, which must at some point have been white. BE HAPPY, YOU'RE IN STADE COUNTY! was written above a jetty on the Elbe, which led to a deserted ferry dock, and on either side of that, frozen flags scratched at their masts.

Anne bought french fries with ketchup and put the carton on the seat between Leon and her. An enormous container ship was coming up the Elbe, nosing its way toward Hamburg. Leon watched it as he chewed and dribbled. Anne wiped ketchup off the seat and went and got some more fries, and after that she got a lollipop for Leon and a plastic cup of coffee for herself that tasted of frying fat. But she would also have drunk Vera's cement sludge as long as she could sit here with Leon, who loved ships, in a car that smelled like a french fry stand.

The sky had turned red and the sun was sinking into the Elbe by the time they reached the "teensy-weensy little baby town" that Leon had told the kids at his day care about during his farewell breakfast with the Beetle group.

They drove slowly down the smooth street past Heinrich Luehrs's perfectly kept lot. His front yard with its tidy flower beds, paved paths, and square lawns was arranged as neatly as a parade ground. Behind the wooden fence, his rosebushes stood in rank and file, covered in burlap sacks to protect them from the frost. They looked like prisoners about to be shot.

Vera's yard was barely visible behind its high tattered hedge, and that was just as well since the sight wouldn't please the locals. For Heinrich Luehrs and every other farmer in the village, symmetry and order were the pillars of their self-respect. Anyone who let their yard degenerate was a degenerate himself—or a very weird person, like Vera Eckhoff.

Anne drove through the high ornamental gate, which hadn't lived up to its name for decades. Since Vera's dogs had mellowed with age, it was left open most of the time. It hung rotting and crooked on its hinges. In fact it was a miracle that it was still standing.

Anne had just lifted Leon and Willy out of the car when she heard scrunching on the gravel behind her.

A green John Deere children's tractor with a front loader was reversing into the driveway. The driver was around Leon's age and was wearing professional-looking overalls and a cap. Slowly he dismounted, approached her with an outstretched arm, and opened his fist to reveal a large dead moth. He snuffled, wiped a string of snot away with his sleeve, and said: "Varmint. A winter moth." He dropped it and stepped on it forcefully once more for good measure, grinding it down with his heel until the moth was completely squashed. Then he tapped his finger on the visor of his cap and pedaled off.

Leon, who had watched the performance in silence, went

over to the flattened moth and mumbled "winter moth," as if learning his first word of a foreign language.

The exterminator had just disappeared behind the hedge again when a red tractor and trailer swung into the driveway, full scale this time. It braked and pulled up behind the white van. The stocky man behind the wheel was wearing a peaked cap with ear flaps. Without turning off the engine, he placed his arms on his steering wheel and looked down at Anne and Leon.

"Right. Those are my trees back there. I need to be able to drive through here at any time. Get that stupid jalopy out of the way."

Leon decided to move his rabbit to safety by dragging the crate across the pavement. Willy wasn't thrilled and Anne, caught unawares, simply stood by and watched.

She'd have liked to have given the driver a parting shot about his stupid cap, or have made some comment about his manners—some statement that would put him in his place.

It would come to her too late, as usual.

She turned around without a word, got into the van, and pulled it off to the side. Then, hoping that the tractor had a rearview mirror, she gave him the finger.

8

Peasant Theater

Dirk zum Felde had had his fill. Totally. There seemed to be new arrivals every day. City slickers running around the place aimlessly and getting in his way.

Just last week Burkhard Weisswerth had shuffled into his yard with some newspaper guys in tow, there to take a couple of photos. He'd called out "Howdy!," slapped Dirk on the shoulder as though they were pals, and blathered on meaninglessly about the weather. This is what people did *in the country-side,* this is why they liked *the folk out here.*

"Dirk, my man, mind if I climb back up on your tractor for a bit?"

Burkhard Weisswerth couldn't drive farm machinery, but he looked real good sitting on it, with his corduroy pants from Manufactum stuffed into his natural rubber boots—effortlessly, it seemed—his shirtsleeves rolled up, and his eyes narrowed ever so slightly beneath the wide brim of his soft hat, as he looked off into the distance. The very picture of a rural man. This is what people with vision looked like.

Two and a half years ago, Weisswerth had been laid off from his job as chief copy editor, been given a reasonable severance package, and had moved from the Isestrasse in Hamburg to a former farm on the banks of the Elbe. He was now writing books about country life and columns for a slow-food magazine. He was frequently being interviewed by former colleagues and having his picture taken for the photo spreads, usually with a lamb, a piglet, or a chicken on his arm. A pitchfork or a bunch of carrots were good too—but he much preferred to use one of his neighbors, such as Dirk zum Felde, this *awkward* farmer with his red tractor.

Weisswerth loved these *totally authentic* guys. And he'd long since joined their ranks! When being photographed, he liked to stand right next to them, shoulder to shoulder, his hands buried deep in his pants pockets, engrossed in a conversation about night frosts or crop rotation. As if there weren't a camera in sight. He'd sprinkle a few local phrases into his speech, such as "Ain't that somethin'?" or "You said it," and when leaving, he'd call out resolutely, "All righty, see ya!"

Weisswerth knew how these *wonderfully simple folks* ticked, all the earthy, reticent, pigheaded farmers he wrote about so wittily, and with a wink, in his books. They really existed! And he also knew country life so much better than all the editors in Hamburg's Baumwall media district, who, at the very most, might drive their SUVs to the nearest Demeter farm on a weekend, so their kids could pet a calf that was being raised in a near-natural environment.

But Dirk zum Felde had no time to pose with farm machinery. He'd already prepared his spray unit, but Burkhard Weisswerth was still sitting on his tractor, staring off into the distance. The photographer must have taken hundreds of shots by this point. The camera lens had been clicking so continuously, you'd have thought they were standing on the red carpet at Cannes rather than on the property of an Altland farmer who just wanted to get back to work.

"All right, Burkhard, off the tractor. I've gotta spray."

Click-click-click. Click-click-click. Click-click-click.

"Hey, we haven't finished up here yet," the photographer had said without taking the camera away from his eyes. "Burkhard, I was thinking, maybe he should join you up there?"

He, Dirk zum Felde, had gotten a bit tense at that point.

He had given the photographer from the slow-food magazine he'd never heard of a kick in the backside to get him out of the way, and had thrown the tripod after him. Burkhard Weisswerth had then clambered down from the tractor of his own accord, pretty fast in fact, and the guy with the black-rimmed glasses, who'd stood freezing on the sidelines the whole time, had had to run back to fetch Burkhard's hat.

Dirk zum Felde had had his fill of idiots in expensive rubber boots who just had to move to the country.

It was only ever those who hadn't made it in the city. B-list professionals and creative types, no longer equipped for city life. Left on the shelf, they wanted one more go-around at the farmer's market.

At first, with the early arrivals, before he knew that a whole invasion would follow, he'd made it clear every now and then that he himself had been a student and had lived in shared apartments. That he wasn't a boor with a diploma from the tree nursery, which was what they obviously thought he and all the other established residents around here were.

It had taken him a while to figure out why they didn't want to hear about that. Because he was spoiling their fantasy. An agricultural scientist with a college degree who worked an Altland orchard using modern technology, sprayed his apple trees with pesticides, and simply chopped them down when they stopped bearing fruit—that was like a four-lane highway in a sentimental film set in the countryside. He didn't fit the mold. He unsettled them.

And they bothered him! These dopey creative types streaming from the towns into the villages, to *ground* themselves, and then bumming around the fruit fields with their golden retrievers and loitering in front of run-down farms and farmhands' small houses. And when it was springtime and somewhere in an overgrown garden an apple tree weakened by age braced itself for its final blossoming, there was no stopping them. They'd tasted blood and burrowed in like ticks, like Burkhard Weisswerth and that wife of his.

These uptight city chicks with their identity crises nagged for ramshackle thatched roof homes just as their daughters did for ponies. It was so sweet! They just had to have it! They'd look after it, always! And then they spent megabucks doing up the old brick ruins, laying out their *farm gardens,* and setting up pottery studios in the old stables.

And if they still weren't over it, they bought sheep and started making their own cheese, and every last one of these newly countrified folks made jelly from heirloom apples, as if under some hidden compulsion.

Then he, Dirk zum Felde, would come along with his tractor and a spray tank full of Funguran fungicide, to spray his overbred apple trees against infestation and would crash right through their open-air museum.

It would be a while before Burkhard Weisswerth in his stupid corduroy pants would sit on his tractor again. Dirk had no intention of participating in this peasant theater as an extra or a stagehand.

And the last thing, the very last thing he needed today was this slowpoke hogging up Vera Eckhoff's yard with her white van, blocking the entrance to the orchard. A Hamburg license plate, of course. A hooded sweater and chunky shoes, what else. He knew the type. Yet another addition to the big peasant theater ensemble.

He gave her three weeks. Then she'd offer him some sort of fair-trade concoction in a shoddy ceramic cup with no handle and ask innocently: "So, what is it you're spraying then?" And of course it wouldn't be a question so much as a way to launch into her little eco-sermon. And after ten minutes tops she'd start singing the praises of heirloom fruits and vegetables.

Then he—the country hick, who couldn't count to three and was mindlessly spraying evil poison onto his poor, poor trees—he was supposed to slap himself on the forehead and say: "Man! I've never thought about it like that before! You're absolutely right! I'm such an idiot! I'll apply for organic certification right away!"

These eco-missionaries couldn't tell the difference between Russet and Jonagold apples and had certainly never eaten a grubby, scabby Finkenwerder Herbstprinz, or they'd know that these crummy old varieties were dying out for a reason. As far as he was concerned, they could feed their brats parsnips, chard, and spelt, and all the other old junk, as long as he didn't have to harvest the crap and could just get on with his job.

Dirk zum Felde passed the white van and turned on his sprayer. In his rearview mirror he watched the woman with the hood disappear in a misty haze.

9

Refugees

VERA ECKHOFF DIDN'T KNOW MUCH about her niece, but she knew a refugee when she saw one. The woman with the pinched face, fetching her few belongings from the van, was obviously looking for more than just a new experience and a bit of fresh air for her son.

Out there in the driveway were two homeless people. And an animal in a plastic cage, which the little boy was now dragging over to the front door.

Anne had wrapped her son up like a grub. The little one could hardly move in his thick snowsuit; his arms were sticking out at the sides of his body, and his legs rubbed to-gether when he walked.

Vera suddenly recalled how it felt to stand in five layers of clothing in front of this house that didn't care for strangers. Whether one was driven away or on the run, with a handcart or in a minivan, it didn't make a whole lot of difference.

As she walked through the hallway to open the door, she could see Ida Eckhoff standing before her. Her furious face on the day the Polacks arrived.

Vera went over to Anne, who was standing next to the van's open door, and they managed an awkward embrace. But how should you greet a young boy? Lift him up and press him against you? Bend down and shake his small, thickly padded hand? Find a bare piece of cheek and kiss it?

"This is Willy!" Leon said, pointing at the crate. Vera knelt down in front of it, looking at the rabbit and then at the child. Blond curls fell over his forehead to just above his nose, which was red and shiny with snot. As far as Vera could see, it looked like all children's noses. No one in her family had had blond hair, but she believed she recognized the brown eyes with their thick lashes. A wink from the East. "Willy. I see. And who are you?" "I'm the owner," Leon replied, scraping the crate across the flagstones toward the front door. "Tell Vera your name,

Leon!" Anne called after him. He turned around and laughed. "You've just said it already, Anne! So I don't have to anymore."

Vera could hear her dogs whining in the kitchen; they hated being confined. But two hunting dogs and a rabbit wasn't an auspicious combination, from the rabbit's perspective at least. She would have to impress upon the child the importance of not letting his pet hop about the place and keeping the door to his room shut at all times. Her dogs would never get so old and exhausted that an overfed city rabbit could escape their clutches.

Vera put the refugees in Ida Eckhoff's apartment.

When Leon finally nodded off around nine in the evening with his rabbit cage on the floor beside him, Anne went across the hall with a bottle of red wine and knocked on Vera's kitchen door.

The smell coming from within took her breath away. Vera was standing at the sink in a white rubber apron and was cutting up a large animal. "Come in, the glasses are over there." Anne, breathing through her mouth, took two crystal wineglasses out of the kitchen cupboard and climbed carefully over the two dogs that were lying on the floor gnawing on bluish bones. "I'm almost finished here." Anne tried not to look over at the pail that Vera was tossing bits of hide, entrails, and tendons into. "The corkscrew's in the drawer," she said, pointing a bloody hand at the old sideboard. Then she sawed a bone off with her ripsaw, threw it over to the dogs, and put a large chunk of meat into a plastic tub. The animal was too big to be a hare, so it had to be a deer.

Anne, who felt as though the contents of her stomach were slowly rising toward her throat, concentrated on the wine bottle and fiddled silently with the cork for such a long time that Vera turned around to see what she was up to.

When she saw Anne's face, she yanked the window open, shoved the bowl of meat and the waste pail into the pantry, and washed the blood off her hands. Then she fetched a bottle of fruit brandy from the cupboard, took the wine bottle and the corkscrew out of her niece's hand, poured a large shot of kirschwasser into her glass, and said, "Down the hatch!" Anne knocked the schnapps back and received another.

Vera pulled her over to the open window and had her breathe in and out deeply ten times. She knew that game always smelled a bit strong, although she no longer noticed it herself.

They left the bottle of wine corked and stuck to the fruit schnapps. Anne thought the pear tasted better than the cherry, even if not quite as good as the yellow plum.

They toasted each other with the crystal wineglasses.

"Down with the ex!" Anne said after the dogs had been snoring under the kitchen table for some time, and because she found it so funny, she emptied another couple of glasses to *down with the ex,* until Vera took her by the arm and dragged her across the hallway to Ida's parlor. The grandfather clock in the corner struck two.

Anne sat giggling in a chair while Vera pulled out the sofa bed, but she fell asleep before the bed was ready.

Vera removed Anne's weird shoes and put her feet up on a footstool. The right sock had been darned—by the boy, by the looks of it. The black fabric had a blue piece of yarn zigzagging every which way across Anne's big toe. Vera threw the duvet over her, then went back to the kitchen to fetch a bottle of water, two Alka-Seltzers, and an empty pail, hoping that it wouldn't all end up on Ida's beautiful old rug.

She left the door to the apartment ajar, then made some coffee, put the rubber apron on again, and went back to the deer.

When Anne came to in the armchair about four hours later, she immediately remembered the dissected animal with the bluish bones—and then its smell as well.

She more or less managed to get everything into the pail on her lap and gagged until her eyes welled up. Vera had left the floor lamp on, but it still took Anne some time to figure out where she was. With a groan, she set the pail aside and tried to get out of the chair, but the pounding in her head forced her back onto the cushion.

She felt around on the table for the tablets and the bottle of water, pressed the two Alka-Seltzers out of their foil, put them into the bottle, and shook it up. She tried to drink the stuff without throwing up again. The first few gulps landed straight back in the bucket, but then it was okay. Anne sat motionless until the sharp pains in her head became a little duller.

When she felt no more than a gentle thumping, she lifted herself out of the armchair, picked up the pail, and went to look for the bathroom.

Where was Leon? She put the pail in the bathtub, tripped over her shoes in the living room, and located the door to the bedroom, which was slightly open. The rabbit was sitting very quietly and pricked up his ears as Anne clattered through the room and bent over the bed. She knelt down next to the sleeping Leon and listened to him breathe.

The house groaned. Anne could feel it sucking in the cold wind through its rotten windows.

I'm completely shot, she thought as she staggered back into the living room. She somehow managed to stuff the duvet into its cover, left the buttons undone, undressed partway, and went into the bathroom to rinse the bad taste out of her mouth.

Then she lay down on the twisted duvet and tried in vain to ward off the thoughts that were buzzing through her drunken skull like a swarm of hornets:

I'm lying completely wasted in a dilapidated farmhouse. I'm living with my four-year-old son in the house of a madwoman, who guns down animals and hacks them up in her kitchen. I haven't held a plane in my hand for five years, and I haven't the foggiest idea how I am going to fix Vera's decrepit windows and beams. Christoph loves Carola.

Why hadn't she brought her Camper boots down on those red-painted toenails? Pressed down hard and crushed Carola's foot by grinding her heel back and forth, as the boy had done earlier with the dead moth?

Varmint!

A woman with bloodred toenails had climbed into her life, lain with her man in her bed, drunk wine from her glasses, and put her hand on her arm in her hallway as though she had a right to do so, as if they were sisters.

And she, Anne, the poor little wretch, had trotted off, speechless and defenseless, into the kitchen. She hadn't been able to say a thing and had hung up with her hands shaking when Carola had had the nerve to call her a few days later to *talk things out.*

Women who shot their rivals in a wild rage, men who finished their rivals off with knives or ran them over with their cars, things like that happened—but not in the civilized, even-tempered relationships of Hamburg-Ottensen. These were wrapped up without any displays of emotion when a feeling called love intervened. Because people were powerless in the face of love. Hey, it just happened! And someone in love could do anything, could develop himself further with an editor who resembled Snow White.

Carola with her white car could run over Anne's life, take her man away, laugh, look great—and even make herself a little more lovable on account of the fact that this thing with Anne was really *getting her down,* because she would *never have wanted that* and hoped that she and Anne could at some point *be cool with each another* because Anne was *a really great woman.*

Christoph was allowed to simply stop loving Anne. He could look through her when she spoke to him, and just walk out of her life. That sort of thing happened. He and Carola weren't breaking any laws.

But Anne, who had lost her man and wasn't allowed to

grieve for him—since Christoph was alive and well, after all, and because he would *always be there* for her and Leon—Anne, who was now supposed to fall out of love, who felt widowed, wounded, and messed with, could be prosecuted if she were to knock out one of Carola's teeth or vandalize the white Fiat. And even worse than that: she'd make a fool of herself.

People didn't get violent when one of the civilized, even-tempered relationships in Hamburg-Ottensen ended. They got a little hysterical, sought out a girlfriend, a sister, or their mother to take long, tearful walks with, and to moan to on the phone at night. They enrolled in a writing course in Liguria, or booked a spa weekend on the island of Sylt, drummed for a while on La Gomera, learned yoga in Andalucia, spent a couple of tense nights with an interim lover, got a haircut, bought a short dress. And if none of that helped, they sat down in a creaking basket chair in a therapist's office and attempted to mend their broken souls for eighty euros an hour.

Or they simply took off—fled to the countryside where the world was still safe and good—and lay sloshed against a damp brick wall, feeling sorry for themselves.

10

Venison Sausage

AT FIRST HE'D WOBBLED ABOUT quite a bit, but now he had the hang of it.

It was just as well that he'd bought a helmet and elbow pads! At these speeds, crashes and collisions couldn't be ruled out, and he really couldn't afford a serious injury, not as a free-lancer! Six weeks without any commissions and Eva could kiss her summer house good-bye.

His severance pay had disappeared faster than the excavator who had dug the drainpipe trenches around the house. The two young families who had bought the plots on either side of them had built their houses without cellars, and now he knew why.

But at least the Weisswerths had a dry cellar for their wine—and for the potatoes that he and Eva had dug out of the heavy marsh soil with their own hands. Their farmhouse had a new thatched roof and new wooden windows, and was paved with original Altland cobblestones that Burkhard had found through an online building material supplier for pickup. What a steal!

Klaus and Erich Jarck had laid the dump truck full of cobblestones at a snail's pace after the previous owner's concrete paving was finally out of the way. For four weeks they'd rattled in at seven o'clock on their moped. Neither of them had a driver's license and only Erich could drive the thing. Klaus had even less going on upstairs than his brother. But what the heck! That had been Burkhard Weisswerth's first big story for *Going Back to Country Life:* the twins Klaus and Erich Jarck, stonemasons, the last representatives of a dying guild. The photos alone! Klaus with his thick glasses, his mouth permanently half-open (and his pants too, for the most part), and red-haired Erich with a cigarette behind each ear and another in the corner of his mouth. And the two of them on their morning break, with Fanta and thick-sliced aspic without any bread, which they ate with their filthy fingers!

Florian had taken photos. "This is awesome!" The editorial team was thrilled with the *wonderfully quirky* guys and wanted more of the same. And Burkhard had been able to use Klaus and Erich again in his book *People from the Elbe—Gnarled Faces of a Landscape*. That's how it was supposed to work.

The bumpy cobblestone courtyard was worth every cent anyhow. It gave their house a raw and honest quality. There was no room here for the urbane, neurotic, overwrought high-heeled life.

WELCOME TO RUBBER BOOT WORLD, Eva had put up a sign on the garden gate for their housewarming party. They had bought twenty pairs in various sizes and colors and the women could exchange their pumps for rubber boots before stepping onto the cobblestones. It was a successful icebreaker. They had all laughed so much.

Burkhard had then called his second book *Welcome to Rubber Boot World*. It had sold well, but Burkhard Weisswerth was capable of more. He was an editor and wanted his own magazine, wanted high circulation figures and success, and for everything to be calm and relaxed at the same time, to be free of fluster and excitement, like a farmhand, laid-back, completely unruffled. That's what would piss them off most of all, those anxious smart-asses on the Baumwall media embankment with their nervous stomachs and slipped discs.

Those who'd tossed him out because they thought he could no longer hack it.

They couldn't have done him a bigger favor.

He'd come up with the title for his magazine a long time ago: *A Taste of Country Life,* a magazine for people who'd had enough, *downshifters* like himself who had realized that less was more, who wanted to jettison the whole ballast.

He had sold his Audi and it didn't bother him in the least. Now they just had the Jeep that Eva needed for driving to the home-improvement store or the garden center. He went practically everywhere by bike. It wasn't until they were living out here in the countryside that he understood what mattered in life.

A man never forgot the first potato that he took out of the earth with his own hands. That had been an initiation. He, Burkhard Weisswerth, had been let in on the big secret of sowing and reaping, growing and blossoming, blossoming and dying off, and, yes, it had humbled him, sensitized him to the wonderful, simple folks out here who were sustained by the work of their hands. Respect! He had the deepest respect for them. He wasn't afraid to make contact and they sensed that. That's why he got so much closer to them than the affected, clueless hacks from the women's and lifestyle magazines who'd recently been unleashed in droves on the poor country folk. They didn't understand anything whatsoever.

Here he sat, Burkhard Weisswerth, fifty-two years of age, just before eight o'clock on a Saturday morning, in the saddle of a custom-made recumbent bike, riding along the Elbe at a fair speed for a man his age.

He was thinking of his former colleagues in Hamburg who would just be struggling out of their beds around this time in order to jog once around the Alster before having to go to the weekly market with their stressed-out wives. *Not me, buddy.*

Burkhard shifted down two gears and rode up the narrow asphalt road that led over the dike to the main street. It was all downhill from here, and he had to watch that he didn't go too fast. He briefly held on to a streetlight to let an Elbe fruit truck pass, then crossed the main street and turned onto the village road.

He stopped in front of a large well-tended half-timbered house and examined its cobblestones. It looked like his courtyard, but this one had most definitely been here two hundred years longer, and the stonemasons back then had obviously been more talented than Klaus and Erich Jarck. His, in any case, hadn't been laid as evenly as this. Perhaps that's how it was with dying guilds—the last representatives were only half as good.

Still, he'd gotten it at a reasonable price. "No more than ten euros an hour!" Eva had said, "they'll just go off and spend it all on schnapps anyhow." And she'd been right. "We normally get fifteen," they'd replied, but they hadn't turned it down. The two of them didn't get many jobs anymore, and he'd given them *cash in hand,* which they didn't pay taxes on for sure!

Burkhard Weisswerth couldn't help smirking at the thought of Klaus Jarck filling out a tax form. He wouldn't even know which end of the pen to write with.

The next house had to be it. Burkhard ducked as he rode under the rotting ornamental gate, then got off and leaned his bike against the wall of the old house. The enormous, mossy thatched roof was shimmering greenish in the sun, and dark chunks of it were lying around the yard. It was obviously coming down in clumps. Oh boy! He knew what his small roof had cost, and this pile was easily three times the size. A rustic cathedral! A northern German hall-house from the eighteenth century at the latest. Burkhard took a few steps into the front yard to get a better look at the facade. Nine windows, decorative plaster infill, and the carved crescent suns up top! You could no longer make out the long inscription on the large crossbeams. Was it Latin?

He turned around and surveyed the overgrown front yard. It must have at one time been a classic boxwood garden. You could still see the remains of the old hedges under the brush.

In lousy shape, but it could be rectified.

He couldn't let Eva see anything like this or she'd hire an architect right away and run to the bank. But this one was a tad too big. Anyone with a house like this on their hands would have to win the lottery jackpot. Or run a magazine-publishing house that was doing extremely well. You never could tell!

So this was where Dr. Vera Eckhoff, dentist and honorary chairwoman of the county hunting club, lived. Up till now, Burkhard had only ever seen her galloping along the bank of the Elbe. "I wouldn't get into an argument with her," Dirk zum Felde had warned him, "she's a heckuva good shot." Burkhard had just given her a call recently.

Vera Eckhoff seemed to be a true original. He had *chewed the fat* with her for a bit and was now being allowed to watch her make her venison sausage.

Venison sausage! No one will believe me when I tell them! The first time around, it would be just him without the camera—that's what he always did. He couldn't come right out with it. You had to let country folks thaw a little, it took a bit of time. But if you had a knack for it, they'd come to trust you sooner or later and eat out of your hand. It always worked for him anyhow. He was on good terms with these people.

Initial contact without the camera, that was rule number one.

And anyhow, Florian was still ticked off about the incident with the tractor the previous week. Burkhard had had to work hard to talk him out of reporting Dirk zum Felde for bodily harm. It had cost him two crates of Bordeaux, which ought to be plenty of compensation for a bruised butt.

"Howdy!" Burkhard walked through the large front door with a spring in his step and made his way toward the noise. He could hear voices and a grinding, crunching sound clearly coming from the kitchen. Knocking on the open door, he saw Vera Eckhoff standing at the table in a white dentist's coat. It looked like someone had just blown themselves up next to her; her coat was splattered with dark blood everywhere, all over her stomach, sleeves, and collar—even her face was speckled red.

"Hey, good morning, I'd forgotten all about you! But you haven't missed anything yet, we're just getting started." Vera Eckhoff pointed to a large older man in a rubber apron who had his shirtsleeves rolled up. He was standing next to her, turning a crank. "My neighbor, Heinrich Luehrs." There was a grating and a creaking sound.

"That's the guy from Hamburg who bought Mimi's little house."

"I see," said Heinrich Luehrs, nodding once and continuing with his cranking.

Beside him sat a small boy whose mouth was covered in chocolate. He was chewing M&M's and watching in fascination as one piece of meat after another disappeared into the grinder and emerged from the other end as red worms, which curled up into a large washtub.

Heinrich Luehrs couldn't kill animals. He didn't even slaughter his own rabbits—when he was a boy, his father had had to do it—but he was an ace with the meat grinder.

Burkhard Weisswerth leaned against the wall, with his hands in the pockets of his corduroys. He tried not to look straight at the grinder, to stare off slightly to the side, but it was all still too much for him. The horrendous crunching, the smell of raw meat and fat.

It reminded him of that awful scene in *Fargo* where the crazy kidnapper with the dyed blond hair stuffed his victim into the wood chipper. But this was awesome. Burkhard thought of the photos that Florian would take of this massacre. He couldn't recall having ever seen anything like it in a magazine photo spread. It was amazing! He wanted the photos raw and totally naturalistic. Definitely not black and white! This wasn't art, it was nature! This is country life, folks, it's completely different from buying a few slices of venison salami at the weekly market!

Vera Eckhoff was using an old kitchen scale to weigh out salt and spices. Burkhard typed the ingredients into his iPhone. Pepper, juniper berries, marjoram.

Heinrich Luehrs began stuffing large chunks of lard into the grinder, and pale worms oozed out of the holes into the plastic tub. When he was finished with the lard, Vera dumped the spices in, picked up a mixer, and began stirring everything into a shiny pink fatty mass.

Burkhard cleared his throat, but the sound was drowned out by the noise from the appliance. A couple of small beads of sweat appeared on his forehead.

Vera turned off the mixer and placed it next to the tub. The pale mass of sausage filling dropped off the dough hooks.

She released the hooks from the mixer, gave one to Heinrich Luehrs, and held on to the other one herself. With their index fingers, they then wiped the mixture from the stirrers and tasted it. "A bit more salt," said Heinrich, tipping a tablespoon of salt into the tub. "Do you want to stir it around?" he asked, pressing a wooden spoon into the boy's hand.

The child stirred with a serious look on his face as his hand sank into the smacking mass of sausage meat. They were exactly the same color. Vera Eckhoff disappeared into the pantry to fetch a bunch of transparent tubes that looked like overly long condoms. Heinrich Luehrs meanwhile had stuffed the sausage filling into some sort of silicone syringe and was now pumping it slowly into the intestines.

Burkhard Weisswerth left the kitchen without saying a word.

"What's with him?" asked Heinrich Luehrs as he lay the sausage stuffer aside for a bit.

"Bad circulation or a vegetarian," muttered Vera with a shrug.

11

Order

HEINRICH LUEHRS HAD LONG AGO stopped wondering about Vera Eckhoff, so he wasn't particularly surprised to see that she now had her niece—with child and rabbit—living with her. "A day laborer of sorts" was how Vera explained the arrangement to him. Free food and accommodation, four hundred euros per month, and free travel in her old Benz. And in return she's putting my house in order.

That had floored him. The word *order* out of Vera's mouth without a hint of irony. *Order* was precisely what Vera's farm had lacked since Ida Eckhoff had hanged herself and her East

Prussian daughter-in-law had walked out on Karl and the child. And *order* was the word Vera had used to tease him ever since they'd been grown-ups. "Hey, Hinni, have you got everything in order?"

When he'd pruned his bushes and trees, trimmed the hedge, pulled the weeds, mowed the lawn, painted the fence, swept the yard, and raked out the molehills, when his flower beds were perfectly straight, the young cherry trees were cut back, and the old ones felled, chopped up, and piled up as firewood, whenever Heinrich Luehrs did the things that anyone who wanted to remain master of his house and farm had to do to stop the place from getting run-down or overgrown, then Vera Eckhoff would sit on her rickety bench with a cigarette, or stand under the barren cherry tree that spoiled her front yard with a mug of coffee in her hand, knee-high in a tangle of weeds, wave over to him and laugh: "Hey, Hinni, have you got everything in order?"

And Heinrich Luehrs had never understood what was so funny about someone's keeping his world in order.

Beyond his fence, the world did whatever it wanted to. Vera's garden was the end of all order, the opposite of *order,* chaos and dilapidation. Vera's place was an example of what happened when you let nature take its course.

And at the end of his cherry orchard, on the other side of

the ditch, there was no longer much order either, because Peter Niebuhr had gone organic and was letting his trees go to seed. He was selling his measly cherries to an organic wholesaler in Hamburg before they'd completely ripened. Heinrich Luehrs would've been ashamed even to hawk those things to tourists at the side of the road. But the organic mob in Hamburg was snapping up Peter Niebuhr's cherries, and he was pocketing a third more than before.

The portion of the world that was still in order seemed to be shrinking by the day.

Three sons but no successor. Heinrich had one daughter-in-law from Japan and one from the city, both nice women as far as he could tell, but they were so alien to him that they might as well have been from Mars.

He had visited Heini and Sakura in their restaurant in Berlin once. Heini, his eldest, had stood at a bare table in a tall white chef's hat, making rice rolls with raw fish, which he then placed on some kind of conveyor belt from which his customers took what they wanted.

Sakura had shown Heinrich how to use chopsticks and what to do with the black sauce. He'd found the green stuff too hot, but the rest didn't taste bad at all.

Heini behind the counter with his long knife, with Elisabeth's blond hair, his joyful, good-natured boyish face. Now he spoke fluent Japanese. "It ain't all that different from Low German, Father," he'd said, and they had laughed.

He was Elisabeth's favorite, even though she'd never have admitted it, and when he'd stood in his kitchen cutting fish into small pieces, he hummed to himself. Now Heini was in Japan. They had a little girl and sent photos, but Heinrich Luehrs forgot time and again the name of the town they lived in.

Jochen dropped by every couple of weeks on a Saturday or Sunday, mostly with Steffi and the twins, but sometimes he came by himself, in old clothes, and they would work together in the barn and get the tractor and trailer ready for spring, or prepare the large nets for drawing over the cherry trees in the summer, just before the starlings arrived. Jochen always took a couple of days off for the apple harvest and drove the forklift when the large crates needed to be taken to cold storage. He would spend the night in his old room and drink a couple of beers in the kitchen with Heinrich. Then they'd make fried egg and ham sandwiches, share the paper, and watch the news together in the evening. Sometimes Jochen would nod off on the sofa before the weather forecast. He wasn't used to working in the fresh air anymore. In Hannover, he sat in his engineering office all day long and never saw the sun.

Steffi didn't like Jochen staying over at his father's place because she then had to deal with everything at home by herself, and she already had enough to do. Steffi was a pharmaceutical rep and earned a ton of money. Heinrich didn't dare ask, but he imagined that Jochen's salary wasn't keeping pace with hers.

He sometimes felt sorry for the boy. Jochen always seemed a bit worn-out, but nowhere near as bad as his wife. When the four of them came from Hannover to visit, Steffi didn't seem able to tolerate the cold. She seldom went out along the Elbe or into the orchards, although that wouldn't have been possible in her shoes anyhow.

Heinrich always took the boys for a ride on his tractor. He assumed they liked it, or Ben did at least, since he always wanted to sit on his lap and steer. Noah usually had a little electronic gadget with him, which beeped when he pushed it, but he'd join them outside so Steffi could take a photo of the three of them with her cell phone. Granddad would then get the picture in a metal frame for his birthday.

Georg was his youngest, his open wound. *Me neither, Father*.

He had just gotten his degree in agricultural science, and

Elisabeth had seen it coming. But she wasn't the type of wife who shared her thoughts with her husband, and he wasn't the kind of husband who listened much to his wife.

The old man decreed, the boy cowered, and at some point—when the boy gathered enough strength and anger—the tables would turn. That's how it worked. There was no other way.

Heinrich's father had often hit him, but he hardly lifted a hand to his own sons.

Georg had gotten a slap once for climbing a ladder half-drunk after partying all night and hacking away at one of his best cherry trees. Otherwise a couple of nudges at most, occasionally a little shove, if he was getting in his way, which rarely happened, since Georg worked really hard. Heinrich knew he had the makings of a good fruit farmer.

But father versus son wasn't a friendly sparring match, it was a battle. The old man obstinate, the boy full of rage, attacking and defending, round after round, fighting for new kinds of cherries and apples, fewer pesticides, larger cold storage houses, expensive machines, more seasonal workers. Heinrich heard himself yelling sentences that he remembered his father saying, and it sometimes made him cringe.

What you inherit from your father must first be earned before it's yours! His great-grandfather had had this quote from Goethe inscribed in the crossbeams of the gable. He hadn't inherited songs of praise from his father, so Heinrich didn't know how to sing them. But Georg seemed to expect one.

"Just one good word for once, Heinrich, is that so hard?" Elisabeth had shouted at him in a voice he didn't recognize when Georg had thrown the pruning shears at his feet without saying a word. But Heinrich had seen that he was crying, sobbing like a child.

Heinrich was almost ashamed of this son who couldn't wrestle him down, or didn't want to, who didn't understand that he, the old man, wished to be defeated by him. Not by old age, or aching legs and a stiff back, but by a strong son who was obliged to throw him out of the ring in a rage.

Me neither, Father.

If Elisabeth hadn't died a couple of days after that, then Heinrich might have been able to sort things out with Georg. But after her death he couldn't see anything, even if it was right in front of him; he drifted around blindly in a thick fog and couldn't find his way back to his sons.

Georg had married Frauke, the only daughter of Klaus and Beke Matthes, who lived only two villages away. Heinrich always passed their farm when he went to get fertilizer or sprays from the cooperative. They'd pulled down the old thatched roof, and it was about time, but they obviously hadn't had enough money for new thatch, as the roof was now covered in red tiles and the entire south side had large solar panels on it. Not a pleasant sight, but it was probably worth it.

At least Heinrich no longer needed to stare stubbornly at the road whenever he drove by. For a couple of years now he was allowed to drop in and have a cup of coffee in the kitchen with Frauke or drink a beer with Georg in the sorting shed if the timing was right. The two girls even came to visit him, cycled over on their small shiny bikes to see their grandfather. Frauke brought them over and then came back to get them again.

But Georg didn't come. He steered clear of his parents' house, seemed to avoid it like a vampire avoids a cross. It was only when Heinrich turned seventy that they all came, even Heini and his family from Japan.

When the others had gone to bed, the three brothers sat in the yard for a while, the sleeves of their white shirts rolled up, shoulder to shoulder on the bench, drinking beer, laughing, being boys again. Heinrich looked out the kitchen window without turning on the lights, saw what his sons were like when their father wasn't there, laid-back and easygoing. Then suddenly Georg jumped up, marched across the lawn like a general, and pointed with jerky movements at the hedge, the rose bed, and the shrubs. "That's all got to be put in order," he roared, "all neat and tidy!" and his brothers cracked up. Jochen even fell off the bench and rolled around on the lawn, screaming with laughter.

Georg would never come again, by the looks of it. Klaus and Beke Matthes had signed their farm over to Frauke a couple of weeks before and were now trekking through South America in a motor home.

Heinrich Luehrs remained behind his white fence, his back straight as a ramrod, so that the trees and bushes could take a leaf from his book.

12

Hunting Accident

THE GUY FROM HAMBURG WITH the bike helmet didn't come back until Vera was wiping down the kitchen. Heinrich showed him the smokehouse, then left him standing in the hallway and headed off.

This visitor didn't seem to be in any hurry. He looked around for a bit. Vera was just taking off her bloodstained work coat when she heard him groan loudly out in the hall. It was a sound of delight.

Burkhard Weisswerth had discovered the old hope chest that stood against the wall next to the kitchen door. He was now kneeling in front of its carved-oak front, running his fingers over the inlay—birds, flowering vines, the finest Baroque craftsmanship. "Holy mackerel!" he said as he inspected the forged metal fittings and the turned feet. He took a couple of photos with his iPhone before shifting his attention to the sideboard containing Ida Eckhoff's crystal glasses. Then he looked down at the terrazzo floor, which was cracked in a couple of places, but what an expanse! Burkhard Weisswerth knew what a floor like that was worth. Eva had been dreaming of one like it for some time, but the cost today was prohibitive. They'd looked into it.

Vera watched the man in her hallway snapping away like a tourist. That was enough!

She went up to him briskly, said "Right!" stretched out her arm and shook his hand, just once, decisively and vigorously. That's what she did in her practice with patients who sat around for ages after their treatment was over and went on and on about their children and grandchildren. It always worked.

Burkhard Weisswerth tucked his cell phone away and thanked her for the *extremely thrilling* morning. He lifted his bike helmet from her hope chest and left his business card on it.

Vera had wanted to ask what kind of a magazine published articles about venison sausage, but he had already rolled off on his bike. Apparently they now cycled on their backs in Hamburg.

* * *

Anne's boy had suddenly appeared in the kitchen shortly before seven that morning, and stepped straight into the blood. "A big boy like you shouldn't cry," Heinrich had said, pulling a cough drop out of a tin for him. "You can sit down and watch. But no more whining!"

Leon didn't utter a sound. He wiped the snot from his face with the sleeve of his pajamas and climbed onto the kitchen bench. Vera fetched the bag of M&M's that had been in her drawer since New Year's Eve. Kids had stopped coming to her door at the New Year to sing songs; not even the neighbor boys for the last few years. Maybe they were afraid of her, the old witch in her crooked house.

As she was putting the candy down in front of Leon, he tugged gently at her sleeve, glanced quickly over at Heinrich, who was turning the crank of the meat grinder, and whispered, "What are you guys doing?"

A large knife was lying in front of him on the cutting board, and beside it were bowls of raw meat and lard. He had just been standing barefoot in a puddle of deer blood and had seen Heinrich Luehrs stuff something bloody into the meat grinder. Perhaps it wasn't surprising that the boy was a little upset.

"Well," said Vera, "we're making sausage. We use meat and

lard for that, and it all has to be ground up, which is why we're turning it through this thing, which is called a meat grinder. That's Heinrich, he lives next door, he won't bite. Unless you annoy him, of course."

"That's when I make sausages out of children!" Heinrich said as he resumed his cranking. Vera wasn't sure how Heinrich Luehrs's humor went down with young children. Leon didn't laugh but he stayed seated on the bench, and later on he helped with the stirring. "Clever boy," said Heinrich, patting him on the shoulder on his way out.

Still no sign of life from Anne. The morning after you got drunk on fruit brandy was always awful, Vera knew, so she let her sleep. She put the coffee on and made breakfast while Leon drew on her shopping pad. "It's a tractor." He obviously hadn't seen a lot of farm machinery before now. His tractor was emitting clouds of smoke and looked like a steam engine.

Since Vera didn't have any hazelnut spread, he was eating bread with honey. "Your mother will have to hose you down later," Vera said. The kid was sticky from head to toe.

They went to the horse barn and fetched hay for his rabbit, but Willy didn't want the stuff that Leon shoved into his cage. In Hamburg there had been carrots and Happy Bunny nuggets.

Willy set his ears back anxiously and turned away. He still had to process all this change.

"Try it, Willy, it's delicious," Leon said, chewing a piece of hay to prove it. But that didn't help either. The rabbit retreated into a corner of his cage and surrendered to culture shock.

Vera suddenly felt that her legs were about to give way. She was dead tired from spending the night in the kitchen, from the sudden commotion in her house, and to top it all off, the guy in the bike helmet that morning. Willy wasn't the only one who needed to get used to all the changes.

A quick peek into Ida Eckhoff's living room revealed that Anne was still out of it. She was lying diagonally across the sofa bed, with her legs tangled up in the duvet cover.

Vera opened the window partway. Since there was no movement on the bed, she went back to the kitchen.

Leon had dressed himself. The straps of his dungarees were twisted and he'd forgotten his socks. He came over with several of his board books and stretched his arms out toward Vera: "Lap."

She pushed back her chair and lifted him up. He weighed no more than a fawn.

Leon inconspicuously pulled his pacifier out of his pocket and shoved it in his mouth. Then he leaned back with his head on her shoulder, and she felt his soft skin against her cheek, and his hair as well. He felt like a chick to her.

The letters swam briefly before her eyes, so she pressed her fingers to her eyelids for a moment, then started to read. "It had already been raining for days. . . ."

How long had it been since she had touched something that didn't have fur?

Her hands knew horsehair and dog fur, dead hares and deer, the velvety coat of the chewed-up moles that Heinrich's tomcat would sometimes bring her. They had known Karl's bony shoulders under his flannel shirts, and the stubble on his cheeks that she sometimes touched when he lay sleeping on the bench. But her hands were almost afraid of this warm little boy.

Vera Eckhoff only had experience with children who were tense with fear, lying back in her dentist's chair, their eyes large and mouths open wide, and for the most part she hurt them.

She could have touched their faces now and again, let her hand pass briefly over their cheeks, before or even after their treatments. And you're only just realizing that now, she said to herself.

Children didn't come to her practice anymore. Their parents now drove them to Stade, to a young dentist couple who specialized in young patients, whatever that meant.

There were probably toys in the waiting room, and the dentists most likely wore T-shirts.

Vera spent only two days a week in her practice nowadays. Her patients came simply out of habit, or because they didn't have a car to drive to Stade. Now and then a fruit farmer would bring her a Kurdish farmhand with bad tooth decay or an infected molar. Word had gotten around that Dr. Eckhoff didn't ask about health insurance or official documents.

Vera carried on reading to Leon. It was a story about a bear, a pelican, and a penguin. The story didn't make any sense, but Leon was mesmerized. He had pulled his knees in to his chest, and Vera placed her hand on his bare foot, feeling his round toes beneath her thumb; it took everything she had not to press the child against her and bury her face in his soft hair.

You're a silly old bat, Vera Eckhoff! But she placed her cheek against his and continued reading the crap about the animals that were searching for the sun.

Still, it was better than the stories she'd had to read to Karl in his final year, when he had to be with her at all times.

Karl, who had never seen the Alps, fell in love with the idyllic world of alpine romance novels after coming across a cheap paperback that a female patient had left behind on a chair in Vera's waiting room.

After that, Vera had bought him a new one at the Edeka store every week when she did her grocery shopping.

The old lady dentist with the alpine doctor novels in her shopping cart. People had probably found that highly amusing, but who was surprised anymore where Vera Eckhoff was concerned?

At that point, Karl already couldn't sit up very well. At night, he kept slipping off the kitchen bench, and his back couldn't take the living room armchair or sofa for very long. So he had to go to bed. Too tired to read and too anxious to sleep, he would just lie there while Vera read him the stories about the doctor from Tyrol.

Dr. Martin Burger with his brown eyes and his steely physique from mountain climbing became Karl Eckhoff's family physician. The doctor had to rescue him every night.

Vera mostly read from midnight until about one in the morning, when Karl finally drifted off into a dreamless sleep. But Dr. Burger's remedy often didn't last until morning, and Vera would hear Karl screaming again.

First like a child, then like an animal.

She'd wake him, sit down on the edge of the bed, and hold him until he calmed down. But sometimes only the medicine helped. PsychoPax, ten hours of inner peace. But he would pay for it the next morning. He'd be numb from the Valium and hungover into the afternoon, and often the next night would be bad again.

What Karl dreamed at night couldn't be put into words. Vera no longer asked him, and she didn't tell him that he called out for his mother in his sleep.

"Help me, Mother," he'd cry.

But Ida couldn't help her boy anymore, so Vera helped him instead.

She'd thought for a long time about how she should do it. Some nights she put Dr. Martin Burger aside quietly once Karl's eyes were closed and took Ida's hand-embroidered sofa cushion in both hands, since it was big and heavy enough for an old man. But then she would lower it because Karl, who dreamed he bled to death in his wet sheets night after night, didn't deserve to die in the bed he detested so much.

Karl Eckhoff ought to fall like a brave soldier, taken cleanly by an unexpected bullet, between the trenches of an apple field, Vera thought, a hero's death. He had earned medals for his bravery, held out on the battlefield day after day, and in all those nights, he hadn't climbed into the hayloft and jumped from a stool. He hadn't abandoned Vera.

It seemed to her that she had practiced for this shot her entire life, each time they'd stalked together through the fruit fields at first light on an autumn or winter morning. Karl, who hadn't fired a shot in ages, still loved the hunt, the absence of human activity, the world as seen through binoculars, the hours spent up in the deer stand, Vera's rough coffee out of the thermos. He couldn't smoke before she fired, of course, because the animals would smell the smoke.

When she slowly and quietly raised her shotgun, aimed at a hare or a deer, squinched her left eye shut, and placed her index finger on the trigger, Karl would stick his fingers in his ears and look down at his feet.

Vera shot only when she was absolutely certain. She almost always hit her target. Then Karl would stand against a tree and smoke while she went and got the car. He still helped with the carrying, so they'd both take hold of the dead animal and place it in Vera's trunk. But after that he'd walk back alone, on foot, a hunter without a gun.

It could be as easy as this: Old Karl Eckhoff shot while hunting, an accident. These things happened.

She watched him limp with his stiff leg through the dull

light of a November morning, saw him clearly and distinctly through her scope, followed him silently through the wet grass. There were hardly any leaves left on the apple trees and Vera could hear the desolate, tuneless song of the whooper swans flying toward the Elbe. Karl stopped and looked up at the birds. He was standing completely still, unsuspecting. Vera placed her finger on the trigger.

And then she couldn't do it and was ashamed of her cowardice.

That winter they hardly slept.

It got better in the spring.

In the summer it was no longer bearable.

When the sun shone, Karl would doze on the swing and sometimes would whistle to himself, but at any moment he might stand up with a start and salute an invisible superior.

And he now screamed during the day too. A couple of times, Heinrich Luehrs had come running over from his garden, even though he recognized the screaming. He heard it whenever they left Karl's window open on a summer night. Heinrich also saw the duvet cover on the clothesline every day—*Just don't look*—and he knew what went on over at the Eckhoffs' during the night.

And what he couldn't possibly know, Vera would tell him when he went to her for his six-month checkup.

When Heinrich Luehrs was lying back in her chair, with two cotton rolls stuffed in his cheek, when her assistant was gone and the waiting room was empty, when Heinrich couldn't speak but could still hear, Vera told him all the things that she otherwise kept to herself.

With his mouth wide open, Heinrich Luehrs heard about Vera's *near hunting accident*, of Karl's hero's death and her cowardice. He just winced slightly when she told him, but once the cotton was out and he'd rinsed his mouth, he quickly left the office. Sometimes she freaked him out.

One day in July, when the cherries were still hanging in the trees, Heinrich and Vera, with Karl in between them, were sitting on Ida's old wedding bench, and Karl wasn't screaming anymore because Vera had given him ten drops of PsychoPax. He was leaning against his neighbor's shoulder, fast asleep.

Karl Eckhoff was a case for the loony bin. He had been for a long time. This was clear to Heinrich, but Vera would hear none of it. And crazy people often outlived everyone.

Karl had to be past ninety by now, and he'd looked like a corpse for a long time already.

Vera pulled him off Heinrich's shoulder and over onto her own without waking him. She put Karl's head in her lap, and since she never cried otherwise, Heinrich didn't notice at first. She wasn't making any sound.

Heinrich Luehrs didn't dare ask straight out. He sat for a while with her in silence on this rotten bench before finally working up the courage to ask very softly, so that Karl couldn't hear:

"Can't you give him something for it, Vera?"

She didn't respond and Heinrich simply got up and left. But a few days later, Dr. Vera Eckhoff drove to her old vet and asked for 100 ml of Narcoren, the amount needed to put a medium-sized Trakehner mare to sleep. "It's not any fun," the vet said, pressing the brown bottle into her hand. Then he packed a large syringe and a couple of needles into a plastic bag and scrutinized her face. "Give me a call if you want me to do it for you." She shook her head.

The following Sunday—a warm day without wind—Karl was sitting under the linden, his white smoke rings wafting up to its crown. He followed them with his eyes until they disappeared and then made new ones. Vera watched him from the kitchen window, with his gray hair all matted, and his back as narrow as a child's, only more stooped. She went outside and sat down beside him; it seemed to her that she had spent her entire life like this, sitting on this white bench with Karl smoking beside her.

"How small you were, Vera," he mumbled suddenly. Then he began whistling softly.

She looked at his profile for a while. His cheeks were so sunken and his eyes were all red with fatigue.

"Karl," she said, "shall I give you something so you can sleep?"

He repositioned his leg, the stiff one. Then he stared at the grass, which was teeming with ants, and reached for his cigarettes.

"You don't mean the drops, do you?" he said.

She shook her head.

In the night, the alpine doctor had to be fetched again, and they needed the medicine later on as well. Karl lay in his bed, small and fluttering like a bird, and his voice was so weak that Vera didn't hear him at first.

When she realized what he was saying, she helped him get dressed, took him by the arm, and they walked as slowly as a bride and groom through the hallway and out into the garden.

Once Karl was seated on the bench, she draped a blanket around his shoulders and gave him his cigarettes. Then she went back into the house and returned with a glass of apple juice from Heinrich Luehrs in one hand and a smaller glass in the other. Karl Eckhoff was a slip of a man. He wouldn't need all that much.

It was very dark with just a sliver of moon overhead. On Elbe island, young seagulls were cheeping, sleepless, restless, hungry all the time. The leaves of the white poplars rushed in the night's wind as if asking for peace and quiet. "Shhhh."

Karl took the glass out of her hand. Vera cupped her hand under his elbows, held his arm very gently, because he was shaking so much, and then he chugged the stuff like he would schnapps, shuddered, and said, "Like a club over the head." Vera quickly slipped him the apple juice.

She couldn't help thinking of Ida in her black costume hanging from the ceiling beam. She took Karl's hand and held it tight. He didn't let go of her until he slumped over to the side. Vera remained seated next to him on Ida's wedding bench until she heard the blackbirds' morning song.

The last Eckhoff, a refugee. She didn't make a sound.

Heinrich then had to help her carry Karl back to his bed and he didn't ask any questions. Old Eckhoff had passed away peacefully, the rest was nobody's business. They sat in the kitchen until Dr. Schuett had completed the death certificate, and Heinrich stayed until Otto Suhr arrived with the hearse.

Vera did the right thing for once. Karl Eckhoff got a grave, *as was fitting*. Otto Suhr knew the routine. An obituary and cards, a condolence book, and a coffee table laden with butter cake. The neighbors all came, as did a couple of Vera's old patients, and two classmates of Karl's, the only ones still living, came from the village as well.

Pastor Herwig kept it short. They sang *O take my hand, dear Father,* and placed Karl Eckhoff next to his parents.

Their buddies from the hunting club stood at the graveside in their green jackets, sweating in the July heat, and sounded the last death-halloo, out of tune as always, but Vera was grateful nonetheless.

In the church, for funerals, Otto Suhr always reserved the front three pews for family members, but the first row sufficed for Karl Eckhoff.

Heinrich Luehrs, who was sitting farther back, got up after the organ started playing and sat in the front row next to Vera, even though he didn't belong there. He imagined that there was now some whispering going on behind him.

But a person alone in the family pew wasn't a pretty sight to behold.

He didn't know that Vera's sister was in the church.

Vera herself discovered Marlene only at the graveside. Then she saw Marlene's daughter too, and started to cry. Up until then she'd held up well. Heinrich Luehrs had never been a hero at funerals. The receptions afterward were the worst. All that jabbering. Now that Vera's sister had linked arms with her and she was no longer alone, he didn't feel like he had to go.

After the funeral, Marlene and Anne stayed with Vera, who looked like a ghost. They sent her to bed, then opened all the windows, cleaned the filthy windowpanes, and scrubbed down all the floors and wall tiles. They dusted the furniture, took Karl Eckhoff's clothes to the dump, and threw out all the old food in the fridge.

Anne drove back to Hamburg the following day, but Marlene stayed and made soups, poured them into plastic containers, and put them in the freezer. She woke Vera up only to eat, kept the bedroom door ajar, watched over her like a sister for three days and nights until Vera was back on her feet and as snappy as a guard dog.

Marlene's soups came with a price, Vera knew, and she didn't want to pay it.

She didn't want to talk about *Us* with her half sister, didn't want to see her walk through Ida Eckhoff's hallway or let her drink from the old gold-rimmed cups.

She didn't want to show her the small black album that contained the photographs that Marlene lacked: Hildegard von Kamcke in her bright dresses and with her beautiful horses. Hildegard Eckhoff on stilts beneath the fruit trees.

Vera didn't want to share these pictures with Marlene.

She'd shaken her hand and continued to give her cherries on those July Sundays when Marlene would turn up with empty buckets, wanting to pick some fruit. Vera had also set up ladders and put coffee and apple juice out on the table in the yard.

She hadn't asked her into the house, but Marlene had gone in regardless, as though it were also her home, as though she and Vera had more in common than their thin, straight noses and their brown eyes.

Vera had buried Karl and then sat by herself on the family bench just eight months ago.

Now she was sitting here with Marlene's grandchild on her lap and Marlene's daughter was sleeping in Ida Eckhoff's parlor.

She didn't know who was calling the shots in her life at the moment.

13

Elbe Frogs

LEON'S SNOWSUIT WAS FILTHY. HIS fingernails, too. Anne didn't even look down at the boots. She knew what they must be like.

The Elbe Frogs looked different. In the parking lot of their day care center, shortly before nine o'clock, they hopped out of their large family cars into their mothers' arms. In the backseats, their little brothers and sisters occupied Maxi-Cosi car seats—Elbe tadpoles, Frogs in the making. The minivans and station wagons in which the three- to six-year-old Elbe Frogs were punctually delivered to the morning circle at the village day care center looked like rolling ads for the multichild family.

Their rear windows bore blue and pink stickers: LASSE & LENA ON BOARD or VIVIENNE & BEN & PAUL ON TOUR—like vehicle inspection stickers certifying good family planning.

Anne let Leon climb out of his stroller and took his hand. He looked serious and pale as they made their way to the entrance through the hustle and bustle. The Elbe Frogs' jackets and snow pants were vibrant and their hats, scarves, and gloves were all color coordinated. The girls' long hair fell over their shoulders in pretty braids, and when they took off their hats you could see that their barrettes matched too.

Anne thought back to Leon's day care center in Hamburg and to the rat's-nest hairstyles sported by the little girls there. If they didn't feel like letting their parents brush out their tousles in the morning, they would arrive at day care with their hair unbrushed. And in Ottensen, the children wore weird clothes—skirts and pants on top of one another, spotted, striped, checked, whatever, unmatched socks and gloves, any old scarves with any old hats thrown any old way onto their heads and around their necks—often the result of an *autonomous decision by the child* in front of the wardrobe, which was respected, of course, even if the child looked like he or she had been dressed in clothes donated after a natural disaster. *Hey, if you think that looks good, you wear it, sweetie.*

Their children's slightly waiflike hobo-look, which could

also be achieved with extremely expensive clothing, was an expression of the Hamburg-Ottensen professionals' parenting style. Nonconformist and creative, wild and insubordinate, that's how they liked their sons and daughters. A solid crust of mud on their rubber boots and fingernails completed the look. The last thing they wanted was clean-cut, obedient children.

Here, Leon was placed in the Bumblebee group. During their interview, the head of the day care center had asked him what his favorite animal was, and now Leon had a picture of a bunny above his cubbyhole—and his name spelled out in blue wooden letters.

Sigrid Pape had set some time aside for the new child and mother. Anne could see her registering key facts: moved here from Hamburg, only child, single mother (with a strange bag made of upcycled truck tarp), Dr. Eckhoff's niece. Music teacher/carpenter, now that was some combination. In response to Anne's questions and answers, she merely raised her right eyebrow a couple of times. Sigrid Pape sat smiling opposite the two new arrivals. Her blond hair was short and *chic,* she had *jazzed up* her beige cardigan with a hand-painted silk scarf, and her eyes behind those rimless glasses were subtly made up. Sigrid Pape had led the Elbe Frogs for over twenty years. She'd seen a lot and had no problem with this slightly mousy duo from Hamburg.

The boy clearly didn't get much fresh air, but that would now change. Otherwise an unremarkable child, cute, somewhat unkempt. She made a shorthand notation in Leon's file just to be on the safe side. *RH4WK*. Her teachers all knew the code and would record his state of hygiene every four weeks. Perhaps the move had simply been too much for the mother; that sort of thing happened and mostly resolved itself.

If not, Sigrid Pape would schedule a little parents' meeting. That usually worked wonders.

Now she just had to discuss the nonsense about the meals. "Frau Hove, you asked if there was a vegetarian lunch option for the children."

That was all she needed! Sigrid Pape and her colleagues already had enough on their plates with all the peanut, tomato, dairy, and gluten allergies that were now all too common among the children in the countryside too. And on top of that there were two little ones with diabetes and, as usual in day care, lots of I-don't-like-this-I-don't-like-that. They managed to feed the Elbe Frogs fish once a week, but they weren't about to start with spelt meatballs and unripe spelt grain mush as well.

Sigrid Pape had as little faith in a vegetarian diet as she had in this chummy parenting style that was becoming increasingly common of late.

Feeding them tofu sausages and letting the children call

them by their first names. They couldn't be serious! As a mother or father you had to keep it together now and again. That's how Sigrid saw it anyway.

"We could have Leon eat only the side dishes. If that's what you'd like."

Anne thought back to the grueling and emotional lacto-ovo-wholefood-kosher-halal-vegan debates in Leon's Hamburg day care and tried to imagine those mothers studying the Elbe Frogs' meal plan, their faces upon seeing *bratwurst, goulash,* or *meat loaf.*

"No problem, that's fine," she said.

Leon took off his boots and put them in his cubbyhole, and they hung his snowsuit up on his hook. The cubbyhole to the right of Leon's had a hammerhead shark sticker on it. Green overalls were hanging on the hook, and above them in blue wooden letters was the name *Theis.*

Anne looked into the Bumblebees' room and saw the little exterminator playing on the mat. He was building a complex intersection out of Legos with two other boys. Theis zum Felde looked as though he had ripped out two or three acres of fruit trees before heading off to day care. His face was rosy, his white-blond hair was cropped very short, and he was wearing a checked shirt with the sleeves pushed up. "Look, Leon, that's the boy who came by our place on his tractor. You know him already."

Leon didn't look very happy. Perhaps he was thinking about the squashed moth. He looked at the builders on the mat, then at his mother. "Anne, stay with me."

"Sure, I'll come in with you for a bit."

The teacher, Wiebke Quast, watched with irritation as Anne removed her shoes, entered the room, and sat on the floor with Leon. Mothers on the play mat—it just kept getting better and better.

Her colleague Elke arrived with the breakfast dishes, saw Anne, then looked at Wiebke and raised her shoulders inquiringly. Wiebke Quast, the leader of the Bumblebee group, rolled her eyes momentarily, then went over to Anne and tried to handle the situation with humor.

"Oh, good morning, I didn't know we had a new colleague!" She shook Anne's hand firmly.

Anne laughed, got up, introduced herself—then sat back down. Leon climbed into her lap, leaned his head against her chest, stuck his index finger in his mouth, and from this safe distance, watched the three boys playing pileup at their

Lego-junction. As their Matchbox cars smashed into each other, the collisions were accompanied by dramatic crashing sounds.

The woman on the play mat was still showing no signs of leaving. It was getting a bit weird. Wiebke Quast made her presence known in the center of the room by clearing her throat, clapping her hands once, and calling out: "Good morning, Bumblebees, it's time for us to have breakfast, so we must ALL say good-bye to our mommies!"

There, it finally seemed to be sinking in. Anne looked up and it slowly dawned on her that the Elbe Frogs' settling-in routine was somewhat different from the one in Leon's day care in Hamburg, where the children parted from their parents very slowly. It was ten whole days before Leon spent an entire morning there without either Anne or Christoph, because he'd been only two at the time, not four.

Anne tried to ease Leon gently off her lap.

But he turned around right away and clung to her. "Leon, I've got to go now. This isn't a day care for mommies, it's a day care for kids, right?"

When she stood up, Leon hugged her right leg tightly and let himself be dragged across the room like a ball and chain. "DON'T GO AWAY!"

Anne dragged her son behind her as far as the door. Then

Wiebke Quast came over, unclasped her new Bumblebee from his mother's leg with the expert touch of a day care teacher, and lifted him up.

"So, Leon, you come with me, and, Mommy, you LEAVE REALLY FAST right now, then we can get started STRAIGHT-AWAY with our morning circle. The Bumblebees can't wait to meet you, Leon. Say bye-bye, Mommy! Bye-bye, Mommy!" She shut the door quickly.

Anne stood in the hallway in her stocking feet among all the snowsuits and wet boots. A janitor was wiping up the muddy puddles on the floor, but Anne was already standing in one of them. She hovered near the door with soaking wet feet and heard Leon shouting.

"ANNE, COME BACK! ANNE!! ANNE!!!"

From her office, Sigrid Pape could also hear the new kid from Hamburg acting up a bit. Oh well, it's always difficult at first, she said to herself, as the boy's mother, slim as a whip, walked past her window with her weird messenger bag. Her clothes were really dark, even her hat was black, and her pants were way too wide. Is that how women in Hamburg were dressing these days?

Frau Hove wouldn't have an easy time settling in here. People who let their children call them by their first names never had it easy. Sigrid Pape could only advise against that.

* * *

At first Anne didn't know what to do with herself. She resisted the urge to look for the window of the Bumblebees' room but checked again to make sure that her cell phone was on.

"If there are any problems, we'll get in touch," Wiebke Quast had said. "You don't need to worry."

But what constituted a problem in Wiebke Quast's world? A four-year-old clinging to his mother's leg and screaming obviously wasn't one.

The trees in people's front yards were still bare. But in the tidy flower beds around the old thatched-roof houses in the center of the village, the first crocuses were blooming, and Anne wished she had a dress in those same colors—yellow and white and violet—colors emblematic of this spring, which was going to be different from previous ones.

She would buy Leon a few gardening tools: a spade, some flower seeds, and a watering can; then he could show little Theis in his green overalls what was what. And sooner or later he'd also need a tractor to pedal around. She hadn't seen any balance bikes around here yet.

The new development in which the day care center was located ended in a farm track, so Anne continued walking along the narrow gravelly path.

On either side of her there were now only fruit trees, end-less, bare rows, apple or cherry perhaps. She hadn't a clue. They could also be plum or pear trees for all she knew. Some were big and gnarled and stretched their twisted limbs out like be-witched people in an enchanted forest might do, but most of them were graceful, delicate little trees, supported by posts to which they were tied by wire cables. Like galley slaves, Anne thought, not trees to be climbed and shaken, and they obviously didn't give their fruit willingly either.

She saw a man in a thick parka pruning branches with a pair of electric shears. He must have just started, since he'd clipped only five or six trees and there were loads still to go. He raised his hand curtly as she passed, and Anne nodded back. It wasn't until she'd gone another few steps that she realized who he was.

She turned around and walked back, but Dirk zum Felde didn't seem to be aware that she was there. He carried on prun-ing the branches of his apple trees in a practiced way until she was standing right beside him. Then he looked at her and raised his eyebrows quizzically. Anne put out her hand, and it took him a moment to realize what she wanted. He hung the pruning shears on a snap hook on his belt, then took off his right work glove and shook her hand.

"Anne Hove." She squeezed his hand quite tightly. "I've

moved into Vera Eckhoff's place. We had the pleasure of meeting briefly already."

Dirk zum Felde almost laughed out loud. He felt as though he were watching a badly dubbed movie. The woman and her voice just didn't go together. She was five foot three at most, looked like Bambi, and sounded as though she'd spent twenty years behind the bar of a harbor dive.

"Dirk zum Felde," he said. "You recently gave me the finger awfully nicely. Do we have a problem?" He was wearing the cap with the earflaps again and his eyes were so bright that they almost looked transparent.

"I don't know what you're spraying on your trees," she said in her scratchy voice. "It's none of my business, but you don't need to go spraying it all over me, and definitely not on my son." She shoved her hands into the pockets of her jacket and straightened up. "The next time you have to mark your territory, you can piss on my car instead. I'll get it."

Dirk zum Felde put his glove back on. He took the shears from his belt and cut off another branch. "Very happy to oblige."

She turned around and went bounding along the gravel track. It took a couple of minutes for her heart to settle down. This, she thought, is what it must be like for people in those courses for social anxiety who are afraid of human contact and get sent by their therapists to the meat counter to buy a single slice of salami.

A few lingering islands of snow lay on either side of the track like the remains of a bubble bath. She heard a tractor and, somewhere in the distance, the aggressive whine of a chain saw. She took her cell phone out of her pocket. No one had called. Had she given the day care center the right number? Maybe Leon was still screaming.

"Frau Hove, everything's all right," said Sigrid Pape in the all-clear style characteristic of all the caregiving professions, which was equally effective with the hard of hearing, dementia sufferers, and mothers, and Anne understood very well what Sigrid Pape hadn't said: as a mother you have to keep it together now and again.

She went home, took a screwdriver out of her toolbox, and started inspecting the thirty-two rotting windows in Vera Eckhoff's house.

14

Apple Diplomas

Dɪʀᴋ ᴢᴜᴍ Fᴇʟᴅᴇ ʜᴀᴅ ᴛᴏ slam on his brakes when Burkhard Weisswerth came hurtling out of the farm track on his bike.

Weisswerth under his tractor, that was all he needed! Him in his hat and suspenders *on* the tractor, posing with farm equipment, was bad enough.

But that matter seemed to have resolved itself. They hadn't come by with the camera since the incident. The photographer probably didn't have the nerve to come back, the chickenshit.

Britta thought the kick in the butt hadn't been called for, but she couldn't stand that type any more than he could. It just took her longer to get mad.

He wished he had her nerves: the kids, all the livestock, his parents, who were slowly getting unsteady, and all the little kids with stutters and lisps with whom she practiced speech therapy. Britta stayed as cool as a cucumber.

"Go drive your tractor, Dirk," she'd say when the brats were driving him up the wall, and by the time he got back everything was fine, and the kids knew that he was never angry for long. If it had been up to Britta they'd have had their fifth a while ago already.

GIMME FIVE! she'd recently written with her finger in the grime on the rear window of their car.

"Wash the car first, Frau zum Felde!"

She'd just smiled and drawn another 5 on the hood, followed by exclamation marks.

He'd gone ahead and ordered soccer tickets online: Werder Bremen against Hannover, VIP platinum seats. The price was ridiculous, but it was their tenth wedding anniversary, and some men spent much more than that.

Kerstin Duewer had gotten a new kitchen from Kai. A Bulthaup, with an induction stove. *You might as well go whole hog,* the old show-off had said. Now you weren't allowed to spill anything over at their place anymore.

"It's like eating in an operating room," Britta had said, "but really snazzy."

She didn't care what her kitchen looked like. They still had his mother's built-in oak cupboards. Indestructible, even by their children.

He had also ordered a Werder hat with a grass-green pom-pom from the fan shop, *green-white for life*. Britta would wear it, he knew she would. There weren't many women who could pull off a pom-pom hat. He didn't know any apart from her. Zum Felde for life.

Burkhard Weisswerth called out "Howdy!" and waved when he saw Dirk zum Felde. He was totally oblivious to the fact that Dirk had had to slam on his brakes and was now pedaling easy as can be in the direction of the dike.

Dirk turned into Vera Eckhoff's driveway, drove across her yard, and switched on the spreader. He would fertilize the apple trees by noon as well.

He'd have to see Vera soon about the lease agreement, which would run out next February. Another fifteen years, hopefully.

But with Karl Eckhoff now dead, she didn't have to think about anyone else. And if she wanted to sell the farm, Peter Niebuhr would pounce. Then Dirk would look pretty foolish.

But if this chick from Hamburg was now fixing up Vera's house, as Heinrich Luehrs had said, then it didn't seem that Vera was about to pack up and go.

Maybe it was merely a form of therapy, supervised work, a

little fiddling about with Vera's ruins in order to *downshift* or *get herself sorted out*. The tree huggers and people searching for *spiritual power places* along the Elbe were the ones he liked most—to kick in the butt.

But if Vera was now planning to set up a sanctuary for female carpenters, then she wasn't intending to pack it in just yet.

His lease agreement with Heinrich Luehrs ran for another five years. After that, anything could happen. Heinrich was almost surely still hoping that Georg would return, but he could forget about that. Dirk met up with Georg, who was only a year younger than him, from time to time. "As long as the old man's alive, I'm not gonna touch a single apple around there." The question was how long Heinrich would carry on. He was already in his mid-seventies.

Grow or give way—he couldn't stand hearing that anymore, but it was true, and he needed the acreage. If he could no longer lease anything from Luehrs and Eckhoff, he'd have to find land elsewhere. His thirty acres wouldn't get you very far anymore, even if his father still didn't want to accept it.

Perhaps he should have done what Georg did. Marrying Frauke Matthes had been worth it. *Beauty fades, acres remain.*

Nothing against Frauke, but she'd obviously had a humor bypass and she couldn't pull off a pom-pom hat, that was for sure.

* * *

A deer shot out of the ditch and jumped right in front of his tractor. It was heading toward the Elbe. Somehow the animals seemed to know when hunting season was over. In any case, they always got pretty bold in the spring.

Please, no game damage to the tractor now. That recent mess with the VW Passat was enough, and the animal had still been alive and screaming.

He hadn't known that deer could scream. "They only do it when it's really bad," Vera had said. She'd come immediately and shot it. "Should I skin it for you?" But after all the commotion, he really hadn't felt up to roast venison. It didn't bother Vera in the least, though. She'd taken the thing with her and almost surely chopped it into pieces as soon as she got home.

He turned to fertilize the next row and saw Peter Niebuhr waving at him from his cherry orchard with his pruning shears. Niebuhr had gone organic a short while ago. He now drove to Ottensen twice a week and set up a stall at the organic market at Spritzenplatz with his apples and cherries, and he did the same again on Friday at the Isemarkt. They were apparently tearing the stuff out of his hands in Hamburg.

Dirk had discussed it with Britta as a possible way forward

for them: less acreage, but organic and marketed directly. But they'd imagined what that would be like: Dirk zum Felde at the weekly organic market with customers like Burkhard Weisswerth and his pesky wife embroiling him in endless discussions about GMO technology and heirloom apples. "Sooner or later you'll kill one of them," Britta had said. "Forget it, Dirk, you're just a simple farmer."

And that was precisely the problem. He saw what his colleagues did when it got too hard just to be a fruit farmer and it sickened him.

Hajo Duehrkopp had turned his farm into a *Parappledise* and pulled tourists behind him in his old harvest crates with his tractor, pensioners in windbreakers, families from the campground, school classes. He explained to them how apples grow, and afterward they could earn an apple diploma and eat butter cake in his farm café. Then, before climbing back into their buses and camper vans, they passed through the farm shop and bought cherry brandy, cherry jam, and elderflower jelly, all homemade by his wife.

Yeah, right! You can bet Susi Duehrkopp stood at the juice extractor and boiled elderberries by the ton!

No way. There was jelly at the local Rewe store. Label off, piece of checkered fabric over the lid, handwritten label onto the front, and presto, two euros profit per jar.

And the Low German labels probably got you twenty cents more. DUEHRKOPP'S ELDERBERRIES.

But why did it bother Dirk so much? The tourists happily spread Duehrkopp's Elderberries on their rolls at home. It tasted like their grandmothers' recipe, 100 percent. And Hajo Duehrkopp and his wife now took a vacation twice a year. Hadn't needed to slog away for ages. Still had five acres directly behind the house where Hajo continued to play apple farmer with his customers.

What he sold in his farm shop, he got from colleagues, from Dirk zum Felde, for instance, so Dirk really ought to simmer down.

But it got his goat when he saw Hajo Duehrkopp decanting his apples and cherries, transferring them from the zum Felde crates into Duehrkopp ones before putting them into the shop. Hajo the magician in his big rustic circus. He did the magic and Dirk zum Felde, his stupid assistant, had to get the rabbit into the hat without anyone noticing.

The good thing was that no one lost out.

The tourists drove back to their rented apartments and row houses with their image of country life intact. The life that was reflected in calendar pictures, everything so healthy. And they came back again and again.

Next year Hajo also wanted to launch an adopt-an-apple-tree scheme. Werner Harms had already been doing it for some time. Forty euros per sponsor per year, and all he had to do was stick a name tag on their tree and they could visit it from time to time and pick twenty kilos of apples in September.

"I'll bet you anything the little baby apples all get names too," Britta said. She'd thought Dirk was kidding when he told her about it.

Hajo fared best as a fruit entertainer; when he was in really good form, he would walk through the farm café and play folk songs on his accordion.

And he, Dirk zum Felde, had a reliable customer in Hajo Duehrkopp.

So, what was the problem?

He turned the tractor and saw Heinrich Luehrs coming out of the barn with his ladder. The recent storm had nearly blown Heinrich out of a tree. Dirk had seen his ladder swaying. But the tree would've had to fall over before Heinrich Luehrs came down.

Heinrich was totally old-school. He still shook his head at the farmers who set up roadside fruit stands to sell apples, pears, or plums to folks driving past. Even though pretty much everyone was doing it now, Heinrich would never dream of it, as he considered it beneath his dignity.

I'll have to ask him whether his apple trees also have godmothers now, Dirk said to himself, and he looked forward to seeing Hinni Luehrs's face.

Doubts about artificial fertilizers and pesticides hadn't yet entered Heinrich's world. His faith in high-performance trees and premium fruit was still intact. He had sprayed mercury and arsenic in the past. They were of a completely different caliber than today's pesticides and had also killed off moles and all other burrowing and scuttling critters, and as far as he was concerned, it could have carried on that way. What good were the vermin to anyone anyhow? Now they were protected species, but in Heinrich's garden that didn't do them any good. And he wasn't stupid enough to get caught when he trapped a mole.

His trees stood in rank and file, his fruit was flawless. He was horrified when he saw a meadow with scattered fruit trees, and he thought organic farmers were screwballs.

Heinrich's worldview was just as well ordered as his lawn.

The fact that some bushy-bearded pomologists had recently been celebrated as saviors of the world for resuscitating the Finkenwerder Herbstprinz and the old Pfannkuchenapfel had passed him by, and he should be envied in that respect. He simply hadn't realized that everything had changed a while back, and Dirk zum Felde wasn't going to tell him that farmers like them were now profit-hungry idiots who simply continued mass-producing goods in their pesticide-polluted monocultures for the indifferent folks who still shopped in supermarkets, while organic farmers like Niebuhr and his pomologist cronies were improving the world with the fruit they were producing for professionals.

Or that, as ordinary farmers, it was best to drive through the orchards only at night, so they didn't get caught doing their dirty work by tourists and *critical consumers*.

"We can rent out," Britta had said when he'd had it up to here yet again.

Kai and Kerstin Duewer had done it. They had converted their cold-storage house into vacation apartments, leased the land, and Kai now had a great job at the Raiffeisen hardware and feed store. A five-day workweek, vacation and sick pay, and they still had enough to buy a Bulthaup kitchen.

"We could do that," Britta said, "no big deal."

But they couldn't really, and she knew that, of course. Precisely because he was a farmer. That was the problem.

But he wasn't the only one. He still had colleagues who understood how it felt to see the trailer drive into the farmyard in the fall with crates full of fruit, and to see his name on the crates, DIRK ZUM FELDE. And the old crates still bore the name of his father, who still helped with the harvest too.

And this: fertilizing the cherry trees on a March day, not a single leaf in sight, the buzzard already circling, and the horny brown hares tearing after each other, nature on the hop, everything new, each year again in the springtime.

How could they bear to stand in the Raiffeisen store selling rubber boots when outside the ground was thawing and everything smelled of new beginnings?

Out on the street in front of Heinrich's house, a tour bus pulled in. It was almost Easter, so the tourist coaches were slowly starting to arrive. They always stopped in front of Luehrs's farm, but fortunately no one ever got out. That's all Heinrich needed, a bunch of strangers tramping over his raked sand. They stayed seated while their guides described through the microphone the impressive decorative plaster infill of the house's facade, the witches' broom, the windmill, and the swan gable. Some of them took photos through the tinted windows before the bus drove on to the apple cider tasting.

At Eckhoff's the bus picked up speed. It could only be hoped for Vera's sake that her niece wasn't as dopey as she looked. The house really needed some help.

But it didn't really make a huge difference.

Heinrich was just as lonesome behind his glorious facade as Vera was behind her drafty windows.

Two old people in enormous empty houses.

To be the last farmer on the farm, like Heinrich, that was a bitch. After that it would become a *former farm*. The phrase alone was enough to make you want to throw in the towel. Former farm, put out to pasture, as in *retired*. And then people from Hamburg would sweep in and finish the poor farm off.

Most of them didn't even have a handle on their children or their dogs, let alone their lives, and then they believed in all honesty that they could take on an old thatched-roof house and make it *cozy*.

The results were clear to see. The entire village was killing itself laughing at Weisswerth's wet cellar (*wine cellar!*), and even more so at his bumpy cobblestone paving. The Jarck brothers had done quite a job laying that. Weisswerth had gotten the workmanship that ten euros an hour bought you, and on top of that, the Jarcks had drawn the work out, *just take it easy, man,* and taken twice as long as they should have.

Right, the last row. Dirk zum Felde turned around and saw the twins and the dog coming toward him. Erik out in front as usual, Hannes in tow, bending down for something or other—a beetle, a worm, a snail. He could use them all for his creepy-crawly zoo in the machine shed.

He stopped and let them both climb onto the tractor. Two laughing, gap-toothed faces. Another six months and they'd be in school.

Pauline was going on ten already. Theis was now five.

Maybe one more.

Full house.

15

Nesting Instinct

NATURE WAS SLOWLY COMING ROUND. Like a patient coming out of a deep coma, it still looked pale. The grass was lifeless, straggly, and the fields looked swollen, as if from crying. The trees were dripping and shivering, but the buds on their bare branches were already starting to swell.

You could now hear the water rushing when you pressed your ear against their trunks. "The sap flow," Theis zum Felde said. Anne tried it but couldn't hear a thing. She believed only half of what the little exterminator said anyway, but Leon hung on his every word.

The boys were out and about exploring Vera's garden. They

had fetched the yellow plastic stethoscope from Leon's doctor bag and were listening to the trees with it. Anne could see them standing next to the linden in their rubber boots, listening and nodding.

Theis zum Felde had been pedaling his green tractor over to the farm almost daily since he and Leon had first played pileup together in the Bumblebee group.

He had suddenly appeared in Vera's hallway in his green overalls. His muddy rubber boots were lying outside the door. He had stood with his hands akimbo, in his Bob-the-Builder socks, not saying a word. When Anne said hi, he just nodded. Leon had arrived and stayed silent as well until Theis uttered an almost complete sentence: "I'm allowed till five."

That evening, after Leon had brushed his teeth, and after the bedtime reading and songs, when he'd rolled into his bed to sleep, his eyes already closed, Anne heard him mumble through his pacifier: "Theis is my best friend ever."

Now, in all kinds of weather, they trekked through the fruit farms and over the farm tracks, Leon and his best friend ever, who explained the world to him in shorthand.

"Crab apple. Inedible," he warned, pointing at a little tree behind Heinrich's barn.

"Turn handlebars!" he yelled when he was teaching Leon how to reverse his John Deere tractor.

And the first time he'd stood in front of the rabbit cage in Leon's room, with his arms folded across his chest, Theis zum Felde had said, "Individual housing. Not species appropriate."

Leon had looked at Willy and then at his mother, shaking his head reproachfully.

Now Theis zum Felde was standing with the stethoscope in front of Vera's linden like the head doctor, and Leon was at his side like his staunch assistant.

Anne could see Heinrich Luehrs in his garden, pruning some defenseless bush that was daring to grow in the wrong direction.

She had borrowed his longest ladder so as to reach the small window that was hanging to one side on its hinges at the very top of Vera's gable.

It must have been decades since anyone had looked through its cracked pane. There were so many spiderwebs on it you could hardly see through it. Anne could make out only a couple of beams of light in the attic—the sky shimmering through where the thatched roof was worn. But once her eyes got used to the dark, she could see a couple of little bones lying on the floor. A mouse, a rat, a marten, some sort of small animal must have perished there a while back. She could also see a flight of stairs, the narrow stairway that led up to the attic, and next to it a dusty bag and a large pair of boots.

Vera hadn't let anyone go up in this attic for a long time, because the stairs and floorboards were giving way.

Anne could press the screwdriver into the rotten wood of the window frame without applying any pressure, and in some spots it went all the way through. The wood was untreated apart from the remains of dark green paint that was left in the corners. The putty was crumbly and yellowed.

She took the narrow chisel out of her pocket and started to lever the little window out of its frame.

She carried it down the ladder with care, went into the toolshed, and used the jigsaw to cut a piece of hardboard the same size as the window.

Heinrich Luehrs had taken the burlap bags off the tops of his rosebushes, a reprieve after the long, anxious winter. Now he was raking their bed.

He should never have lent her the ladder. If anything happened, he'd be in for it. Heinrich kept a close watch over the top of his boxwood hedge as Anne lifted her hammer, stuck a couple of nails between her lips, clamped the board under her arm, and climbed back up the wobbly thing.

He couldn't bear to look. She'd never stood on a ladder as tall as this one before and now she was brandishing tools thirty feet above the ground. It was sheer madness.

He put down his rake.

Anne watched Heinrich Luehrs walk over to the bottom of the ladder and hold it firmly with both hands. She nailed the hardboard over the gap in the window, waved down to him, and waited until he was back at his roses. Then she dropped the hammer onto the lawn, climbed down a couple of rungs, and tried to decipher the weathered inscription on the large crossbeam.

"Oh, something in Low German," was all Vera had said.

It wasn't easy trying to discuss the house with her.

The deal was that she'd *put the house in order*. But whenever Anne picked up a tool, Vera would come up behind her and want to talk through everything she planned to do.

Whether the windows were really so shot that they had to be knocked out. Whether the roof couldn't be patched instead of ripping off all the thatch and the old beams in one go.

It took a while for Anne to realize that money wasn't the problem. Vera had piles of it.

"I'm not going to destroy anything around here," Anne said, "you can take my word for it."

But that wasn't it either.

* * *

Vera Eckhoff turned white when Leon hit the vase that stood on the table in the foyer with his Super Ball. There was a gorgeous, crystal-clear sound and the large vase tottered briefly, then stopped, but Vera caught the ball right away and tossed it out the front door like a hand grenade.

Leon started to cry and scoured the entire yard with Theis zum Felde, but they couldn't find it. "In the ditch probably," Theis said with a shrug. "Good throw."

Leon cried himself hoarse. Anne pulled him onto her lap and sent Theis home. "I'll buy you a new one, Leon."

Behind Vera's kitchen door, she could hear the pots rattling and clanking.

Two women, one stove. That never works. Vera had made that clear shortly after Anne moved in. They didn't cook together, seldom ate with one another, but Leon had gotten used to shuttling between them.

He no longer woke Anne up in the mornings. He dressed himself and ran in his slipper socks through the cold hallway and into the kitchen to Vera.

Vera never sent you back to bed just because it was still dark. She didn't want to *sleep in for once* or *for crying out loud* have some peace.

Vera was always up already.

Early in the morning, she fixed his twisted trouser straps and the sleeves of his sweater, spread honey on bread for him, and eventually bought him a plastic cup. It drove her nuts when he waved the thin old cups with the gold rims around the place.

Vera found a child's cup with a mole on it at Edeka, and they teased Heinrich Luehrs with it when he came over for coffee.

"Hey, look, Hinni, your buddy," said Leon, pointing at the mole, and Heinrich looked as though he wanted to toss the cup with the *stupid-ass mole* out the window.

When Anne heard Leon laughing in Vera's kitchen in the morning, she knew they were telling the hilarious mole joke again.

The morning after the incident with the Super Ball, Vera had gotten into her old Benz and driven off at high speed to buy saddle soap and oats. At the cash register there were small toy animals, impulse-buy items for the farmers' children, and Vera had bought two of them, a Trakehner mare and a foal. Theis zum Felde had dozens of these animals, which he drove around in his trailer, but these would be Leon's first ones.

"No more rubber balls in my house," Vera said. Leon nodded,

took the horses, and shuffled through to the kitchen with her. Then she made breakfast.

Ida Eckhoff's old cupboards were still hanging in Vera's kitchen; SAGO, PEARL BARLEY, and MALT COFFEE were inscribed on the ceramic drawers; and Vera cut her bread with a cast-iron hand crank.

Everything in her house was old and heavy. Vera didn't appear to ever have purchased a chair or a tablecloth or a cupboard.

She'd inherited everything, but she lived with the things as though they didn't belong to her.

She was house-sitting, nothing more than that. It seemed that she didn't even dare disturb the old flowerpots that her mother had placed on the windowsills decades earlier.

When Anne removed the curtain rods in the front room so she could get at the window frames, Vera ran around aimlessly, clearly on edge, before finally starting to clear the sills.

She lifted the flowerpots one at a time and carried them with both hands as though they were her relatives' urns, took them into her bedroom and locked the door, because children with or without rubber balls had taken to parading through all the rooms lately. Then she disappeared into the kitchen and started banging cupboard doors and slamming drawers.

Anne heard her crashing about and was reminded of her

mother, who would do exactly the same: set her face, not say a word, and let objects cry out in pain instead.

Marlene could be preparing vegetable soup and make it sound like a massacre, hacking off cabbage heads, snapping beans, scraping the skin off carrots while making horrendous noises.

As she had done the evening that her daughter had taken her flute back up to the attic and put the sheet music in the recycling.

Anne imagined there were other ways of reacting. That instead of abusing a cabbage with a knife in the kitchen, you could have gone to the living room and lain down next to your child on the parquet floor.

You could also perhaps have pulled her toward you, taken her in your arms, and held her for a while. You could have shaken her or cried. You could have said, "I'm sorry."

Sorry because you couldn't have a broken child around you, because you could only cope with a bright, perfect child.

You had to leave this one lying on the floor, unfortunately.

Marlene didn't cry, she wreaked havoc, and Vera did the same. They started wars when they didn't know what else to do.

Hildegard von Kamcke's daughters in their armor of rage.

* * *

Vera never seemed to sleep.

If Anne woke up at one in the morning because Leon was looking for his pacifier or his stuffed toy, Vera would be sitting in the kitchen with her dogs.

And at three or four, if Anne awoke with a start from a dream or was shaken awake by a storm, Vera would still be sitting on the kitchen bench.

Anne could see light under the door. She could hear Vera's radio. String quartets and piano concertos until about six in the morning, *Classics for Night Enthusiasts*. But Vera didn't enthuse through her nights, she sat in the kitchen as though riveted to the spot, and waited for another night to be over.

She didn't seem to possess her house. It was more the other way around. Vera belonged to this house.

This hoose is mine ain . . .

You had to feel the letters on the gray, exhausted beams. She needed a scaffold. It wasn't possible with the wobbly ladder. And Heinrich Luehrs looked as though he wanted to pull her down with his rake right that minute. He was shaking his head and edging closer again.

She could see the Elbe from up here. One sailor—the first—had ventured out. Small as a paper boat, his vessel bobbed up and down in the wake of a massive container ship. The first ewes were standing on the dike, bleating after their lambs. The shepherd came daily, counted the new arrivals, and collected the dead. He moved the electric fence and drove the herd on as soon as the grass on the dike had been eaten down far enough.

Shaggy clouds, gray and thick as a fleece, moved across the sky as though someone had inflated the sheep and let them rise.

The clouds were moving eastward as though they had appointments to get to.

Seagulls were circling above the Elbe island, surveying breeding sites, looking for partners, heading off rivals, building nests, all as though on command. Everything according to plan.

Dirk zum Felde was driving his forklift over the farm track. It was carrying two plastic sacks, each one reaching about head height, because he knew that it was time to spread the potash fertilizer under his apple trees, and how much, and why.

Even Vera's stunted cherry tree still understood that it ought to produce blossoms now.

Everything was rehearsed down to the supporting roles. No one missed a cue, no one forgot their words. They had all mastered their parts.

Except for Anne Hove, who was standing on a tall ladder, ignorant of the script.

In fact, she didn't even know the play, knew even less than Willy, who, in the third spring of his pygmy rabbit existence, suddenly began plucking his belly fur and piling up straw in the corner of his cage in the hope of offspring.

Heinrich Luehrs had taken a look at the agitated rabbit and shaken his head.

"If that's a buck, then I'm a girl."

Theis zum Felde then removed any remaining doubts. He took out a pair of work gloves from the pockets of his overalls, pulled the struggling, scratching rabbit out of his cage, examined it, and nodded. "Girl."

Leon looked at Willy, baffled. He needed time to digest the news.

"Nesting instinct," said Theis, and Leon nodded now too, as if he had long suspected this to be the case.

Anne climbed down and took the ladder back to Heinrich Luehrs. He gave her a look that would make you cower.

"The ladder topples, then what? All hands on deck and general panic!"

Another one who almost toppled over when he spoke.

Another one with a tendency to knock people down a peg or two.

Get down from the ladder, get out of the driveway, varmint!

She wondered how someone got to be like that. If it was the landscape that did that to them, the trees, the river Elbe. If it might be because their fathers' fathers had tamed a river, cut it down to size, directed it with dikes, driven their ditches and canals into its soft foreland. That they hadn't simply discovered the land on which they lived, they had *made* it.

And then built their enormous houses, hall-houses like cathedrals, and in so doing extolled themselves as creators of the marshlands, not gods, not farmers, but something in between.

Perhaps that's why men like Heinrich Luehrs and Dirk zum Felde stood like that in front of you, half-gods with rakes and pruning shears. And why five-year-old boys from the Altland, who wore size 12 rubber boots, trampled varmints into the ground.

Perhaps it was handed down. If you were born into one of these marshland families, if you were part of a timber frame from the start, you knew your place and your position in this landscape, and it always went according to age: first came the river, then the land, then bricks and oak beams, and then the people with the old names who owned the land and the old houses.

Everything that came after that, people who'd been bombed out, driven away, those weary of the city, those without land

and looking for a homeland were nothing but wind-borne sand and washed-up scum. Travelers who should stay on the road.

Down from the ladder, don't block the access, varmint.

Anne wondered how long you had to stay here so as not to be considered a stranger. A lifetime clearly wasn't enough.

"Thanks for the ladder," she said, "just don't look next time!"

16

Drift Ice

VERA HAD SLEPT LIKE A child for three nights. No dreams, no Dr. Martin Burger, no old man crying. Inner peace without PsychoPax. She hoped that Karl had found it too. She missed him.

Karl Eckhoff had *gone home,* Pastor Herwig said, he now lay next to the little half-timbered church. When there wasn't any wind and her windows were open, Vera could hear the clock in the church tower chiming. Not celebratory strikes, it was more a kind of clanging, as though someone were hitting a pot with a wooden spoon. She thought of Karl, who had gone home with his stiff leg.

She had had his name engraved on the Eckhoffs' head-stone and asked whether there was enough space for a fourth name. "Plenty," Otto Suhr said. "Let's take care of it at the same time." And so under *Karl Eckhoff* they'd also written *Vera Eckhoff. *1940–*

"That's sorted then." Otto Suhr thought practically. You didn't get far as a mortician otherwise.

There wasn't a word for what Karl had been. Not a father, nor a brother, nor a child. Her comrade perhaps. Her fellow man.

Vera had driven Marlene to the station in silence. They had rubbed each other the wrong way in the three days and nights that they were sisters. Or pretended they were.

Hildegard von Kamcke's daughters, her war child and her postwar child, fourteen years between them—and the Elbe. Vera had pushed little Marlene in her swing in the large garden in Blankenese and played Trap the Cap with her at the round table in Hildegard's living room, three or four times a year on a Sunday when the head of the household wasn't around, because Hildegard kept her life in order.

Vera was her guest, invited to lunch, and there was tea in the afternoon as well. Hildegard's last name was now Jacobi.

She would send her driver to collect Vera from the ferry, and he would take her back to the pier in the late afternoon.

The man that Vera never saw had gotten rich from the apartment complexes and row houses that he'd built in Hamburg. Thin walls and small windows for people who never got anywhere after the war.

Personally, he loved art nouveau, stucco facades, arched windows, and oak floors. His own home had all these features in spades, and Hildegard knew how to live in these big houses. The villa wasn't a mansion, Jacobi was no aristocrat, everything wasn't quite *comme il faut*, but it was close enough.

Hildegard never set foot in Karl Eckhoff's house again, nor in the village on the dike, nor in the Altland. She left it all behind as though this ground had also been ravaged and scorched.

She also left her war child there as if she had lost it along the way.

Just like the other one, the little one that had frozen in his swaddling clothes. That she'd left at the side of the road in his baby carriage.

She had covered him one more time, smoothed out his blanket. Most of the mothers did this before they left their dead children behind and then carried on past all the other silent baby carriages standing in the snowdrifts.

It had been too cold that January. The little ones perished first.

Some of the women had sat down in the snow long before they reached the lagoon, leaned against their baby carriages, and trusted in the cold.

Some had jumped from bridges, holding their children by the hand.

Some had gone into the woods, hanged their children in the trees, and then hanged themselves.

Some, only sometime later, had employed straight razors, a rope, or poison, because they could no longer find themselves in the miserable wretches they'd become.

The majority, though, hadn't allowed themselves to die and remained homesick wanderers for the rest of their lives.

They had marched off as Prussians and arrived as riffraff. You could get used to that. You could live in an apartment or a little house in a development and be thankful that you no longer had to live in a damp barrack or a Quonset hut.

They had cultivated wax beans, planted potatoes, and not thought back, not looked east except in their dreams and on holidays, when they cried and didn't tell their children why. And their sons and daughters got used to the fact that their parents were drift ice.

Hildegard von Kamcke had brought her elder child to

safety. Her child had become a farmer's daughter, but Hildegard hadn't become a farmer's wife.

She'd had no intention of acclimating. Of settling for a few acres of cherry and apple trees and a wounded man on a bench in a house where she'd slept on straw and had to steal milk. Where she'd stood in front of the ornamental gate in her stockinged feet, with a child who was freezing and had snot all over her sleeve. *Refugee pack, lice on your back.*

She would have remained a stranger in this village, a nobody to the straddle-legged farmers with the timber-framed farmhouses, who thought they were aristocrats and had never seen an East Prussian wheat field or the grand tree-lined avenues that led up to manor homes.

She wanted to become once more what she had been before. She wanted to have her old life back, all of it.

Including her little boy.

But when she had a baby with Fritz Jacobi, it was a girl, and no boy came after that.

Vera always polished her shoes and cut her fingernails before she went to the Jacobis'. She wore her best clothes but noticed that her mother still furrowed her brow when greeting her. They would shake hands; Vera didn't curtsy. She'd decide on the ferry ahead of time that she wouldn't bend her knees and almost always succeeded.

Marlene was like a puppy whenever Vera came. She'd jump around her excitedly with dolls and balls, pull her into the nursery, show her the miniature shop, and fetch games and picture books from the cupboard until Hildegard called them for dinner.

Every meal was a test—the white tablecloth, the stiff napkins, the overly large silver spoons. Little Marlene always passed, and Vera inevitably failed. She was almost twenty the last time and got tomato soup on the damask.

"Tell me, do you eat in the barn at home?"

Hildegard didn't see Vera flinch. Marlene put down her spoon. They finished the meal in silence.

That was Vera's last visit to the Jacobis'. She never went again when Hildegard summoned her, but she still read the letters that her mother had been writing to her since she had left Ida Eckhoff's farm.

She wrote about oak woods and stork nests, cornflowers, kingfishers, and cranes, about swimming in the lakes of Mazuria, and skating on black ice.

She recorded the names of her horses and dogs, and the names of her three siblings, none of whom were alive anymore. She wrote down the words and the music to the songs of her homeland, including "The Land of the Dark Forests" and "Annie of Tharaw," all seventeen verses, and she drew hollyhocks, globeflowers, white-tailed sea eagles, and the von Kamcke family's manor home.

She also put recipes in the envelopes, for beetroot soup, potato dumplings, and blintzes.

My dear Vera, wrote Hildegard Jacobi to the farmer's child she couldn't stand to have in her Blankenese house for even half a day. And each time the child stood right in front of her, Hildegard only inspected Vera's shoes and fingernails and kept her at arm's length.

Hildegard wrote about baby Vera, who had sung when she could barely speak, who wanted to sleep in the kitchen in the big basket with the puppies.

She sent Vera a photo of a man with a broad smile, sitting on a horse with a child in front of him. *Friedrich und Vera von Kamcke on Excelsior.*

Hildegard wrote as if she were trying to keep a Prussian Atlantis from sinking.

My dear Vera. She could be affectionate as long as the Elbe lay between her and her daughter.

Vera had filed the letters in a document folder. They were stored in the oak chest and were no one else's business, not even her half sister's.

But she no longer even had Karl and sat by herself on the family bench. Too much solitude, even for Vera Eckhoff.

So, on the second day after the funeral, she fetched the letters from the chest, placed them on the kitchen table, and went off to bed.

The letters were still there the following morning in the closed folder, but they'd been read. Marlene's eyes were red and puffy. They drank their coffee without a word, even had a second cup, but then Marlene took the breadbasket and threw it against the wall. The cutlery followed. "DON'T YOU DARE!" Vera shouted as Marlene reached for a cup. Marlene rushed outside, ran through the garden and into the cherry trees, and started to scream. The last few starlings that were still looking for cherries flew off in alarm.

Leaves and whole branches were broken off, tree trunks got roared at, dandelions were crushed and beheaded by feet that could no longer kick Hildegard von Kamcke, since she had died without saying a word. Like drift ice, always cold, something you couldn't get a grip on. Marlene didn't know a single children's song from Prussia, she had no photos of a manor home, and she had never heard of a dead child by the roadside. She knew absolutely nothing.

A mother like an uncharted continent, the daughter sent out without a compass, without a map, in a country with deep ravines, in which the earth shook and wild animals lurked. You didn't come through that in one piece. Marlene had fallen into every gorge, come crashing down again and again from smooth, cold walls. It hadn't been nice being Hildegard Jacobi's child.

To Marlene she'd bequeathed her musical talent, her voice, her ear. There were singing and piano lessons, and Marlene played very well.

But not well enough for Hildegard Jacobi, who'd raise her eyebrows as high as they could go, give a thin-lipped smile, and exhale briefly whenever Marlene played a wrong note in an impromptu, as though she'd known in advance that it would happen.

And if Marlene didn't make a mistake, if she had mastered a difficult piece, played it perfectly, then let her hands fall, was content for a brief moment, Hildegard liked to cite the German humorist Wilhelm Busch.

If a frog, who on hands and knees barely made it up a tree, were to think he's now a bird, he's erred.

Her chronically cheerful father, seldom found without a brandy snifter, would then sit next to his daughter on the piano stool, laugh, and pull her toward him.

"Oh, don't let that bother you, little Marlene. Come on, play another nice tune. . . ."

She was a frog in a tree to Hildegard Jacobi.

The older, faraway daughter who had gotten straight A's in school, gone off to college, then opened a dental practice and owned the Trakehners, *My dear Vera,* was the bird.

And Vera had never said anything about these letters, not in all the summers that Marlene—with her pigtails and her backpack—had spent in the Altland, vacationing at her big sister's. She'd begged for it every year, just for a week. She had loved Vera so much, even her scary house, even the old man with the limp who quietly whistled songs on his white bench.

Not one word about the letters, not even later, on any of the July Sundays when she'd visited the farm with her husband and children to pick cherries. Vera had kept her at arm's length, starving.

Snails died, molehills were trampled under Marlene's feet, field hares fled.

Vera stood at the kitchen window with her binoculars and watched Marlene wreak havoc, creating a scene for the trees, like a woman who had been deceived.

Vera regretted it already. Wished she'd left the letters in the chest and burned them at some point.

That's what happened when you offered *Us* just because you were tired and relented out of loneliness.

Marlene was now out of sight. She had to be getting close to the big ditch. Vera called the dogs and went after her.

She found her on one of the little wooden bridges, slumped over, and no wonder, after that terrible frenzy. "Move over," Vera said. The dogs lay down on the grass, and she sat down next to Marlene on the bridge, at arm's length. But it wasn't about the letters anymore.

Marlene sat howling in the blazing sun because the ice just wouldn't thaw.

Because Hildegard Jacobi's daughter, herself frozen to the core, was now letting her own daughter freeze.

"I'm treating Anne the same way! Everything just carries on unchanged."

She didn't have a Kleenex, so she used her sleeves. Her face grew blurred from crying like a child, with her eyes squeezed shut and her mouth wide open. "I didn't want that."

She was bawling like a girl who'd accidentally broken her doll's arm or ripped off its head.

Vera didn't understand such things, but she could see Marlene's sweat-drenched hair, her face that was like a fuzzy photograph, and her blouse hanging on her like a wet rag, stained with dirt, grass, and tears.

She pulled her up and they stumbled back to the house, two soldiers exhausted by battle.

Marlene lay down on the bench under the linden, and Vera went inside to get her some water, but Marlene had fallen asleep by the time she got back.

Vera drank it herself. She looked at Marlene on the bench and didn't know where to sit.

That evening, they drank too much. The wine and apple brandy gave Marlene Dutch courage, and she asked questions that she would never ask Vera Eckhoff if she was sober.

"Why did she leave you here on your own?"

"Why don't you have any children, no husband?"

"Why do you have no one?"

Vera got up and cleared away the bottles and glasses. "I had Karl," she said. Then they went to bed. The next morning she took Marlene to the train.

On the way back she dropped in at the graveyard. It was still hot outside and the gerbera flower arrangement from the hunting club was already flagging.

She heard the gate creak, and saw Heinrich Luehrs coming down the sandy path toward her. When the weather was like this, he drove to the graveyard every day to water the flowers on Elisabeth's grave. He noticed Vera, turned off the path, and came over to her. He put down his watering can and pail. "Hi, Vera."

They stood for a while in the sun.

"It's all behind him now," said Heinrich as he watered the gerbera on Karl's grave. "No need for tears."

He watered the cornflower wreath from Vera and the flower arrangement with yellow roses from the neighbors. The remainder, just a few drops, he poured over Vera's head. Then he widened his eyes in mock horror, slapped her on the shoulder, and left.

She wiped the water from her hair and watched Hinni Luehrs march the watering can back to the faucet, then over to his wife's grave.

He crouched down stiff-kneed and started to feel around for dead heads on the two daisy bushes that stood to the right and left of the headstone. He snapped them off, tossed them into his pail, then did the same with the six rosebushes that stood in two rows parallel to the perfectly straight flagstone path. The flowers were cut to the exact height of the headstone, glowing soldiers at roll call.

Heinrich wasn't prone to compromise when it came to looking after graves either.

WHY SO SOON? In the case of sudden deaths, the Suhr firm

always recommended this inscription, and mostly an angel on the headstone too.

But Heinrich Luehrs was through with angels, and the question on the headstone wasn't meant as pious whispering. It was best roared out loud: *WHY* SO SOON!

Vera watched him kneeling in the graveyard, plucking the flowers with a punishing hand.

He'd carried her himself with his three sons. They had heaved the coffin onto their shoulders, Heinrich and his eldest in front, Jochen and Georg at the back, in their new black suits. The four of them had schlepped the heavy oak coffin through the entire graveyard, soaked to the skin, their black ties and sharply creased trousers waving like flags of mourning in the wind. It had rained and stormed, but at least that weather suited Heinrich's furious face at the side of the grave, when there was nothing else to carry, nothing more to do than stand empty-handed next to his sons, none of them daring to cry.

None of the mourners were crazy enough to go up to Heinrich Luehrs at the graveside and press his hand. They all took off.

Karl then hobbled across to Heinrich and held the umbrella over his head while Vera took his drenched sons home.

When she got back to the graveyard, they were still standing under the broken umbrella. Both of them were dripping wet and shivering, and Heinrich was still too stubborn to accept a ride.

It passed, even for a man like Heinrich Luehrs, who was very precise about everything, who would never say an Our Father in his life again because he'd discovered what it might mean: *Thy will be done.*

Who didn't like to be pushed around and was finished with angels.

Vera watched him water the roses and daisies carefully with his watering can. At least the flowers and bushes complied. They grew as he wished them to. On this grave, the will of Heinrich Luehrs alone was done, even though it was God's Acre.

17

Rural Plagues

THE FEATURE STORY WAS ALREADY in place. "From Quarry to Sausage," an opulent photo spread, but nothing quaint. He wanted it raw, honest, bloody, hard. He just had to ask Vera Eckhoff when he could go out hunting with her. He wouldn't mention a photographer at this point. He still wasn't sure that Florian was right for the job. After he had been thrown out of Dirk zum Felde's place, he'd called in sick for two weeks and said that he would *definitely be psychologically scarred by the incident.* The man was in his mid-thirties and was acting like a little girl.

But his magazine, *A Taste of Country Life,* would never be

one of these country kitsch rags, not another of those magazines with cute songbirds and lambs and little wildflowers on the cover, and with recipes for parsnip soup and instructions for absurd woodworking projects, tea warmers, nest boxes, or crap like that, and above all NOTHING with felt, God forbid. Felt was so last year, for heaven's sake.

Burkhard Weisswerth shifted down a gear and turned onto the small farm track. He took the curve a little too tightly, his back tire swerved a bit, and it almost went very wrong. It could've been quite ugly, with a bottle of single malt in one saddlebag and a jar of Eva's zucchini-apple-chutney in the other. He slowed down a little. The streetlights ended, so it was pitch-dark, and the farm track was muddy and slippery.

He'd seen Dirk zum Felde only a couple of times since the kicking incident, just in passing. They had waved at each other from a distance. Dirk could have stopped and said something, since he had clearly overreacted, although Florian's tone wasn't optimal either, admittedly. Best just to let it go!

Burkhard Weisswerth wasn't a cheapskate. He had just gone out and spent fifty euros on an eighteen-year-old Glenfiddich that Dirk zum Felde would appreciate. He was a farmer but no idiot. Eva had given him the chutney for Britta, along with an invitation to the spring festival at her jelly factory. This was the third year in a row that she'd organized it, and always on Pentecost Monday. When the weather cooperated, and the day trippers came from Hamburg, she sold quite a lot.

Her single-variety apple jellies did best of all. Eva had the heirloom varieties delivered by a pomologist, a brilliant guy who had previously studied Asian cultures. You could see immediately that a man like that had a different outlook from your run-of-the-mill Altland farmer. It would take a lot more persuasion before someone like Dirk zum Felde would finally realize that modern fruit production with its overbreeding and overfertilization as well as its monocultures and all that GMO technology was completely insane. Total lunacy!

As a journalist he also had a role to play, of course. He was planning a portrait of pomologists for the autumn edition of *A Taste of Country Life*. And last year already, Eva had planted a few of the heirloom varieties in her garden, Ananas Reinette, Horneburger Pfannkuchen, and Marten's Gravensteiner apples. Just three of each sort to begin with, but a start at least.

When he rode into the yard, Burkhard Weisswerth had to slalom around a scooter, a children's tractor, a go-cart, and a tricycle. All the vehicles looked as though kids had dismounted them in a terrible hurry. The scooter was lying on its side, the go-cart and tricycle appeared to have gotten wedged together in a collision, and the tractor was standing crossways in front of the entrance to the house.

A rope ladder was dangling from a large buckeye tree. Someone had started building a tree house in its crown. A couple of laths had been nailed together every which way, and a John Deere flag had already been hoisted.

In a small wheelbarrow, a stack of farm animals—cows, pigs, and sheep—were piled atop each other as if they'd been culled following a pandemic. A wooden sword was sticking out of a flowerpot. How many kids did Dirk zum Felde have?

Burkhard Weisswerth looked for a free space to park his bike, took off his helmet, fetched the bottle of single malt and the jar of chutney from his saddlebags, and walked up to the door.

He'd drink a pretty good scotch with Dirk zum Felde, *no hard feelings, chew the fat* man to man, and they'd gradually open up to each other a little. Establishing contact with neighbors wasn't unimportant if you wanted to make it out here. He was very pleased that he had a knack for it, that he didn't fear contact with others.

And you always got a lot back as well.

The nameplate above the doorbell was handmade, a large ceramic egg with a cracked shell. ZUM FELDE was written on the egg, and brightly colored lizards curled around it. Or dragons? Or maybe dinosaurs? And their little tummies had names on them: *DIRK, BRITTA, PAULINE, HANNES, ERIK, THEIS.*

Burkhard put the bottle down, pulled his iPhone out of his jacket pocket, and took a quick photo of it. Eva just had to see it! She had a great weakness for the monstrosities made of ceramic, salt dough, and terra-cotta that the folks here in the village used to *decorate* their houses and front yards.

Gesine Holst's concrete lighthouse with the flashing light would be hard to beat, but this might be a worthy runner-up. He couldn't wait to see Eva's face. He put his iPhone away and rang the doorbell.

There was an edgy barking behind the front door, followed by the patter of bare feet on stone. A little boy in pajamas opened up, looked briefly at Burkhard's expensive work boots made of fine leather, and said, "Shoes off!" before disappearing back inside.

"Who's at the door, Theis?"

"Dunno!"

Burkhard tried to get rid of the big dog that was weaving around him, wagging its long tail, slobbering all over his trousers, and sniffing the jar of chutney. He couldn't stand it and called out, "Howdy!"

Britta zum Felde came to the door. She was wearing a

Simpsons T-shirt that reached all the way down to her knees and a pair of neon-green socks, and she had a towel wrapped into a turban around her head.

"Oh, hi there, Burkhard. Schnuppi, leave him alone, come on, off to the kitchen with you!" She slapped the dog gently and he trotted off as though he were now finally allowed to call it a day.

"D'you wanna come in?"

"Hopefully I'm not disturbing you," Burkhard replied.

"We've just eaten, come on in. You can leave your shoes on the mat there."

On the way to the kitchen, Burkhard stepped in something wet. He very much hoped that it wasn't from the dog, which was now lying like a Flokati shag rug on the tile floor, next to the boy in the pajamas, who was loading a small grain transporter with corn. He had laid out a farm with a large fleet of vehicles in the middle of the floor, but it didn't seem to be bothering anyone. The kitchen was enormous.

When Burkhard saw the table and the long bench, he was reminded of youth hostels and houses in the countryside he'd stayed in on school trips. On the plates were the remains of supper: eggshells, cheese rinds, sausage casings, and a piece of buttered bread with a bite taken out of it.

There was a roll of paper towels on the table, and next to that was an enormous bottle of ketchup and a pan containing leftover cocoa with a skin on it.

A girl with long blond pigtails was sitting on the corner bench. She had her chin cupped in her hands and was reading a thick book. She raised her head briefly when she saw him, mumbled, hi, then went back to her reading. Next to her, two boys who looked completely identical were trying to explain a complicated magic trick to their father. They were both talking at the same time and were waving a dish towel through the air above a saltshaker that was supposed to disappear but obviously didn't want to.

"Howdy, Burkhard," said Dirk zum Felde, shaking Burkhard's hand without taking his eyes off the saltshaker. "Just a minute, I need to concentrate right now."

He was sitting at the table in a thermal undershirt, wearing thermal long johns as well, as far as Burkhard could tell. It was the first time he'd seen Dirk zum Felde without his overalls, and he found it somewhat embarrassing. He felt like a Peeping Tom.

"Take a load off," said Britta, putting a cup down for him, and then she poured something red into it, which was steaming and smelled of gummy bears.

The magic trick finally appeared to have worked, and the

twins were now grinning, revealing more gaps than teeth. "Again! One more time!"

Two ash-blond kids, gap-toothed magicians—Burkhard had another idea for *A Taste of Country Life:* rural fathers! Dirk zum Felde with his four children in the field, in the sorting shed, up on the tractor, building a tree house. And Dirk's father was still alive as well, so he could even make a three-generation story out of it. Gender roles in the countryside, masculinity and gender in a farming context, now there was a topic.

It was astonishing. Since he'd moved out here, the ideas were simply coming to him, they were practically hunting him down! Because he was no longer strung-out from the hubbub of the city, or distracted by posers and windbags in editorial conferences, tapas bars, theater foyers, and art galleries—the money alone that he was saving! And the time! He had all the time in the world out here, stress was passé, stress was history!

He was a man who had cut to the chase, had gotten down to the bare essentials, was at peace with himself, grounded. He didn't need all that nonsense anymore.

And Eva too would reach this point of equilibrium.

He had caught her looking at apartments in Hamburg online. She'd quickly closed the page when he'd entered the room, but he was able to check it out afterward, since she hadn't cleared her search history: *3-Rm Condo in HH-Eppendorf.*

After that he had gone out on his bike, down to the Elbe, all the way to Stade and back, doing an average of twenty miles per hour, and that had calmed him down a bit.

She hadn't been looking for rental apartments at least, and there wasn't a *1-Rm Apt* for singles among them, so she didn't seem to be thinking of leaving him. That would just be . . . well, he'd have noticed that.

Other people Googled recipes, beautiful hotels, or old schoolmates. Eva simply Googled apartments in the city with a yard. It was just a hobby for winter evenings, nothing more.

He would happily admit that this winter hadn't been easy out here: hardly any snow, not much frost either, just the constant westerly wind whipping perpetual rain.

Freezing rain, sleety rain, heavy rain, drizzles, showers. A sky like a gravestone, hardly a clear day from November to March. That could get you down if you were the least bit so inclined.

And Eva's so-called friends hadn't been any help either. They didn't come in winter, not a damn soul came in winter.

At the outset, sure, they'd all come then, wanting to have a look at what the two pioneers were getting up to, all alone out there in their *rubber boot world*.

The first winter the place had been packed in the evenings and on weekends. They'd taken walks, never-ending ones, in breathable jackets, along the Elbe and around the fruit farms.

They'd eaten Eva's *sensational* apple cake and sat for hours at the crackling woodstove while the rain lashed against the windowpanes. *Simply fantastic.* They'd raved about the tranquillity, the picturesque houses, the dreamy river-scape. They'd talked about writing books, of a life *devoid of makeup*, fantasized about dropping out, about little organic cafés beneath thatched roofs that were guaranteed to take off, about the *spirit* of these old farmers' cottages.

That first winter they'd all wanted to pack in their *cerebral* jobs, wanted to do something with their hands! "Hey, I could live out here. I mean it," Sabine, Eva's best friend, had said, "keep an eye out for me, will you? Doesn't have to be anything big. Something like your place would do."

Nothing but hot air. The second winter Sabine had come only once, for Eva's birthday at the end of January, and they had the same rain, the same cake, the same log fire in the stove. "Hey, in all honesty, Eva, I'd go nuts out here. How the hell do you stand it?" The optimal thing to say to yank a friend out of her seasonal depression. Thanks a lot for that.

But their friends still came in the spring when the flowers were in bloom, or in the summer when the black currants, raspberries, and gooseberries ripened and Eva had to pick them, extract their juices, and boil them down from morning till night. Then they suddenly appeared with their bikes at the garden fence, ding-a-ling-a-ling, a little excursion. "Don't you country folks have any coffee?"

If you were lucky they'd call on their cell phones beforehand, on the ferry to Finkenwerder. Then Eva would have time to whip up a couple of waffles and get some cherries out of the freezer.

She hated it when she had only a packet of butter cookies. It made her feel like she was being exposed as an imposter. Cookies from the supermarket in rubber boot world was downright embarrassing.

With a little advance warning, she could at least run into the bathroom, put in her contact lenses, smack on some mascara, scrub the worst of the garden dirt from under her fingernails, and pack Burkhard off quickly to Nodorps farm shop for a few pounds of asparagus.

Because once their friends were there, they simply relaxed. They had time, they were in the countryside. They wandered through the garden, picking strawberries here and nibbling on a few cherries there. "It's like living in paradise."

They sat under the apple trees, took off their shoes, told stories about impossible colleagues and unbelievably bad writing, complained about the antics of those with image complexes in their morning conferences.

"Consider yourself lucky you don't have to put up with all that any longer, Burkhard!"

They never turned down a small glass of white wine. Eva then went into the house and prepared asparagus for everyone. "But then we'll have to head off!" Ding-a-ling-a-ling back to Hamburg. They had tickets for the opera, wanted to catch a reading, attend a gallery opening in the Kaispeicher or a garden party on the Alster river.

Sometimes Eva would cry on evenings like that, when she was putting the plates and glasses into the dishwasher, when she had to rush back out into the garden to pick the ripe berries before it got dark, when the juicer was still bubbling late in the evening, and she was stirring pots of jelly and jam until just before midnight.

When at one o'clock in the morning everything in the kitchen was sticky—the stove, the floor, the tiles—and when the stuff wouldn't set yet again, *son of a bitch*!

She used agar, which was absolutely not as idiot-proof as canning sugar. Eva's jelly factory produced only vegan spreads, jellies, and preserves.

The idiots at the countrywomen's club didn't even know that such a thing existed! They were still merrily tossing canning sugar into their jellies—and turned up their noses at Eva's zucchini and pumpkin jams. *What the farmer doesn't know, he doesn't eat!*

No, Eva hadn't fully acclimated to the country yet. Burkhard could see that quite clearly now. She needed a bit of support, a bit of distraction, especially in the dark season. It didn't have to be the twelve tenors in the Stade culture center, or the Black Sea Fleet Naval Choir. But driving now and then to a morning jazz session in Agathenburg for brunch, or catching a Low German play in Ladekop—why not? That was worth doing!

But yesterday evening hadn't been successful. They'd gone to the Italian restaurant for no particular reason, in the middle of the week, just to get out of the house. But people in these parts went to bed very early.

At nine thirty they were the last diners there. The waitress had already put the chairs up on the tables and had said that if they could maybe pay, she'd give them a grappa on the house. Eva's response was out of order.

"If your grappa tastes as shitty as your Chianti, you can go clean the john with it."

Even a big tip couldn't set that right.

Burkhard was hoping for a sunny Pentecost Monday and lots of visitors at Eva's spring festival.

He wasn't very optimistic otherwise.

* * *

"Yuck, what is THAT?" One of the twins had discovered Eva's jar of chutney and was holding it up with both hands.

"Looks like Schnuppi puked in it," the other crowed.

"Really?" Britta took the jar away from them. "And what does Nutella look like?"

They shrieked, "Urgh!" and ran upstairs giggling.

Burkhard Weisswerth was very drunk when he pushed his recumbent bike home a couple of hours later. He was also very sober. It was, he realized, possible to be both at the same time. A drunken sober person and a sober drunk. What did that make you? Whatever! Not a good mixture.

First ice cubes, then Coke. Dirk and Britta zum Felde had made a *nice mixed drink* out of an eighteen-year-old Glenfiddich. And when the Coke was gone, they'd moved on to Sprite. Glenfiddich-Sprite on the rocks.

How dim-witted could you be?

At least it was dark enough on the farm track that you could pee against one of the apple trees. That was something anyway.

18

Looking Away

ƒN THE WINTER, HE IRONED only the collars and the cuffs. He wore sweaters over his shirts, so no one could see whether the rest was done or not.

He put the ironing board up in the kitchen, close enough to the window that he could look outside, but not so close that he could be seen from out there. Heinrich Luehrs preferred not to be observed when he was ironing.

It was now getting warmer out. Soon he wouldn't need a sweater. He would just wear his work jacket over his shirt. So then he'd have to iron the entire front, for he might well open his jacket a bit when outside in springtime. But he wouldn't bother with the back. He'd do that again only in the summer.

Here he was, standing in the kitchen, smoothing out his wrinkled shirts as though he had nothing better to do.

Leni Cohrs could do the ironing, she had offered to. She dropped by once a week, cleaned the windows, vacuumed, and mopped the floors. But he wouldn't let her anywhere near his laundry. Just the thought of a strange woman fiddling around with his shirts and pants! Not to mention his bedclothes and his underwear. *That'll be the day!*

There were now shirts that didn't need to be ironed at all; the sales associate at Holst had shown him one last summer when she'd noticed that he was on his own. A man buying shirts for himself at Holst had to be a widower or a bachelor.

He had taken one, to please the sales associate more than anything else. It looked completely different from his gray-and-blue-checked shirts. It was striped.

And Vera had noticed it right away, of course, had wolf whistled at him with her fingers. At first he'd thought she was whistling for her dogs, until he saw her grinning and giving him two thumbs-up.

Vera had always been like that. She got up to stuff.

Like the time she dove off the Lühe bridge—simply took off her clothes and dove headfirst into the river in her underwear.

She was twelve at most at the time. And then, without drying herself off, she'd gotten back into her clothes and ridden home on the old bike Karl Eckhoff used for the milking.

Nobody jumped headfirst from the Lühe bridge. They jumped feetfirst or cannonballed at the very most, and girls didn't even do that. Only daredevils dove headfirst. And Vera Eckhoff.

Then, later, she had shown him how she had learned to do it: from practicing in Eckhoff's hayloft. Jumping down from the hayloft onto the little ledge and then headlong into the big haystack. The ledge was pretty high, but that wasn't so bad.

Heinrich just couldn't stop thinking of Ida Eckhoff the entire time.

He wondered what it looked like when someone hanged themselves. He had never seen anything like that.

"Like someone who's fallen asleep while dancing," Vera had said, then gave him a demonstration. Let her head slump to one side, and turned back and forth with her arms dangling at her sides. Then she climbed back up onto the beam and jumped into the hay.

Heinrich jumped then too. He sometimes wondered if Vera Eckhoff was all there.

* * *

The flat bits didn't take long to iron. He used the water sprayer to dampen pillows and sheets a little. You had less fuss and bother with the large items than with the shirts.

From his window, he could see Vera riding home from the Elbe. Yessiree, always straight over his raked sand! He ran to the window, rapped on it, and wagged his finger at her. She lifted her riding crop briefly. She seemed to be coming back around at last. It had taken a while.

You'd think she had lost a child, not a man past ninety who was tired of life.

They'd dragged Karl Eckhoff's stiff body back to his bed that July morning. Vera was still quite normal then, a bit pale of course, understandably.

But when the sister left after the funeral, she had crawled around the house, and the practice was *temporarily closed*. Then, as winter approached, she got to looking like a ghost.

Even so, she still fed her horses.

Heinrich had gone to check at some point, and she came shuffling along. In her bathrobe, at five in the afternoon.

"Well, Hinni, come to see if I've hung myself?"

She could be mean. And how!

He had just left her standing in the horse barn in her bathrobe and rubber boots. He didn't have to take everything Vera Eckhoff dished out.

"Just go and die then, you nasty old hag."

Later he noticed that the light was on over at her place all night long again.

You had to grow into an empty house at first. In the beginning, you were much too small.

After Elisabeth's funeral, the neighboring women had come by with goulash casseroles and plates of cake every day. They took turns. They meant well.

They gave him their leftovers and almost finished him off.

Widower's meals warmed up and eaten in silence. It was so quiet he could hear himself chewing and swallowing.

Some things tasted quite different than Elisabeth's, which wasn't so bad.

If a dish tasted just like hers, he'd get upset while eating it. It was like the dream he'd had repeatedly in the early days. That she was still alive.

And then waking up.

In his first winter as a widower, the land behind the house also lay there as though it were dead. Silent, dark, and odorless.

In December, he thought the trees were going to stay as they were, skeletons, their branches bones that had been stripped, forever this time.

But they stirred themselves in March. They really did bud again.

Then some hard frosts came in April, but most of the buds still managed to hang on.

And by July, there were black cherries on the branches.

Many split open in the heavy rain and hail.

Then the apple trees produced a good crop in August, although many were broken by the September storms.

But, all in all, his harvest hadn't been bad in the first year without Elisabeth.

He wondered how others did it, townsfolk, people without land, office workers who weren't pushed through the first year by nature. Or thrashed. Who had to march through it without a taskmaster.

Vera hadn't brought him soups or cakes, and she didn't make any jellies either. Vera didn't put her hand on his arm.

She looked away when he kneeled in the flower beds, his eyes all red, and she didn't listen when he spoke to himself in the cherry tree.

Vera banged on his windowpane with her fist at six in the morning if he wasn't able to get out of bed, when he didn't want to enter the deathly quiet morning, when he lay in bed like a stone because he was so horrified by the single cup that stood on the kitchen table like someone bereaved.

Hinni, get up! Every morning for nearly half a year, Vera Eckhoff had banged on his bedroom window and waited until the light came on.

She wrote him a note to stick on the washing machine:

Shirts, pants, sweaters, socks 104° F
Bedclothes, underwear, towels 140° F
Wool by hand, lukewarm (don't wring out)!

She drove with him to the Edeka store, showed him what got weighed and what didn't, where to put his empty deposit bottles and cans, and where to find the oatmeal and the jars of little sausages.

But she noticed quickly that it wasn't working. He was ashamed of his shopping cart, of the few paltry items he pushed before him, an old man who no longer had a wife. Everyone who looked in his cart could see that he was on his own. He was a man with something missing. He felt like a man with only one leg, like someone with scars all over his face.

Heinrich Luehrs didn't want young mothers with massive amounts of family shopping to let him go ahead of them at the checkout. It was none of their business which toothpaste he used, or what he washed his hair with, what he had for lunch, or that he liked chocolates filled with brandy.

"Write me a list," Vera said finally, and since then she'd picked his stuff up for him twice a week.

He never complained when she bought the wrong thing, which rarely happened anyway. And occasionally he'd find something in the bags that he hadn't written down, white marshmallow mice, port wine, or cheese sticks perhaps, and he'd put them on the table when Vera came over to play rummy.

He pulled the iron's plug out of the socket and folded his bed-clothes. He had overlooked a crease in the center, but he didn't give a shit.

At first he had kept changing both beds, and had also washed and ironed Elisabeth's bedclothes. But he didn't do that any-more. It was nonsense. Her pillow and her duvet now lay in the cupboard, had done so for several years now. What was the point?

But going to bed in the evening, turning on the light and seeing her side empty, you didn't get used to that. It remained something that had to be confronted every night. And a bitter awakening every morning.

The little zum Felde kid came pedaling around the corner

on his tractor. He steered clear of the raked strip of sand. Farmer boy, Heinrich Luehrs said to himself.

Dirk zum Felde had three sons, and all of them wanted to be farmers. What else? He often saw them driving to the orchard with their father. But he'd also had three like that himself at one point.

Me neither, Father, and then you were left here on your own.

You raked the sand, pruned the trees, fertilized, sprayed, harvested, put everything in order in the winter, and it started all over again in the spring. You painted the windows and fetched the roofer because the thatch had to be mended in one corner, and you painted your fence for no reason at all, because there was no one to succeed you.

But the house wasn't built to have one solitary last person living in it.

Fathers built houses like these for their sons, and the sons took care of them and preserved them for their sons, and a son didn't ask himself whether he wanted it. When had the wanting begun? When had the fault crept in? When had the misunderstanding arisen that farmers' sons were allowed to choose a life for themselves? Simply select one that was nice and colorful and comfortable? Go to Japan and cook fish, move to Hannover to sit in an office. And Georg, who was a farmer, the best of the three, had simply left it all behind and looked for a farm someplace else, just because his old man didn't suit him. As if at any time in the past a father had ever suited his son!

This was no longer the world that Heinrich Luehrs knew. He'd raised three sons, lived as he was told, *what you inherit from your fathers,* and yet he was all alone in the end regardless.

No better off than Vera next door, who had never done the right thing, had only ever been ornery. Indeed, two people couldn't be more different than he and she were.

And now they were suddenly almost identical. Two old people in two old houses.

He could simply quit, *sell it lock, stock, and barrel,* and get a mobile home, like others did. But what were you if you didn't have a house? The houses remained standing even if the people left—or didn't take care of them, like Vera Eckhoff. A half-timbered house didn't fall down. It stayed standing.

Heinrich Luehrs wouldn't be standing for long without his half-timbered house. He knew that for certain.

Nothing much had been done to Vera's house yet, as far as he could tell. Still the same old dump.

Apart from the fact that the niece had fidgeted around hazardously with the facade atop his forty-foot ladder.

Just don't look!

The saying must run in the family.

If living next to Vera Eckhoff for six decades had taught him anything, it was just that: *Don't look.*

Heinrich Luehrs hadn't looked when the Stade police had driven onto the Eckhoff farm because Ida was hanging in the hayloft in her traditional costume. And later, when the hearse had arrived, he hadn't looked then either.

Neither had Vera. They had played Sorry!, his mother stoking up the stove especially for her so late in the evening. "Play with her," she'd whispered to him in the kitchen, "go off and play, Heinrich." His brothers had played as well.

Vera loved knocking you out of the game, especially when you had three pieces already home and only had to throw a final six in order to bring your last one in. Wham! She'd won almost every game that night. "My lucky day!"

Back then he hadn't yet started wondering about Vera. That had only started once she showed him what people looked like after they had hanged themselves. As though they had fallen asleep while dancing, like Grandma Ida.

But there were others too, she explained, who looked like big black scarecrows. They hung in the trees by the roadside.

But just where she had come from, not here in the Altland. They didn't hang the dead outside here.

"Just don't look, Heinrich!" Two or three summers after Vera dove headfirst from the Lühe bridge, his mother had pulled him away from the kitchen window when a dark-blue Opel Captain had driven onto the Eckhoff farm, brand-new, six cylinders, 60 HP, if not more. And Vera's mother had come out of the house in high heels with only a small suitcase in her hand. "Stop looking over there!"

But Heinrich had run after the car as it was leaving the farm, to get a quick look at its rear end. You could only dream of a car like that.

And Vera was standing next to Karl's shed, slightly bent over, with her fist in her mouth. Don't look.

Word soon got around that Hildegard von Kamcke was over the hills and far away with her knight in the Opel Captain. That she had left her daughter to Karl like a consolation prize.

But if you didn't look very closely, life at the Eckhoffs' seemed totally normal. Vera got straight A's at school and cycled along the main street on Karl Eckhoff's old bike without holding on to the handlebars. And when Heinrich rode alongside her without holding on too, she'd clasp her hands behind her head or stuff them deep down into her jacket pockets. She would have closed her eyes when riding as well, if he'd agreed to compete.

"What on earth's the girl going to do?" asked Minna Luehrs when February came and Hildegard still hadn't come back for her child. Confirmation was in March; the youngest Luehrs and Vera Eckhoff were the same age. Where did a girl get a dress from if her mother wasn't around?

"I've got everything," Vera said when Minna Luehrs went over to the Eckhoffs' and inquired.

Four weeks later, everyone in the church could see that no one had made a dress for Vera Eckhoff, or bought one either. She was wearing a dress that was much too large for her. The sleeves hung loose and were fastened at the ends somehow so they didn't slip down over her wrists.

When Vera lifted her hymnbook later on, you could see that she had secured them to her arms with rubber bands from canning jars.

"Oh my Lord," whispered Minna Luehrs.

Heinrich noticed too that Vera had used shoe polish to turn her brown ankle boots black, and he quickly looked away.

But his father, Heinrich Luehrs Senior, didn't look away when they were streaming home after the service. He turned to Karl and Vera, who were walking along behind them, since they were all heading in the same direction.

"Here comes gammy leg with his gypsy!" He'd had a drink before church already, so he said it very loudly.

Heinrich's brothers chuckled, but their mother suddenly started walking faster. She almost ran home in fact, and Heinrich stayed at her side.

When the guests were seated in the parlor at the white-covered table, she sent Heinrich over to the Eckhoffs' with soup royale and a large plate of cake. She had baked and cooked for days.

Standing before Karl and Vera with his humble offerings, he wanted to sink into the ground or die. He should have known.

They were sitting in the kitchen with a cream cake from Gerde's bakery in front of them. The paper was lying on the table and they were eating the cake with big spoons and drinking red soda pop.

Karl, who was drowning in an enormous suit, and Vera, who must have found her dress in Ida's or Hildegard's wardrobe, were sitting like two children playing dress-up. Two orphans playing house.

"From Mother," Heinrich had said. Vera had stood up, looking horrified, and not looked at him. She'd simply eyed the big dessert plate quizzically as Heinrich placed it on the table. Then he'd put the pot of soup beside it and made a quick exit.

"Tell your mother thanks very much," said Karl.

Heinrich Luehrs had learned a lesson that day.

You could be without a mother, without guests, without a white tablecloth, you could sit alone in the kitchen with a crooked little man and eat cake with soup spoons. All that wasn't bad.

It was bad only if you were seen doing it. Then it was very bad.

Don't look.

Heinrich had abided by this dictum when the Eckhoffs' house and farm became run-down, when they let the garden go to seed and didn't paint the fence or windows.

He had only looked occasionally later on, when Vera was long grown-up, and he had a family of his own. When she walked along the Elbe with strange men, he sometimes wondered what might have been.

If he hadn't lain in the heap of broken glass at Vera Eckhoff's, bleeding and howling like a little kid because his father had hit him. And if Vera hadn't chased his old man out of her house with her shotgun.

She'd swept away all the shards that night. He had heard her when his brothers were already asleep, and the girls from

Stade were sleeping as well. He could have gone out into the hallway to help her.

But that's what she'd been waiting for, Hinni Luehrs, the crybaby.

"That's none of our business, Heinrich," Elisabeth had said when Vera Eckhoff strolled by yet again, hand in hand with some guy from Hamburg. "Stop looking over there."

19

Collapsible Crates

CHRISTOPH TOOK THE COLLAPSIBLE CRATE containing Leon's things from Anne—pajamas and rubber boots, clothes for two days, and his stuffed animal. He appeared to fleetingly consider kissing her on the cheek, but decided to skip it.

He put the crate in the hallway, lifted Leon and kissed him, and just pressed Anne's arm, as if she were his aunt.

It was their second handover after a month's separation. They were still getting the hang of it. Shared custody, naturally, no longer a couple, but parents who wanted the best for their child.

They'd been having coffee together every other Friday to

discuss what needed arranging—new shoes, pediatrician appointments. Civilized dealings with one another for the sake of the child, as was standard practice when relationships ended in Hamburg-Ottensen. They began with abandon and ended with handovers, went from kisses to collapsible crates, were reasonable almost to the point of asphyxiation.

Anne was just a guest in this apartment now, not even that actually, a delivery person, nothing more. She hoped she would get used to it at some point.

Leon ran to his room. Anne could hear him rummaging through his toy chest, his treasures, which he had almost forgotten. Every other Friday, he discovered his old room anew.

There was a loud hammering coming from the corridor. It sounded as though old tiles were being knocked off the wall. "The Udes moved out last week," Christoph said, "now everything's being renovated." He shut the door and took her jacket from her.

"I had a look at the apartment yesterday. One more room than ours, a bigger bathroom."

"Why, are you looking to move?"

He cleared his throat, and she realized what was going on as soon as she entered the kitchen.

The photo on the bulletin board had seemingly been lying in wait for her; it pounced like a beast of prey. A fuzzy black-and-white image. You couldn't make much out yet, something bean-shaped in a bubble.

One more room, a bigger bathroom.

"Yeah," said Christoph with a shrug, "ten weeks." He grinned at her. "Sometimes it goes fast. You had to be the first to know, that was important to me, Anne. Coffee?"

Christoph naked at the kitchen table, Carola's red toenails. How long ago was that? Certainly not ten weeks ago . . .

It had started much earlier.

Something snapped in her. She could feel all her strength seeping away, everything was slipping away from her, she was dissolving at the edges. Everything she had been, all that had been solid and whole, was streaming out, and a cold flood rose up around her very fast, knocked her feet out from under her, appeared to be sweeping away the chairs, the table, the cupboards, the kitchen, the entire house. The world was sinking, and only this man was swimming on top, his head, his gaze, his happiness completely unscathed.

She could hear Leon rummaging through his CDs of children's songs, looking for his favorite, most likely. Christoph closed the kitchen door. He poured the coffee and pushed a cup toward her, said, "Have a seat," and leaned back in his chair without looking at her, looking instead out the balcony window into the yard, past her, shaking his head and smiling. "It's all kinda crazy."

Oh to take a knife, stick it in his grin until he drowned, him too, finally, in his own blood.

She was beginning to feel woozy. There was a bitter taste in her mouth, like poison.

She barely made it to the bathroom, gagged like someone who'd almost drowned. Finally, there was only bile. Then she sat on the edge of the tub and leaned against the tiles, sobbing. She didn't open up when Christoph came to the door. "Anne, jeez, are you okay?"

His happiness was like a thick pelt. He was in love and invulnerable, warm and packed watertight, no ex could get under his skin, and collapsible crate sickness didn't permeate it at all.

The phone rang and she heard Christoph go into the kitchen. She washed her face with cold water and went into Leon's room. He had taken the cars out of his crate and lined them up on the carpet. "Look, Anne, what a traffic jam!"

She sat down beside him, wanted to grab hold of him, take him with her, run away with a little boy who didn't belong to her.

Who'd have a country life and a city life, two beds, and a calendar with *daddy-weekends*.

And soon he would be a brother. Father, mother, two children, *one more room, a bigger bathroom.*

And somewhere far afield, in a farmhouse that was falling apart, was another mother, who appeared to be merely tacked on to the family carpet, who wasn't needed anymore. She didn't go with the rest of it, which was beautiful and intact. A piece added on, a pastiche, a badly sewn *patchwork.* The stuff misery was made of. Parents keeping it together at children's birthday parties, gulped-back sadness at family celebrations. Handing over collapsible crates to Carola in a civilized way. Then dreaming of knives and blood at night.

Knowing that Carola with her red nail polish was lying next to Leon in the evening, reading to him, singing him songs, kissing him.

It was a crime for which there was no punishment, not even a word.

They hadn't gotten married, never promised each other a thing. Two people and a child, loosely crocheted, three chain stitches. It just hadn't held.

Carola had only had to pull very gently at the yarn.

Anne kissed Leon quickly. "Until the day after tomorrow, big guy."

She put on her coat and boots, took her bag, ran out of the apartment, and stumbled down the stairs. She bumped into Carola at the door and instead of pulling herself together or stopping, she pushed her off to the side, with her belly and her crappy organic leeks from the weekly market. Then she slammed the entry door so hard that its glass panels rattled.

She managed to maneuver Vera's Mercedes out of the parking space without ramming into another car, without running over any passers-by, managed to arrive accident-free in Hamburg-Barmbek, where the Drewe firm was waiting for her with lunch.

When Hertha saw her she turned off the stove, and Carsten and Karl-Heinz scurried back over to the workshop.

Hertha helped Anne out of her coat, guided her over to the table, then sat down on the corner bench, pulled her onto her lap, and pulled a Kleenex out of her sleeve. She couldn't make out very much of what Anne was saying, but one thing was certain: the world was ending.

It would also most likely start up again. Hertha Drewe had been through her share of Armageddons. What you asked, what you said didn't matter. Just rock a little. "Oh, dear me."

She had seen him only two or three times, Anne's joker in the white shirt, the book writer.

Once would have been enough. It was immediately obvious that nothing good could come of it. Someone like that didn't stay. A child here, another there. He wasn't the faithful type. That was too restrictive for the likes of him.

Hertha could see that in a man right away. But she hadn't said anything because there wouldn't have been any point. No one ever wanted to know.

She had also known from the start that Urte wasn't right for Carsten. *I think, I think* all day long, and she always had to have the last word. And a picky eater too: she didn't want meat and couldn't have milk, and she didn't like coffee, just endless amounts of ginger tea, which she brought from home whenever she came over. As though she thought Hertha wanted to poison her. And if you were honest, you'd have to admit she wasn't anything to look at either. Even Karl-Heinz had conceded that on one occasion, and he was normally very reserved: "A bit of a frump." She wore shaggy, musty old knits all the time and skirts that almost dragged on the ground, never anything halfway fashionable.

Carsten now seemed to be noticing it too. You didn't hear anything about Urte these days, and Hertha didn't ask. She asked nothing, nothing at all!

But they could forget about grandchildren.

They now had Rudi, which was better than nothing.

She was completely opposed to the idea at first. A dog wasn't a substitute after all. But he was some consolation, the little glutton, and Karl-Heinz always laughed when Rudi waddled over with his rubber duck or jumped up onto the sofa next to him.

He hadn't been his old self since the stroke. He was just getting in the way in the workshop because the left side of his body wasn't good for anything anymore. Carsten didn't say that to him. He was very patient with his old man. But Karl-Heinz could see it himself. There wasn't anything wrong with his head.

His speech was improving now, although he sometimes had to fish around for words for a long time and would often still choose the wrong one. "It's like doing a jigsaw puzzle, Father," Carsten said, "how long do you sometimes spend looking for a part that fits?"

The good thing was that they hardly argued anymore. Why would they? Karl-Heinz couldn't saw particle boards any longer, and Carsten had put a stop to the laminate and vinyl window frames. There weren't any more apprentices either. Carsten built only furniture now.

And every Wednesday, a crowd of thirteen- or fourteen-year-olds would come to the workshop from some teen rehab center or other. Carsten showed them how to build shelves or little stools. Karl-Heinz was up in arms at first, *delinquents* in the firm, but they looked much wilder than they actually were and he realized that fairly quickly.

Now they called him *Grandpa Drewe*, and they called her

Grandma Bee Sting Cake because she always invited them over to the house for coffee.

There was no need to go around worrying all your life. Carsten didn't need much, that had always been the case, and right now he was living above the workshop, in his room full of stuff, and he'd come over to eat and shower and do jigsaw puzzles in the evening, if he wasn't planing one of his walnut dressers, each of which was custom-made. He also designed them himself. "Best not to count the hours!" Karl-Heinz would never understand, not a scrap of ambition in the boy, not a spark of business sense.

Previously they could've argued for three days about something like that. It had gotten much more peaceful in the Drewe firm. Growing old wasn't all bad. You gave up hope but also fear.

"So, apprentice, are we almost there?" Carsten came into the kitchen and took a burger out of the pan. "Dad asked me to tell you that if this goes on much longer, we'll be having Rudi as an appetizer."

"Journeyman, you mean," Anne corrected him on her way over to the sink to wash her face. Hertha turned the stove back on.

* * *

Later, Anne fetched the window she'd pried out of Vera Eck-hoff's wall from the trunk of the car and took it across to Carsten's workshop.

"Thirty-two of these," she said. "This one here's the small-est. I can e-mail you the measurements, but I'll need your expert eye for the doors and the beams."

Carsten raised his eyebrows and smiled. He pulled tobacco out of the pocket of his corduroy vest and rolled himself a cigarette.

She would have preferred to take him with her right then in Vera's old Mercedes, Hertha and Karl-Heinz too. Even the dachshund if need be. She was dreading traveling by herself, arriving at that large, empty house, spending the evening alone with Vera, who felt the cold every bit as much as she did—her hands were permanently blue.

She wasn't looking forward to seeing the rabbit squatting in Leon's room either, all alone in her cage. *Individual housing, not species appropriate.*

Carsten placed three roll-ups and a lighter on the passenger seat. He knocked on the roof of the car twice, then went back into the workshop. Hertha was standing in the yard, waving to her with both hands.

After the Elbe tunnel, Anne turned on the radio and tuned

in to the golden oldies station. Kate Bush singing "Don't Give Up." She turned it off.

She stopped at the ferry dock, got herself a coffee, and smoked Carsten's cigarettes on a bench by the water. BE HAPPY, YOU'RE IN THE DISTRICT OF STADE. Flags were hanging on the masts like wet rags.

A seagull was bobbing up and down stubbornly in the ferry's wake, the only one far and wide. It looked as if it were testing its courage. Perhaps it just hadn't realized that it wasn't a good place for a seagull to be.

Anne felt sick while smoking the third cigarette, but she kept on smoking anyway.

Marlene had known from the start, of course.

"A man with zero potential!"

But she was clever enough to say it only after they had separated.

"I know you don't want to hear this right now, Anne . . ."

"No, I don't."

". . . but as long as he lives, Christoph will only ever write half-baked crime thrillers and wear out women. That sort of man isn't capable of anything more than that. He's all show. You should be glad he—"

"I am, Mama. I'm incredibly happy. I can hardly contain myself."

"Good Lord, Anne. Every time I . . . express an opinion."

The worst thing was that she was spot-on.

Marlene's sure feel for a man with *potential* had led her to marry Enno Hove, a farmboy who'd earned a scholarship to study physics. The foundation had even funded his Ph.D. afterward.

The German National Academic Foundation. That was enough to convince even Hildegard Jacobi that he had prospects. And Enno Hove hadn't let anyone down. Not a palatial life, but a solid one. A full professor, a grand piano in the living room, two gifted children, a beautiful wife.

The house was already paid off when Enno Hove died, the grand piano as well. He was dependable.

A heart attack in his mid-fifties in a full lecture hall was the only dramatic moment that this quiet man had ever granted himself.

Anne had her baby too late. Three months after he died. She would have liked to have shown him Leon, the only thing in her life that was a success.

Marlene grieved for Enno Hove violently and tearfully, but not all that long. Her crying wouldn't bring him back after all. Now she often traveled with Thomas and his wife and their two children, and looked after the kids in the evening if their parents had orchestra rehearsals or concerts. Thomas at the conductor's stand, Svetlana at the piano. Marlene's life still had a touch of glamour.

In fact, there was recently a horn player, Thomas had told Anne. *Mama's got a love interest,* he had written in his last e-mail, *but you didn't hear it from me* ☺.

A hornist with potential, I'll bet.

Marlene, master of the telephone pause, had swallowed audibly when she'd learned that Anne had moved in with Vera.

"You could've come home, Anne."

Pause. "There are a lot of empty rooms in this house too." She sounded as though she meant it.

"Both of us under one roof, Mama." Anne had tried to laugh. Marlene had hung up.

Anne dumped what was left of her coffee into the Elbe, then got into the car and drove to Vera, to the cold, obstinate house.

20

No Sound

THE HOUSE HAD BEEN AS tranquil as a deeply submerged whale. It had held its breath for three days and three nights until Marlene had left.

Vera had tidied up the kitchen, stripped Marlene's bed, and returned her mother's letters to the oak chest.

Then she sat outside on the bench drinking the wine that was left over from the night before until clouds of mosquitoes came out of the ditches. It was still bright when she sat down in the kitchen. She ate Marlene's soup and watched the moon rise in front of her kitchen window.

She almost trusted the calm.

She didn't want to hear the crunching sound at first. She summoned her dogs.

An old beam or a bone breaking or being broken.

A scurrying above her head.

An animal or the wind, and tired dancers scuffling their heavy feet across the floor.

And then silence that lasted until she counted to a hundred.

A flapping in front of the kitchen door, a whispering from the walls. Or a breath.

Heavy chairs being pushed across bare floors.

A choir of old voices quietly warming up.

You weren't allowed to be alone in these houses. They weren't built for that.

He that follows. But there was no one to succeed her, she was falling.

Under the old voices was a stillness that was even older, as old and dark as the sea or the universe. The falling no longer ceased, a falling out of the world, as though she'd been released, as if no one was holding her anymore. Impossible to find Karl in the deep darkness. He had sunk to the bottom, if there was one, if the falling wouldn't simply carry on.

Something rolled, something small—a ball, a bobbin.

Or a silver button off an old costume.

Or she herself, who was only a toy, a little spinning top that the house twirled within its thick walls.

A child crying. Or cats yowling outside, night birds screeching. Vera could no longer leave the kitchen or go out into the hall, where there was a line of angry voices.

Where the soldiers went whom Karl had marched with for decades during the night. He had left them all there for her. And Ida was dancing in her sleep above her head, and all the others she didn't know who had breathed and died here.

This hoose is mine ain and yet no mine ain . . . She couldn't get away from here. She was a moss that clung only to these walls. That couldn't grow here or flourish, but still remained.

She was a refugee who had almost frozen to death once and had never gotten warm again. She had found a house, any old house, and stayed there, so she wouldn't have to go back out into the snow.

The Elbe had frozen in her second winter in the Altland, and the children went out onto the ice—Hinni Luehrs with his brothers, Hans zum Felde, and the chubby Pape sisters. "Vera, come along."

She had gone with them as far as the dike, but not out onto the ice. And she didn't do that later either, when Karl gave her ice skates for Christmas and all the other kids raced along the shiny trenches.

Vera never put the skates on.

The ice wasn't to be trusted. She had seen it give way, and people sink.

Some had slipped down under the ice without a word. They hadn't made sound, as they'd grown so accustomed to suppressing their screams along the way. The horses' screams had been the worst.

You could forget everything if you really wanted to. Vera Eckhoff could do it as well.

She forgot the crunching of shoes in the deep snow, the droning of the airplanes, the heads of the pilots that were visible as they flew over the ice. Forgot how red and bright the villages burned, forgot the scarecrows with their necks askew that had hung in the trees, and all the contorted, quiet bodies in the roadside ditches.

Forgot the little brother in his cold baby carriage, and even the doll, *her* doll, lying next to him on his white pillow, that she wasn't allowed to go back for after they abandoned the baby carriage because Hildegard just kept pulling her along. Simply pulled her away from her soft doll with real hair, which Kris Kringle had just brought her.

You could forget everything but you never forgot the horses' screams.

Vera sat in the kitchen and tried to make herself invisible. She didn't make a sound. That way you might not be discovered.

Then they'd move on, Karl's soldiers and all the broken, frozen figures with their crunching steps and their baby carriages. The forgotten ones. What did they want from her after all these years?

The birds redeemed her early in the morning, the raucous awakening of a summer's day. When the sun rose, she made coffee and let the dogs out.

She must have fallen asleep in her kitchen chair, just dreamed it all, simply been scared of the bogeyman, like a child afraid of the dark. In the cold light of day, her nightly dramas were nothing but soap operas, and the demons were no more than haunted house specters.

The following evening, she turned on the lights in all the rooms before it got dark. She switched the kitchen radio on. Then she took a stack of travel magazines from the shelf, made herself some tea, and sat down at the large table in the hallway, with the doors to all the rooms open. She heard music coming from the kitchen. The dogs wandered back and forth. They were confused at first, but then they lay down at her feet.

She read about ice fields in Patagonia, antelopes in Namibia, monasteries in Engadine. Shortly before midnight, she went to bed. She kept the lights on, and the radio, pretended she couldn't hear it this time, the whispering, the wailing, the dancing, the footsteps of the forgotten ones in her hallway.

She simply listened to the music, tried to think of Namibia and Patagonia, dropped off for half an hour, and woke with a start thinking of Prussian villages that were burning.

She pulled the covers over her head and didn't make a sound.

She fell asleep when she heard the blackbirds' song, woke up with the midday sun streaming through the window, and wanted to laugh at the soap operas and the haunted house specters but wasn't able to.

On the third night, she slept at her office, on the old couch she'd bought for Karl, allowed herself to flee this one time, and dreamed of her house going up in flames. She woke up with a start in the gray of the dawn and drove home. It wasn't burning; she went to the Elbe with her dogs until the sun rose and thought of Hildegard von Kamcke: *Chin up even if your neck is dirty.*

Her mother's Prussian lessons had sunk in. Vera had learned early that you had to become a hunter if you didn't want to remain a hare, that you had to gallop on horseback through these village streets, looking down on the marsh farmers' sharp hair partings, if you didn't want to remain rank-and-file.

She wouldn't let herself be driven out of this house, not by the haunted house specters, not by the cold walls. *This hoose is mine ain.*

Finally she did what Karl had done—she sought relief in PsychoPax and Dr. Martin Burger. Her nights got quieter, the days were dull. She saw her patients only in the afternoons; she didn't have many left anyhow. She barely managed to tend to the horses and dogs. This would be the time to give up the animals, but who would want two ancient Trakehner mares and her worn-out, slobbery hunting dogs? The young Vera Eckhoff would have shot them. That's what she had done with her first two dogs when she'd seen that the end was near. The one had lived to twelve, the other to sixteen. She had found it hard but had done it nonetheless.

The old Vera Eckhoff, who had buried Karl, didn't want to kill any more animals. She still went out hunting but no longer fired any shots. She did what Karl had done.

The dogs slept next to her bed every night.

On good days, the horses still went through their paces with her. They were almost thirty years old. East Prussian warmbloods, they were tough and remained stubborn.

In her first winter without Karl, she thought about the small bottle of Narcoren. There was still enough of it left, and it wasn't all that difficult, as she'd seen on the bench in July.

It was certainly good to have a hand to hold after you had drunk the stuff, but it was also doable without that. Whom could she have asked anyhow? Not Hinni Luehrs—he would never have held her hand and watched her die. She couldn't ask that of him.

She hadn't asked him to bring her his paper every morning either, after he was done with it himself. He just started doing it all of a sudden. At ten on the dot, he'd appear in her kitchen. His day was half over by then. "Any chance of a cup of coffee?"

And in the evenings, there was always rummy. If she didn't go over to his house, he would come by.

Until ten, then he had to go to bed. His alarm went off at five thirty. Heinrich Luehrs, regular as clockwork, dictated her rhythm that first winter.

He probably thought she hadn't noticed. They played rummy until January.

Then her refugees arrived.

"It's Anne." It took Vera a moment to realize who was calling that evening in the middle of February. At Karl's funeral, she had recognized Anne only because she was standing next to Marlene. They would have passed each other in the street and been oblivious.

Now they were sharing a house, and Anne Hove was working her way through Vera's rooms, taking stock of cracks in the beams, damp spots in the masonry, unsound steps, rotten window frames, and cracked panes of glass in the old cowshed.

Vera watched her inspecting the house for damage, tapping and measuring it, recording its dilapidation. Mine as well, Vera thought. Her life was a list of deficiencies, and she found it hard to bear that Anne realized this. Anne knew nothing about this house, she had no idea what could happen to a person in it.

There were so many other houses—solid and well heated—that you could flee to, but this one in particular seemed to attract mothers who compressed their mouths into straight lines, with thickly wrapped-up children on their hands. Anne must have sensed that Vera wouldn't leave two homeless people standing in front of her green front door.

You didn't choose refugees, and you didn't invite them in either. They simply came, covered in snow, with empty hands and muddled plans.

They brought chaos.

It remained to be seen whether they could also sort things out. A couple of windows or beams, or a person who was lonely to the bone. Who had no idea how she might get through the second winter, all the long nights, without a fellow human being.

There was something about Anne that Vera recognized right away. It was the way she brought both hands down fleetingly over her eyes, nose, and cheeks. She did this when she put down the crate to greet Vera.

And later, when they were sitting at the table, she did it again. When you were listening to her, when she stopped speaking and you looked at her, she made this swiping motion, as though she wanted to erase something from herself, a thought or a facial expression. Vera recognized this gesture; she had seen it at this kitchen table many years before, in Hildegard von Kamcke, who had the same slender hands.

But Anne didn't roar her anger through the whole house and didn't go throwing the gold-rimmed cups. She was always very quiet, and when her boy was at his father's, she seemed to fall completely silent. She remained in Ida Eckhoff's apartment, poring over some construction drawing or other, or reading her gory crime novels. Endless streams of deranged serial killers. The cover copy alone made Vera feel weak in the knees.

Sometimes she saw Anne walking through the rows of cherry trees, smoking and listening to music through headphones. Mostly she moved in time to the music, you could tell. And on one occasion she danced, quite clumsily. Vera had looked away quickly. It wasn't the type of dancing that was meant to be seen. It was the way you danced when you had completely forgotten yourself.

Both of them were glad when Leon returned on Sundays.

Easter with his father, Pentecost with his mother, equity all the way down to the holidays. It was customary today to have equal custody as soon as the love was over.

Divorce—a clean cut—that no longer happened, it seemed. They were now attached to one another forever, all the couples who'd made a mistake and wanted to go their separate ways. They wanted out but that wasn't possible. They were joined at the hip because of the children.

People had done it differently in the past. They resolved the question of guilt and got divorced. One had screwed up, the other one got the child. It was much simpler.

The thought alone of Karl and Hildegard having had to see each other every other weekend!

They had never seen each other again. If you wanted a divorce, then you took the consequences, you didn't cry over your child. Hildegard Jacobi, divorcée Eckhoff, hadn't done that anyway. A clean cut. Better for everyone.

It certainly wasn't very easy living as a couple. People were rarely happy with one another. Vera hadn't even tried it. Now and then she'd borrowed a married man for a couple of months, once even for a couple of years, a fine specimen.

But not a good enough liar. His wife almost hadn't wanted to take him back when she found out.

A clean break, then he'd cleaned up his act and it was okay. Vera didn't want him around.

But she could have had a child, a fatherless one, why not? No one in the village would've been surprised. At times she was sorry that she had thought of it too late.

How could anyone forget that she wanted a child?

21

Iceland

IT WAS IMPORTANT TO REMAIN emotionally detached. You had to stick to the facts, avoid any hint of accusation. Sigrid Pape preferred to pick the phone up herself. She had held telephone conversations like this often enough, her *soft skills* could be relied on.

She dialed the number, sat up straight, and smiled.

"Frau Hove, good morning." (continuing to smile) "Sigrid Pape here, from the Elbe Frogs." (still smiling)

What she personally thought of the revolting creatures, how hard it was for her to understand how a mother could possibly not SEE THEM CRAWLING around on her child's head, that had nothing to do with it, nothing at all.

Head lice weren't a sign of bad hygiene, for heaven's sake. Lice could strike any family. They weren't anything to be ashamed of. That was the broadly held consensus among the experts, the accepted doctrine. That was the theory at least.

In practice, however, child care workers could always identify those who were likely to get them. Naturally, they didn't say this, but they knew it to be true.

The fact that the new kid from Hamburg-Ottensen had them all over his head didn't surprise Sigrid Pape in any case. Perhaps his mother would finally cut his long hair; sometimes some good came of it.

Aside from the lice, he was doing well in the Bumblebees. He was still a little whiny, a typical only child, but that was also improving. And he always wanted a second helping when there was goulash. So much for him being a vegetarian.

"Exactly, you can get that at the pharmacy here. See you shortly then, Frau Hove." Sigrid Pape hung up and gradually relaxed her smile.

Anne's head began to itch. She ran into the bathroom, held her head over the sink, ran her fingers through her hair, and rubbed her scalp, but nothing suspicious fell into the wash-basin.

The pharmacist had very long hair, braided into a thick ponytail. Anne couldn't understand her very well, since she was speaking very quietly. "I'll put that into a bag for you." There were always a lot of customers in the pharmacy at this time of day. She pushed the bag over the counter quickly and seemed to take the money from Anne's hand with her fingertips.

Leon was already standing in his jacket and rubber boots outside the Bumblebees' classroom. He was carrying his hat, scarf, and stuffed animal in a plastic bag, which had been tied up tightly. He was scratching his head and could hardly wait to tell Vera what had happened.

"You might have them as well," Anne said, but she didn't find any on Vera. You didn't have to look for long in Leon's hair. That wasn't sand or dandruff on his head. It was crawling. Anne took the lice comb and the pump dispenser out of their bag and began reading the instructions.

"Give me that," Vera said. "I know how to deal with lice."

Then she sprayed the oily stuff all over Leon's head and massaged it into his blond curls.

"I also had lice when I was your age."

* * *

Anne stripped Leon's bed and then her own. You never knew. She gathered up their pajamas, hats, and scarves, and stuffed everything into the washing machine. She poured hot water into the basin and tossed in their brushes and comb. Stuck all the stuffed animals into a big plastic bag, tied it up, and put it in Vera's storeroom. Three days, Sigrid Pape had said, and then she'd have to get a doctor's note stating that Leon was free of lice.

"And would you please be so kind as to let the zum Feldes know? Theis wasn't at day care today. If Leon has lice, Theis might very well have them too."

Vera sat Leon on the kitchen table, placed a towel around his shoulders, and combed the lice out of his hair, strand by strand.

"Refugee pack! Lice on your back!"
Their heads were crawling with them. They had been on the road for weeks, lain on teeming mattresses, on old pillows in abandoned homes, and pulled blankets belonging to others over their heads, other people's coats, and at times it was so cold they had taken hats off the dead. The itching never ceased. They scratched until they bled.

The hair came off later, really short. They looked like criminals, felt like it too, like a pack, like a *refugee pack,* like *stinking Polaks,* even later when their hair grew back.

What should they have said, the Polak children, when the others had teased them?

That they hadn't committed any crime?

That they were children who'd had to walk over the dead? And that this was better than climbing over the dying, because dead people no longer made a sound?

That they'd seen villages burn down?

That they threw up when chickens were singed because the scorched feathers smelled like burned hair?

That you shouldn't bother giving kids like them ice skates?

That it wasn't good to find Ida Eckhoff in the hayloft, because then you started dreaming again about those you had forgotten, who had hung in the trees with crooked necks like birds that were much too large?

But what could people who'd never had to leave their timber-frame villages know about the lice-ridden foreigners who were driven into their barns and houses, in increasing numbers, endless herds like mangy cattle.

"Refugee pack, lice on your back."

You couldn't blame the kids with their rosy apple cheeks.

"Tell me a story," Leon said.

They had had little puppies back then. They were born just

before Christmas and Vera hid them in her coat pockets, so she could bring them along. But Hildegard found them right away. They were whining quietly, and she pulled them out of Vera's pockets and took them away from her.

Hildegard had shot the old bitch before they'd set off. Vera had known that. But the puppies too? What did you do with young dogs that were so small they fit into children's hands?

"How small?" Leon asked. "Show me."

Anne knew where the zum Feldes lived. She passed their farm on her way to the day care. Sometimes she saw Britta in the parking lot next to the Elbe Frogs center and wondered how they were possibly compatible, the bad-tempered Dirk zum Felde and this woman in the grimy VW bus, who was constantly laughing and had her bus packed with children. Theis and the twins, and a sister as well, Pauline. Leon had told Anne about her with wonder. She allegedly knew even more about pygmy rabbits than Theis.

"She's got a whole lot," Leon said. "Not just one."

The zum Feldes' house was big and old. It must have been handsome before, but it now looked as though it were scared. The picture windows gaped in the walls like open mouths. Dirk zum Felde's father had gotten tired of transom windows, thatch, and half timbers—*out with the old crap*—sometime in the seventies, when the historic preservation people didn't yet have a say, and it was only the old and those behind the times that still wanted to live in poky, dark rooms.

He had whipped the house into shape, installed a wide door with glass bricks, had the roof tiled, and extended it out with big dormers. There were a lot of houses like that in the villages along the Elbe.

"Renovated to bits," the Realtors moaned when they were commissioned to find buyers for these abominations. Progress looked very ugly in retrospect; most of the old farmers regretted their renovations already.

They would have preferred to get rid of the clinker facades they'd applied to the framework, and the concrete they'd poured over the cobbles. They mourned the old tiled stoves and carved doors that they had thrown into the ditches as if they were garbage, thirty, forty years ago. And they missed their old language, which they hadn't spoken with their children because it sounded too much like the barn and the countryside, and like stupidity.

Some were now trying to compensate for that. They were teaching their grandchildren a smattering of Low German, as though with a few words, a few phrases, a few songs they could save the language that they had wanted to let die out, as if it weren't long since too late.

Sometimes their children restored the houses, at great expense. They almost looked old again.

And if they didn't have the money, they came to terms with their houses, with their bland bad face-lifts. After a while you didn't notice it anymore.

A large dog almost wrenched Anne from her bike. It barked, jumped up at her, and ran in front of her tires, making her swerve and topple over.

Britta zum Felde came running out of the barn in green overalls, with a stopwatch in her hand. She pulled the dog away by the collar. "Did he hurt you?"

"It's okay," Anne said, as Britta helped her up. The light on the handlebar was now a bit off-center, but everything else seemed to be in order. "You really are a stupid dog," Britta said, giving him a slap. "I'll be right back." She disappeared into the barn again with the dog in tow. Anne leaned her bike against the wall and went after her.

A brown pygmy rabbit was sitting in a pen. It was tethered with a leash as though it were on duty, as if it had to rescue avalanche victims or help blind people cross the street.

Or as though it had to jump over hurdles like a show jumper. In fact, in the sand of the pen, there was a show jumping course, little hurdles with red-and-white bars. "Rabbit show jumping," Britta said, "a pretty new sport. This is our champion." She took the leash. "Come on, Rocky, one last lap." She put the rabbit down in the sand in front of the first hurdle and started the timer on the stopwatch. With its ears flowing, it cleared the first hurdle but remained seated in front of the second one, pressing its paws into the sand. Then it started to dig as though it had buried something very important.

"Shame," Britta said, "he can actually do it." She shoved the stopwatch into her pocket and let the rabbit off the leash. "He jumps better for Pauline."

She gathered up the hurdles, packed them away in an old plastic shopping bag, then took her champion out to a large open-air pen. Anne realized what Leon had meant by *a whole lot of rabbits.* "I know." Britta laughed. "I always have to have the place filled to the brim with everything, children and rabbits, it doesn't matter what. I've also got chickens and I've stopped counting the cats around here."

She also laughed when she heard about Leon's lice. "If Theis has them, my in-laws will be thrilled. They've taken him to Hagenbeck Zoo."

They went into the house, took their shoes off in the hall,

and placed them on an old towel that already had a large pile of shoes on it. The dog picked up a blue children's boot and dragged it over to its basket beneath the stairs.

A hissing sound came from the kitchen, an iron gasping out the last of its steam. "Oh, shit," Britta said as she pulled out the plug.

"Cappuccino?"

Anne didn't notice that it was instant until it was too late. She had said yes, and Britta was already reaching for the kettle. She stirred the cappuccino around until it was frothy, then licked the spoon, threw it in the sink, and sat down on the bench next to Anne.

Two women and two cups of coffee. That's how it always began.

Revealing and confiding at kitchen tables, talking about everything, about nothing whatsoever, about kids, jobs, and husbands, my life and yours. Anne hadn't been able to do it at the Fischi in Hamburg-Ottensen with all the other mothers on the playground benches. These conversations functioned like barter deals. You tell me a secret, and I'll give you a confession; you comfort me, and I'll praise you.

The mothers would sit on the bench, passing the time with this spiritual Ping-Pong, playing at being therapists while their kids were digging around in the sandbox or pushing each other off the swings, the *strong-willed* little rascals.

Mothers with coffee cups wanted to *warm up to each other,* they *thawed, let themselves go*—but Anne clammed shut. She was shy with strangers in the way that some people stammered.

She had no talent for this talking, would lose the thread, stall and stutter, and then get stuck in the middle of her sentences, like an insect caught in a spiderweb. She hadn't had any practice after all.

Since she was a little girl, she had only ever practiced scales, piano sonatas, pieces for the flute. You didn't need to speak if you could play, you just had to know the notes and let your fingers do the work. You also didn't need to listen to anyone. You just paid attention to the music. You didn't have to come out of your shell, you were plenty warm inside it.

"You don't like that one bit." Britta smiled, pointing at Anne's cup. "I'll go get us some beer." They clinked their bottles. Then Britta went and got some potato chips, ripped the bag open, and tipped the contents onto the kitchen table.

She definitely wasn't the type who played spiritual Ping-Pong.

She asked questions that didn't sound like questions. She said, "I'd like to hear your flute sometime. Leon says it's made of silver."

Britta said, "You must be really brave to move in with Vera Eckhoff. Or mad." Then she grinned and left the choice to you. To laugh, remain serious, talk, keep quiet, take a drink.

Anything was permitted in Britta's kitchen, which was as large as an arrivals hall.

They drank their second beer in her workshop, where she was making clay dinosaurs. "The brachiosaurus's killin' me," she said. "The long neck keeps breaking off."

A white delivery truck pulled up outside. Britta caught sight of it through the window, went to the door, and came back with a large box from Iceland Frozen Foods. She opened the freezer, plunged large bags of chicken drumsticks and french fries, pizza boxes and packets of lasagna into it, then kicked the empty box out into the hallway.

Someone kicked it back.

Suddenly a wiry woman appeared in the kitchen. She had white hair, was wearing a dark-blue quilted jacket, and had Theis by the hand. "Here's your son. He doesn't need to go to the zoo, he's already got creatures on his head!" Theis had taken some candy out of his backpack and started eating it. He was holding a chocolate bar in one hand and scratching his head with the other.

"Father's had it, I'm telling you."

Helga zum Felde was standing in the kitchen like a witness

at a crime scene. Beer bottles and chips at eleven in the morning, unironed laundry, dirty windows, dust bunnies lurking in the corners, and an Iceland Frozen Foods delivery in the freezer.

A child with head lice and a strange woman at the table, who obviously had nothing better to do than get drunk on a bright, sunny morning.

Nothing like this had happened here before, not in this house, in this kitchen, which was kept shipshape for thirty years, when it was hers.

"Come and sit down for a bit, Helga," Britta said. "I'll make you a coffee."

"Never mind. Enjoy your meal." She vanished as quickly as she'd appeared.

Anne almost fell off the bench laughing.

"My poor mother-in-law," Britta said, "she really doesn't have it easy with me." She knocked back the last swig of her beer, then laughed as well. "I'll tell you!" she said, turning to her son, who had been scratching his head the entire time they'd been talking.

"And Leon?" asked Theis.

"He's got them too, sweetie pie," Britta said. "Vera's getting rid of his right now."

* * *

"Smaller than Willy," Leon mumbled, "tiny baby dogs." He put his hands together as though he were about to scoop up water. "They fit in there."

He remained silent for a bit while Vera pulled the fine comb through his hair, strand by strand. Then he turned around suddenly, stroked her cheek, and said, "My poor little baby."

Anne always did that when he fell, if he grazed his knees or skinned his hands. When the bleeding had stopped but it still hurt, she'd caress his cheek and say *my poor little baby*.

Vera was so taken aback that she laughed.

Much later that night, she pulled the covers over her head when the forgotten ones were parading through the hallway again. She put her hand on her own cheek, just once and only very briefly, and said, "You poor little baby." Just once and only for a short time, and then never again. She was ashamed of herself for a long time after that. Vera Eckhoff, you maudlin old woman.

22

Resurrection

SHE SAT IN HER BLACK coat under the sailboat that hung from the ceiling of the timber-frame church. The old organ sounded a little hoarse. She had last heard it at Karl's funeral.

Vera Eckhoff went to the church every year on Good Friday, not because she was pious but because she loved the passion hymns.

Altland organs could sound as harmless as barrel organs at street festivals, and then a couple of bars later they would be pounding people into the pews. Uproarious, thunderous, they could put the fear of God into you, probably also make you a believer. But they calmed Vera down, consoled her. You could hear three hundred years of breathing and breathe along with it, as though things carried on forever.

Anne was sitting next to her. A childless Easter weekend stretched out before her. She put on a face suitable for Good Friday.

Weep, mine eyes, with tears o'er-flowing . . .

The choir ladies' soprano voices climbed cautiously up to the high notes—not all of them made it—while farmers and master craftsmen rumbled around in the bass range. Vera saw the guy from Hamburg sitting two rows in front of her, with his bicycle helmet on his lap. He grimaced when there were shaky notes, nudged the woman next to him, and they'd both grin. Two people who didn't have a clue. Who didn't understand that these songs needed to sound just as the apprehensive little church choir sang them.

Anne almost fell apart right there in the church pew. She seemed to cry from the first note to the last. Vera didn't look, and she pretended that she couldn't feel her quaking next to her. A couple of times Vera even nodded off briefly, her back ramrod straight, her head still upright. She only closed her eyes, and never for long.

Vera Eckhoff slept like an animal in flight, even in church on Good Friday, when the organ was supposed to soothe her.

On the way back, they called on Karl. Otto Suhr was keeping the grave in good order. He had planted daffodils and small blue hyacinths. He knew what his clientele expected at Eastertime. There were many graves in the graveyard with daffodils and small blue hyacinths.

"Doesn't that freak you out?" asked Anne, "having your name on the headstone already?"

Vera didn't know what she was talking about. "That's where I'll be buried, and I've got it in writing. It's good to know where you belong."

Easter was late that year. The cherry trees were already in bloom and there were dandelions between the trees, anarchic yellow under obedient branches. Plastic Easter eggs dangled from ornamental cherry and magnolia trees in people's yards, and wooden bunnies with large-toothed grins leaned against fences and flowerpots.

Anne didn't want to get on the horse at first. It had been so long since she had ridden. "Just at a walk and trot," Vera said as she saddled Hela, the calmer of the two horses. Even Trakehners mellowed with age.

Tourist buses edged along the main street, toward the market square. The village walking tours always departed from the church and ended in the only café.

They found a gap between the buses and family cars. The horses knew the way to the Elbe, so Anne didn't have to do very much. "Back straight," said Vera. "Heels down."

Anne let Vera overtake her and observed her perfect posture that she didn't need to strain herself to maintain. She sat like that on a chair or a garden bench too.

They stayed on the grass. There was no wind, the river was calm. "It can also be otherwise," Vera said, "now it's just pretending it's harmless."

Only people who had no idea about water trusted it—and young people who no longer knew what it was like to have the dear Elbe suddenly in their front room, whipped up and voracious on a stormy night.

But even Vera, who didn't trust the river, could see how beautiful it was when it was bathed in the spring sunshine.

Anne followed her onto the dike, and they trotted in the direction of Stade. Endless rows of fruit trees extended from the luscious dike all the way to the arid hinterland, little trees without crowns, spindle trees, which didn't require much space and bore a lot of fruit. And between the rows of trees were ditches and canals that looked as though they'd been cut with an ax.

The river and the land on a tight rein. A landscape that

appeared to be bridled. Vera seemed a perfect fit for this land. Anne saw the large farmhouses—ornamental gables with impeccable timber frames, their front yards full of flowers, each flower bed well conceived and thoroughly weeded, all the lawns cleanly edged, every yard neatly swept—and she wondered why Vera's house didn't look like that. Why someone who held her world on a tight rein would let chaos reign in her house and her backyard.

There was one stretch of sandy shore along the Elbe, the last that the river still had left. The rest already lay as if in a plaster bed, heavily graveled and straightened.

Anne's horse suddenly gathered speed and she couldn't get it to stop. Vera had galloped off ahead of her; then Anne's horse too fell into a gentle, rocking gallop.

She dropped the reins and clung tightly to the saddle. Her feet were slipping out of the stirrups. She cried out briefly, then swore at Vera, but the horse appeared to love this stretch of beach. It snorted, rocked, and did nothing to hurt her. It slowed down, trotted for a few meters, then fell into a steady walking pace. Anne was able to angle for her stirrups, and then took up the reins again.

"Your posture needs a bit of work," Vera said.

Heinrich Luehrs saw Vera's niece laughing as they rode

past his house on their way back, without a riding helmet of course, either of them. They greeted him like lady knights and arced around his yellow sand. Turning a new leaf, it seemed.

Anne slept like a stone that night. Not even the collapsible crates kept her awake, or the house with its creaking and strange mutterings.

The birds woke her in the morning. They sounded hysterical, they were going nuts. It was springtime.

Her muscles were so stiff that she barely got out of bed. She went into the bathroom and heard Vera coming in with the dogs. They always took their walk at dawn.

Dirk zum Felde drove by on his tractor with Theis next to him. They were taking a trailer full of wood to the dike, old apple crates, branches, and pallets—a load for the bonfire on Easter Saturday. And they weren't the only ones. Half the village seemed to be ferrying firewood around.

Vera didn't care much for the spectacle. In every little hick town, piles of wood were set alight, and it was just as pointless as the pumpkin nonsense in the autumn.

Children in hideous costumes, frightening people to death and then expecting candy in return. But no one came to sing at New Year's anymore. People were tired of the old customs and were borrowing new ones.

She didn't understand why large fires were even allowed in

a thatched-roof area. She had already phoned the mayor, Helmut Junge, an old hunting buddy.

"Vera, my dear, the fire department's running it! Drop by and have a bratwurst on me. The entire village will be there, and safety comes first, I can assure you."

She didn't go. What did Helmut Junge know about flying sparks and thatch? His bungalow had a good flammability rating. You could probably pour gasoline all over it and it still wouldn't catch.

She would once again spend half the night walking around the house with her dogs, watching for fires until the flames and sparks above the dike disappeared, the volunteer fire department switched off its hi-fi equipment and dismantled its grills and beer stands, and the last Easter fire fans hobbled over to their cars as straight as laths, or propped themselves against her hedge to pee. Although they never did that more than once, because there was still no command that Vera's dogs liked better than *Attack!*

Heinrich Luehrs didn't care much for the bonfire either. That was something for the young. He himself didn't go along. He had enough to do.

Jochen always came to visit with Steffi and the kids on Easter Sunday, because they didn't have a yard in Hannover, and Heinrich had to be the Easter bunny.

It used to be that Steffi would bring the eggs and chocolate bunnies and Jochen would hide them. The children weren't allowed to see what they were doing. They had to go into the house and be kept busy for fifteen minutes until Jochen was finished, and they managed to wreck his place in that short length of time.

Now they were both so big that they weren't interested in Easter eggs. They just wanted to look for candy, which Heinrich Luehrs could hide himself. He did it very early in the morning, long before they arrived.

He even set the table ahead of time. They brought rolls from Hannover, along with most everything else. They didn't like his things. The ham couldn't be smoked, his butter cheese was too fatty, and there was also something wrong with the juice last year. "Don't stress yourself out, Father. We'll bring everything!" And his napkins were awful, hares on Rollerblades juggling brightly colored eggs. He sometimes thought that Vera did it on purpose, always bought him the worst Easter napkins that she could find at Edeka. "That's all they had left, Hinni."

She'd said that last year as well, and they were just as bad then—sheep in skirts pulling an Easter cart. He wondered whether he just shouldn't put them out. Steffi would tease him again. *What great napkins Granddad has!* But then he thought of Elisabeth's beautiful white Easter tablecloth. He didn't want

Jochen's kids making even more of a mess of it than they had last time, so in the end he decided to place the ludicrous napkins next to the plates after all. It was best if you just didn't look.

Last year Anne had bought an egg coloring kit at the organic supermarket, and brown eggs because there were no white ones left in the whole of Ottensen. When they were finished, the Easter eggs looked like washed-out clothes—reddish, greenish, yellowish, hideous. "Jeez," Christoph had said, "no kid wants to find that in his Easter basket." So they'd snuck into Leon's room for his paint box and touched up the sad eggs all evening, drinking wine and looking forward so much to Easter with their little boy.

Anne walked through the rows of cherry trees as fast as she could with her stiff muscles. She smoked way too much on her child-free weekends. It still hurt so much and it wasn't getting any better.

They'd be going to the Fischi again to hunt for Easter eggs. Without Anne, with Carola, no worries. Just as with becoming a father. Without Anne, with Carola, no problem.

The only problem was her, the bitter one, the killjoy who couldn't delight in the happiness of others. "For goodness' sake, Anne, Carola's doing everything she can."

She was reaching out to Anne, had called her, wanted to talk things out with her, clear things up.

They already had pretty much everything, and now they wanted the rest. Absolution, reconciliation, the blessing of the abandoned woman, who was now supposed to remove the final blemish on their happiness.

Anne had no intention of letting them off the hook.

She picked up speed, tried to outrun the self-pity, but failed again.

The Edeka store stocked only one kind of red wine that she liked. She was going to buy two bottles and drink them this evening so she could sleep.

Then throw up tomorrow at the mere thought of an Easter egg.

"The Easter bonfire," Britta said on the phone, "it kicks off at seven." Again she didn't ask, she just hung up.

Dirk zum Felde was selling beer in a dark-blue volunteer fire department jacket. They all wore their uniforms when on duty at the Easter fire. He tapped his finger against his outrageous cap and pushed a bottle of Jever to her across the counter.

"The first beer's on me. Britta's over there somewhere."

It seemed as if, with the exception of Vera and Heinrich,

the entire village was at the dike. The fire department had turned out in force. They'd parked their fire truck within sight and had already set their stalls up in the morning.

Anne found Britta at one of the little bonfires that had been lit especially for the children. She was standing among her pack with a pom-pom hat on her head and a large plastic bowl under her arm.

Anne recognized Britta's mother-in-law next to her. They were laughing together, and the man next to them had to be Dirk zum Felde's father.

Theis was the first to see Anne. He ran up to her.

"Where's Leon?"

When he realized that Leon wasn't going to be coming at all, his bottom lip started to quiver. "We made more bread-on-a-stick dough mix especially," his sister explained, pointing at the plastic bowl.

Britta pressed the bowl into her mother-in-law's hands, lifted Theis up, smacked a kiss on his cheek, and wiped his face quickly with a Kleenex. Then she went over to Anne and did the same.

Britta's father-in-law took Theis over to the bratwurst stand. They brought a round of Thuringer sausages back. Anne wasn't asked and didn't ask any questions. She just went off and got a round of beers.

"I'm Helmut," the father-in-law mumbled. He was wearing a Prince Henry hat and said nothing but "Cheers!" for the rest of the evening.

When it turned cold, people started huddling around the fire. "And afterward we'll all stink like smoked eels again." Britta's mother-in-law sighed. It didn't seem to bother her, though.

Children marauded back and forth in large gangs, poking the dying embers with long sticks, pressing the charred bread-on-a-stick into their parents' hands, and asking for money for french fries.

The grown-ups gradually lost track of things. They were alternating between cold beer and hot apple punch. Everyone knew everyone else and they were all chatting. Anne learned names and got to know faces, and then forgot them again.

RESCUE—EXTINGUISH—SAVE—PROTECT was written on the firemen's jackets. They were mostly blond, but only one had a dimple in his cheek.

"Woman with curls," he said, "I'll buy you a beer. And is there anything else I can do for you?"

It was already late. She'd have taken him without a dimple too. He could do a whole lot for her.

Vera heard unusual noises coming from Ida's apartment. She shut the kitchen door, and the next morning, before it was completely light, she met a man in a fireman's jacket in her hallway; he was carrying his boots and wishing her a happy Easter.

"Woop, woop, woop," she said, disappearing into her kitchen with a grin on her face.

Heinrich Luehrs was standing out on the lawn. From her kitchen window, Vera could see him clenching his fists behind his back as his grandchildren trampled his flower beds, rummaged under the hedge, and bent the branches of his forsythia bushes.

Jochen was standing beside his father with an Easter basket in each hand, which the boys were throwing their loot into: bunnies, chickens, eggs, and beetles.

"Ben and Noah, stand still!" shouted Steffi, who was taking photos with her iPhone. "Look over here! Hold the bunny up, wontcha? One more time, dammit!"

The boy snapped the Easter bunny's head off, then held both parts up to the camera with a sneer. His brother found a chocolate chick behind a tub of flowers. He was fed up with this *easy-peasy, stupid-ass hiding game*. He took the chick and threw it at his granddad's head.

"Always a treat," Vera said. Anne stirred her coffee and

watched the spectacle in silence. The parents gave their sons a proper talking-to.

Heinrich left the whole lot of them standing on the lawn and went inside.

"We'll cheer him up again this evening," Vera said.

Heinrich arrived at seven thirty on the dot in a white shirt. He brought a bottle of Moselle pinot noir, and they ate roast rabbit, of all things. "We don't like lamb."

They toasted one another with lovely old crystal glasses. The tablecloth was a bit thin in spots, but it was white.

Anne suddenly wondered whether she was in the way.

When Vera woke her up the following morning, the sun had just come up. "Come on," she said, "I want to show you something."

They went outside, past the cherry trees and over the ditches to the apple trees that Dirk zum Felde had planted only a couple of years before. They were still small but had already started to blossom.

Now they were covered in ice. The branches, leaves, and

blossoms looked as though they'd been cast in glass. The trees were like candelabras, sparkling brightly in the early morning sunlight. It was like walking through a hall of mirrors. They walked in silence and couldn't hear a thing except for their own footsteps on the icy grass and the seagulls overhead. Large drops of water were dripping from the trees because the ice was melting in the sun.

"You don't get to see that very often," Vera said. They stopped, their hands in their pockets, and looked. It was very beautiful.

"Everything's shot," Anne said.

Vera shook her head.

They called it frost-protection sprinkling. The farmers did it on cold spring nights. They sprayed the blossoms with fine water droplets that then formed a thin layer of ice during the night. Frost protection through icing up. Coats of ice for the blooms.

"What do you mean?" Anne was too tired for physics. It wasn't even seven o'clock yet. They went back inside and made coffee.

She asked Dirk zum Felde about it when she bumped into him on the farm track a couple of days later. "That's called solidification heat," he said, "never heard of it?" He started his tractor up again. "We've got a few things to teach you yet."

He tapped his cap with his finger and took off. God forbid he should say too much. It was as if he had only a small supply of words that had to last him till the end of his days.

23

Man Oh Man Oh Man

CARSTEN HAD ALREADY PLACED THE window in the trunk. The frame and sash were made of oak, and it was painted white and dark green and was double-glazed. For the smallest facade window, all the way at the top, under the ridge of Vera Eckhoff's house, single glazing would have sufficed, but master carpenter Drewe didn't do things by halves.

"Let's just hope your measurements were right, journeyman," he said, tossing his old Adidas bag onto the backseat of the Mercedes as he climbed into the passenger seat.

He took his tobacco out of his jacket pocket and rolled a

few cigarettes. They drove in silence as far as Finkenwerder, and then he said, "The Lechtal Alps puzzle, a thousand pieces. I hope they can manage without me for two evenings."

It had been a long time since they had bought any new jig-saw puzzles. They now did the old ones over and over again. It didn't bother them, though. Karl-Heinz always started with the edges, since that was the easiest part, but even that took him an eternity now.

Hertha had deteriorated even further. She blamed it on the *stupid energy-saving bulbs,* grumbled about bad lighting and her new reading glasses. But it was her head. She was getting senile. She sometimes tried to force two puzzle pieces together that *couldn't possibly* fit. Even a blind man could see that. It cut Carsten to the quick, but it also really got on his nerves, so he'd pop outside for a smoke whenever that happened.

Hertha was also getting the days of the week mixed up, and she'd read the paper in the morning and then read it again in the afternoon as though she hadn't seen it yet. "Quite handy," Anne said, "that way you get more from your sub-scription."

Carsten smiled, and they didn't say anything more until Borstel.

"The detox is over, eh?" asked Anne.

He nodded, cranked down the window, and tapped the cigarette ash onto the street.

Willy had to move into the living room of Ida Eckhoff's apartment for the weekend. "It's him or me," Carsten said, pointing at the cage. "I'm not sharing a room with a rat."

He put his bag next to Leon's bed and went out into the hallway where Vera was. "I just have to hear that gnawing," he said, "scrape, scrape, and it's already more than I can bear."

Anne heard Vera let out a loud guffaw. It was such a surprise that she almost dropped the rabbit.

They spent nearly an hour showing Carsten around the house.

"Man oh man oh man," said Carsten. He tapped on the timber framing and examined the carving on the wedding door, the worn-out wood of the large front door, and the window frames. He stood in front of the ornamental gate for a long time and then again in front of the facade. "Man oh man oh man." When he asked about the inscription, Vera read it out to him. So, when Carsten Drewe asked it was okay. "And what does that mean in German?" he said, pulling a cigarette out of his pocket. Vera took it out of his hand, pointing at her thatched roof.

"This house is mine and yet not mine, he who comes after me will call it his."

He nodded slowly, then looked at Vera and grinned.

"Nothing rhymes with *hers,* eh?" He shook his head. "Those guys were something else back then."

They showed him the inside of the house. Carsten went through the rooms like a birthday boy, finding surprises in every corner. Those closets! Those chests of drawers! That ceiling panel! *Man.*

"Solid hardwood galore . . . ," said Anne. "Master Drewe's in heaven."

They sat down in the kitchen to plan things out. Carsten sat at the table in his corduroy vest and sharpened his carpenter pencil with his pocketknife.

"So, when's the scaffolding gonna be here?"

They managed to *talk turkey* with Vera. They spoke about money and time, and the heritage conservation regulations, about masons, cabinetmakers, carpenters, thatch, stone, and wood, and Vera didn't jump up once the entire time. She just ran her hands over her table now and again as though reassuring an animal or a child.

They made lists and did sums. Vera remained seated, didn't make any faces, and even served sandwiches and pear brandy later on.

They drank to the house. Then Carsten lay down on Leon's bed, and Anne sat a while longer on the carpet in Ida Eckhoff's room, stroking the lonely rabbit.

Vera stroked the kitchen table.

At the beginning of May, they brought the scaffolding. Men in undershirts, who already had sunburns, tossed heavy pieces of steel around all day and roared orders at one another. Then they all disappeared, leaving Vera's house standing like an old man on crutches.

Anne drove to Hamburg and returned with young men in journeyman outfits. They wore earrings and black hats. "Respectable journeymen," Anne said, but Heinrich Luehrs wasn't so sure. They looked like gypsies—traveling folk—to him and he wouldn't have let them into his house, but Vera had to know what she was doing. It was none of his business.

They rolled out their sleeping bags in the farmhands' rooms, and when it got warm they hung hammocks in the trees. They came and went as they pleased.

Some stayed for only two days, others for a few weeks, and then they moved on and others took their place. Anne stood on the scaffolding with them, kept track of their hours, and paid them.

Vera kept an eye on the house, day and night. Sometimes she couldn't stand the hammering on the walls, the creaking and cracking of the old window frames, the grating in the joints on the weather-beaten windward side.

It felt as though her head were being beaten, her bones were breaking, her teeth were being scratched away, ever deeper, down to the nerve.

Then she started beating her pots again and slamming drawers in the kitchen. She turned white and treated Leon unfairly, scolding him when he made a mess with his bread and honey in the morning, then buying him little animals by way of apology, and grumbling again the next morning.

Anne knew the reason for Vera's kitchen battles. They would have to take their hands off the walls for a couple of days, leave the house alone. She let the journeymen go.

It needed to be quiet for a while. Vera seemed to listen to her house's chest with a stethoscope, as though it were a patient with a heart condition. She took its pulse and paid attention to its breathing.

And she needed to get some sleep but wasn't able to. It was much too loud with the journeymen around, and too quiet without them.

It was best when Carsten was there. Every other Friday, when Anne drove Leon to his father's, she brought Carsten back with her from Hamburg. He arrived with new windows, which he'd built in peace, one by one, in his workshop. Karl-Heinz Drewe had lost it when he saw this.

Carsten did his rounds every other Friday. He walked around the outside of the house with Vera, and through all the rooms, taking note of what had changed and then taking out his tools, "Because I can't stand shoddy workmanship." He always found things that he had to finish off because no journeyman was as finicky as Master Drewe.

He was the only one who didn't see any problem with Vera's house. It wasn't a ruin or a disaster in his eyes. All he saw was an old hero who needed to get himself together. "A tad damaged, but nothing that can't be fixed."

They sat in the kitchen in the evening and tried to play cards, but it didn't work with Anne, as she lacked talent and inclination. "Journeyman," groaned Carsten, throwing the cards onto the table, "I don't like to say it, but my dog can play better than that."

They fetched Heinrich Luehrs and he forgot to go to bed at ten. They played until one in the morning.

Heinrich's favorite tune on the piano was "Für Elise." If it had been up to him, Anne would have played it in an endless loop every evening.

The piano in Vera's hallway was hard to miss. But Anne had managed to give it a wide berth for almost three months.

Then, on a rainy day in June, when Vera was out with the dogs, she removed the old books that were lying on top of the walnut lid and the dusty pile of travel magazines that were twenty or thirty years old.

The house was quiet, because the journeymen weren't around. The keys looked like bad teeth. Yellowed ivory, a little loose, but they felt really good beneath Anne's fingers.

The piano was so out of tune that it invoked a harbor bar. It was a honky-tonk piano that turned every piece of music into a children's song, harmless and off-key, perfect for someone who had run away from the resonant tones of a Bechstein grand piano.

Chopin's preludes sounded like popular tunes on the piano in Vera Eckhoff's hallway. They didn't scare Anne because no matter how often she played a wrong note, it couldn't get any worse.

Vera stood in the doorway in her rain-soaked jacket, and one of the dogs howled briefly when it heard the strange tones.

Anne took her fingers off the keyboard. "It's been a long time since anyone played this thing," she said.

Vera looked at her and mulled it over. "Your mother was the last."

Marlene had had to practice for three hours every day, even when she was vacationing at Vera's. Hildegard Jacobi made no concessions. She would call in the evenings and inquire. But she obviously didn't know her daughter very well. You didn't need to prod Marlene. She played until her fingers seized up. On one occasion, Vera had asked her, "Is that fun, Marlene?" and realized right away how stupid her question was.

Vera had taught Marlene how to ride, first on the longe, until she sat firmly in the saddle and was no longer afraid, then along the Elbe. Finally she had galloped along the beach. Vera could hardly keep pace with her at times.

"Doesn't sound like her," Anne said. Vera took off her rain jacket and wet rubber boots. "You don't know Marlene at all," she said. "You only know your mother."

What did daughters ever know about their mothers? They knew zip.

*   *   *

Hildegard von Kamcke had never mentioned a man with a wide smile, and she had never told anyone what she had felt for a man with a stiff leg. Or what she'd felt at the sight of her mother-in-law, whom she had tormented with music until she'd hung herself from an oak beam.

Nor had she said whether, when she lay awake at night, she sometimes thought of her children, the little one left cold in the roadside ditch, or the big one that lay under a thatched roof.

Or if she was one of those homesick wretches who, in their beds at night, dreamed of tree-lined avenues and wheat fields.

Vera had no idea whether Hildegard von Kamcke had always worn a coat of ice, just as other women sported fox fur or mink, which they'd inherited from their mothers, and whether this coat had also been an heirloom, or if she had worn it only from the moment when she was driven through the snow with her children.

All daughters knew that their mothers were also daughters, but they all forgot this. Vera could have asked questions. You could ask mothers anything.

You just had to live with the answers.

They had never told Hildegard Jacobi that her youngest daughter could ride as wild as a hussar. "She won't believe it anyhow," Marlene had said.

Then she fell off her horse on the last day of her vacation and broke her wrist.

In a cast for six weeks, no piano for eight, no more vacations in the Altland. And no more letters for *My dear Vera*.

24

Miracles of Light

MARLENE MUST'VE SPENT WEEKS preparing. She had maps and travel guides that she had read from cover to cover, as was clear from the yellow Post-it notes that were sticking out between the pages. And she also had a folder in her bag stuffed with papers. She had borrowed her mother's letters from Vera and made copies of them. Anne saw her flipping through them in the lobby of their Danzig hotel and already thought of taking off, and their trip hadn't even started.

"My greatest wish, my only one." It was Marlene's sixtieth birthday. Thomas had a good reason for not being there. He was traveling to Melbourne for a concert, and nothing could be done. But Anne didn't have an excuse, so she cursed and went along.

Single rooms at least. Ten days of sharing a room and they'd kill each other.

She'd almost forgotten what it was like to travel with her mother. Marlene's mode of walking was a working canter. She didn't travel as other people did. She slogged, plowed through landscapes and cities until she'd seen and knew everything there was to know.

So now they were going to East Prussia, Mazuria, by mini-bus, and even Marlene was too young for this journey. Born after the war, she couldn't be homesick for the *land of the dark forests*. Anne had no idea what Marlene was looking for.

It was Vera who ought to have made the journey. Marlene had almost begged her to accompany her, but Vera didn't travel, since it would mean leaving her house, which was out of the question. "And I'm certainly not going there!" Vera was happy when she could forget. The last thing she wanted was to be reminded.

Marlene made a list of villages and towns that her mother had described in her letters to *My dear Vera*. She wanted to look for the manor house of the von Kamckes and drive in the minibus through the tree-lined avenues that Hildegard had trudged through with her children in the deep snow and at minus four degrees in January. And then go to the lagoon, of course. They all wanted that when they traveled through Mazuria in German buses. They wanted to stand at the edge of the water in their sand-colored windbreakers, refugees with white hair who had stood there once before, chilled to the bone and driven away along with their mothers.

The tour guide knew his clientele, the old folks with their broken souls, hoping for a little healing. He drove them to the lakes and the storks and the amber-stone beaches, to Nikolaiken, Heiligelinde, and Steinort. He knew that at some point during the ten days, at some lake or other, in front of an old house or in a church, a trembling voice would sing "The Land of the Dark Forests." Someone started it off on every trip, and then he'd hand out the words, five verses, and he always joined in himself, *miracles of light across wide fields*. Then the whole bus would sing along and everyone would cry.

He drove them to the houses they were born in. Some were too shaken up to get out of the minibus; others worked up the courage and knocked on the door, and the interpreter accompanied them. The Polish families were friendly for the most part, asked them in, showed them around, posed in the doorway for a photo with a smile, shook their hands, and waved at the strangers as they climbed back into their buses.

The old people then sank into their seats and didn't look as though they'd been healed. They looked to Anne like people who'd undergone surgery again, been cut open and sent home too early, at their own risk.

Marlene sat in the window seat, commented on every poppy and every street sign, and made notes in her travel journal like a model student. She sighed at every pothole and let out a moan every time they passed another vehicle. She was constantly taking her water bottle out of her backpack, and every few minutes she would dab her forehead with her handkerchief and fan herself with a sheet of paper, creating so much of a breeze, you'd think she was the only one who was sweating and being jostled during this journey. Anne closed her eyes and turned up the volume on her iPod.

And Marlene watched her daughter travel through this landscape in total silence. Anne seemed completely cut off from her, boarded up, bolted and barred, intent on showing no emotion, on sharing nothing with her. It was driving her crazy.

It was hard for both of them to bear.

Everything they did, they did to one another.

Then Marlene's day came. It was a hot day in July, and the tour guide had ordered a taxi to pick them up from the hotel. Anne climbed in the back and Marlene got in up front with her map in hand.

They had to search for a long time, took wrong turns onto

rough tracks through little villages between Rastenburg and Loetzen, which now had different names than those on Marlene's old Prussian map. She'd added the Polish names in red but soon had trouble deciphering them.

The small places lay in the sun as though in a daze. Only the storks seemed to be awake, and a sluggish breeze leafed dreamily through the old trees. When you traveled through the tree-lined avenues, it felt as though you were in another time, another world. At some point they came across a gate made of stone and wrought iron. It looked like the one that Hildegard von Kamcke had sketched, and 1898 was engraved on the gable.

The gate didn't seem to lead anywhere. All they could see was green undergrowth. They pushed past the rusty iron.

The taxi driver stayed beside his car, smoking in the sun.

Anne struggled through the undergrowth with Marlene. They climbed over fallen trees. Nothing remained of the tree-lined approach that Hildegard had described. They now had a direct view of the ruin.

A birch was growing out of the roof of the large manor house. The house's walls looked as though someone had ripped the skin off them. There was hardly any light-toned stucco left, and the rough stonework was exposed. The high windows were boarded up.

Marlene stood in front of the curved gable. She'd wanted

to take photos but forgot. Anne took the camera, left Marlene standing, and went to look at the back of the house. There were still large, long stables there. It was very quiet. A forest, a river, the sky, a lake. You couldn't imagine anything bad happening here, no shooting, no bleeding. It couldn't possibly have taken place here in this landscape that cradled you like a child.

They must have felt invulnerable in this house, *Chin up!*, and then they were out in the snow, running for their lives.

Anne took photos of the gardens, the stables, the house, then returned to the crumbling outside staircase, where Marlene was still standing. She had said nothing since they'd arrived.

Anne watched her mother take a bag out of her backpack, then a plastic spoon. She scraped some soil into the bag along with a few bits of gravel, then went over to the wall of the house, broke off a couple of pieces of stucco, and took them all with her.

Anne turned away quickly. She didn't want to see Marlene with her plastic spoon in front of the ruined manor house, a sixty-year-old child looking for her mother.

Hildegard von Kamcke wasn't to be found here. She didn't want to be found by Marlene, and the house didn't give anything about her away. It disclosed absolutely nothing. It just stood there with the birch growing out of its roof, like a wounded soldier who'd had a flower placed mockingly in his helmet. It too would soon fall.

Anne asked Marlene if she wanted Anne to take a photo of her standing in front of the house. She shook her head and went over to the taxi without looking back. Yet another person who'd undergone surgery.

They nonetheless drove on down the streets that Hildegard had described and looked for the place on the map where she had drawn a small cross. *Gregor von Kamcke (11.10.1944– 19.1.1945).*

They stopped somewhere on a street that led to Heilsberg, "Lidzbark Warmiński!" said the taxi driver patiently. He knew that the Germans could never remember the Polish names, but he thought they should hear them at least.

He didn't get out of the car with them.

There were a lot of mosquitoes here, and flies. Marlene thrashed the map around, and Anne sought shade under an oak tree.

What had they done with all the dead children who had been left lying at the side of the road? Who had buried them when the earth had finally thawed? The hosts of baby carriages, the slumbering dolls, what had happened to them?

You could no longer believe in the beauty of the Mazurian avenues when you started to ask questions like these. If you thought that under every oak tree and in every green ditch there were still bones, and that there were buttons and little shoes under the poppies.

They went to Frauenburg by minibus. It was the last day of their trip. From the cathedral's tower, they looked out over the Vistula Lagoon. The homesick tourists stood there a long time, fumbling around with their handkerchiefs. Then they got onto a ferry that was to take them to the Vistula Spit.

The captain looked grim, and who could blame him? Dealing with all these distraught old people all the time, perhaps he felt like the mythological ferryman who continually transferred the dead to Hades.

That's it, I've had enough, Anne said to herself. She was going to stay on the jetty.

But Marlene had already gotten on board. She seemed to have shrunk over the course of this trip.

Anne stood next to her mother at the railing. Marlene was wearing sunglasses, and even on the ship, she was holding the guidebook in her hand, with the map open and fluttering in the wind, totally useless.

There was nothing to be found in Mazuria, no answers and no solace, no trace of Hildegard von Kamcke. A mother like a strange continent, that's how it remained. There were no adequate maps for this part of the world.

Anne stood next to her and looked at the choppy water. She put her jacket on.

Then she told Marlene what the farmers did with the blossoms when the night frost came. "Frost protection through glaciation," she said. "It really works. You see?"

Marlene's sunglasses were very large, and Anne couldn't make out what she was thinking.

The women had had to become either heroes or animals. There was no other way to get across the ice with children.

How could they have sung songs to them and laughed with them after that?

They couldn't be mothers like that anymore. They didn't let you speak to them, told you nothing, explained nothing, and didn't even look for a language for the unutterable. They practiced forgetting and got good at it. Trundled on in coats of ice. You didn't need to tell them what solidification heat was.

Marlene didn't say a thing. In Kahlberg, they disembarked for three hours, took off their shoes, and wandered along the beach. They looked at the shops, ate ice cream, and felt each other's pain.

It was inconceivable that they'd ever walk arm in arm or make each other happy again. But ten days together without blood and tears was almost a miracle.

No healing took place in Mazuria, but Anne had seen

Marlene with her plastic spoon in front of the manor house. A daughter who had nothing, who had to scrape sand and plaster and stucco together, as though it were possible to make a mother out of them. She wasn't miserly but poor. What Anne wanted from Marlene, Marlene clearly didn't have to give. Anne could tug at her, rummage around in her pockets, shake her down as though Marlene were a drug dealer, and she wouldn't find anything on her of the stuff she still craved.

Anne could stop searching. It had to be possible to live without it. It *was* possible.

Vera picked them up at Hamburg's central station in her Mercedes, and they drove to Marlene's for coffee. There was some dust on the black Bechstein, and a stack of music too. "I'm just getting started again," Marlene said. "There's no one to hear me play the wrong notes."

They were out in the hallway already and managed an embrace of sorts. Marlene then pressed something cool into Anne's hand and closed the door behind her and Vera.

A little amber heart on a silver chain. A child's necklace from a shop on the Vistula Spit.

Vera took it out of Anne's hand and looked at it for a while, until Anne had finished with her Kleenex. Then she helped her put it on. "I had one like that once too," she said, "it must still be around somewhere."

They drove to Ottensen and picked up Leon. Vera just stayed in the car. Christoph was in the new apartment next door, which still had to be painted.

Carola handed Anne the collapsible crate containing Leon's clothes. "My little brother's in there," Leon said, pointing at Carola's stomach.

Anne nodded and took him into her arms. "Come on," she said, "we're going home."

Vera had nodded off in the car. Nine nights in the house on her own; she hadn't gotten much sleep.

Anne told her to get into the back with Leon. Shortly after the tunnel they were both asleep and Leon's chubby hand was clasped in Vera's blue hands.

25

Brain Drain

You couldn't walk around barefoot in the garden anymore. The slugs had taken over the terrain—the fat brown ones. Burkhard had stepped on one of the critters once, and after that he kept his shoes on.

Eva's hatred of snails was greater than her revulsion to them. She cut them in half with her snail shears. Burkhard didn't like to watch. She didn't even scrunch her face up when she did it.

Eva no longer carried spiders outside to set them free either. She now turned on the hot tap and aimed the showerhead like a flamethrower at the fat ones she found in the bath, rinsed them away, and then pressed the stopper into the drain so they couldn't escape.

Thatched roofs were full of spiders, which got into the rooms through open windows, and some then crawled into the beds. You discovered them when you pulled back the covers in the evening. They were as large as children's hands and frequently they made off very fast. Then you couldn't sleep because you didn't know where they were lurking.

Summer in the countryside was like war. Nature sounded the attack and took no prisoners. You couldn't negotiate with it.

The fly and wasp bottle from Manufactum, handblown in the region of Lusatia, was still down in the cellar. They had placed it on the windowsill during their first summer here. A little sugar water to detain the insects until the strawberry cake was eaten up, and then they'd set them free again. Live and let live, reverence for all creatures, peaceful coexistence of man and animals. That's what they'd believed! What naive refugees from the big city they had been! Almost touching when you looked back on it.

Mosquitoes wanted blood, and so did the horseflies and biting houseflies that came out of the ditches. In the beginning they had still treated the stings with tea tree oil, but now they acted preemptively with DEET. They weren't taking any prisoners.

In that first summer they had laughed, found everything funny. They found so much material in rubber boot world for op-ed columns, and Burkhard had written his first book effortlessly. About the snails and insects, the pellets that the wild cats threw up in front of their door, about voles in the flower beds and molehills in the freshly seeded lawn. About the farmers who couldn't take a joke and eradicated everything they termed vermin. About stonemasons who arrived on mopeds and ate aspic with their fingers.

It was a good book, even by his own exacting standards—ironic and witty and still selling in its fourth printing. He'd like to see his ex-colleagues do that.

He watched Eva yanking out nettles outside. In the winter she struggled with depression, and in the summer it was weeds.

The seagulls that perched in the trees in front of the house screeched constantly, and his neighbors' frogs reached peaks of eighty decibels. He had measured them himself. Tractors, lawn mowers, and electric saws were constantly droning. The entire Altland appeared to be getting deforested. It was a wonder there were any trees left.

Sudden deafness plus tinnitus. "Cut back, my dear man," his family doctor had said, "no stress, no noise." He was now using earplugs when he needed to concentrate, but it did nothing to reduce the cheeping, especially on the right side.

"That's what all your downshifting nonsense has brought you!"

Eva's reaction wasn't quite what he'd expected from his wife when he returned home with high-frequency tinnitus.

Her jelly factory was finished, and they weren't going to refurbish it again. Eva had thrown fruit spreads, chutneys, and jellies worth a thousand euros at the wall. In fact, nothing much remained intact after her spring festival. It had started out bad. Thick clouds, much too cool for Pentecost, and rain showers—not weather for an outing—and no one from the village ever came anyhow.

The point was that the limit had already been reached before that, not just for Eva but for him as well.

He had buried his project.

A Taste of Country Life had died, beginning with the feature story "From Quarry to Sausage." Vera Eckhoff had failed to tell him that deer season didn't start until September. He found out only in April, when he called to make an appointment with her. She had a good laugh about it, and oh, yes, she had now given up hunting, by the way. *By the way.*

Florian wanted a cancellation fee from him for his photos right away. He claimed to have definitively scheduled the job already. Well, he could just go ahead and sue him! His best bet would be a class action suit. He could join forces with the Jarck brothers.

Burkhard had almost fallen off his chair when the letter had arrived from the Jarcks' lawyer in Stade. His clients felt *unfavorably portrayed* in Burkhard Weisswerth's coffee-table book *People from the Elbe—Gnarled Faces of a Landscape*. The photos had *at no point been authorized.*

Violation of privacy: ten thousand euros compensation and a motion for a preliminary injunction. Dumb as stumps, the two of them. They couldn't even spell *injunction*!

Yet they went off and hired a lawyer. Unbelievable! Peasant cunning, that's probably what it was. And their odds of succeeding with the lawsuit were pretty good.

The whole thing really got to Weisswerth. He'd been open toward the people around here and that was all the thanks he got.

But he had also romanticized a few things. He'd realized that in the past few weeks. However much sympathy he had for the bizarre characters he had met out here, the *brain drain* was undeniable.

Anyone with half a brain, anyone capable or who wanted something, didn't stay in this hick town, staring at the Elbe until he croaked. Those who stayed behind were the bottom feeders, remaindered goods. Minnows, poor suckers, odd birds. Extremely stupid stonemasons, social phobics like that Vera Eckhoff, and simpleminded farmers like Dirk zum Felde.

Dirk had apologized to him for the Glenfiddich stunt a couple of days later, with a grin on his face. The *nice cocktail* of scotch, ice, and Sprite was just a joke. "No offense meant, Burkhard." It was still a mystery to him what exactly was funny about it. But okay, let it go.

He didn't want to think about these people anymore, or to write articles or books about them. He'd said all he had to say. He was sorry, but he couldn't do any more, he just had to move on, he had outgrown rubber boot world.

And he was finished with journalism too.

Burkhard Weisswerth was ready for a change. He would steer his life in a new direction, back to the source. A villa in Hamburg-Othmarschen, an excellent address with a view of Jenischpark.

For the first time in her long, fulfilled life, his aged mother had had good timing. The housekeeper had found her at the beginning of June, in her bed as though asleep, the kind of death you'd wish for from a fairy godmother.

He could now call himself wealthy. The house alone was worth four million euros, and the rest was priceless. A Hanseatic upper-class life, the Overseas Club and Patriotic Society, a berth for his boat at Muhlenberg. He would sail again and maybe play polo again too. He was going back to his roots after all these years. He had been a rebel all his life, an *angry young man,* never let himself be bought, never conformed, never used his old man's influence. Now he had nothing left to prove.

It would make their friends in Eppendorf sick. Sure, they lived quite comfortably in their apartments at the Isemarkt; the location on the Alster wasn't bad. But the real, old money was to be found in the Elbe suburbs, and they all knew it. A villa in Hamburg-Othmarschen was simply in a different league.

He was looking forward to their tight-lipped smiles.

Eva was still straining at the weeds out there. He wondered why she was so angry now that everything was looking up.

There had been something with that pomologist. Burkhard wasn't blind. No drama in and of itself. They granted each other freedom in that respect, allowed themselves little side trips. You shouldn't be begrudging. It had never done their marriage any harm. Quite the opposite, in fact.

But they had clear rules: adventures yes, but romance was a no-no. He'd adhered to that up till now. Little biochemical affairs, carried out with discretion—a nice evening or two and then adieu.

He just wasn't so sure about Eva.

26

Shut-eye

THE SUMMER STORMS ARRIVED IN August. The wind gusts dug their claws into the roof and tore at the walls, which whined like old men, like Karl on his worst nights.

Vera stood at the window and watched the trees in her garden hunch over like people who'd been beaten. They appeared to be waving frantically at her, as if they wanted her to let them in.

You couldn't stay seated on nights like this, never mind lie down. You had to stand with your legs apart like a helmsman, waiting for the breakers and the flashes of lightning, and hope that the ship wouldn't go down this time either.

* * *

They were making good progress. You could hardly recognize the facade with its new windows and sound timber frame. Nothing had been plastered yet. They were finishing the side walls first, and by the spring they wanted to be up on the roof.

Vera had grown accustomed to the journeymen with their black hats, their long hair, and the rings in their ears, noses, and eyebrows. A couple of them had tattoos on their arms like sailors, and that's what they moved like too. Always calmly, as though they had all the time in the world.

When their pace slacked too much, Anne revved them up again. They stood head and shoulders above her, but woe betide any of the tattooed guys who got lippy with her.

The house held its ground beneath the hammer blows.

At first Vera had expected an accident every day, reckoned there would be blood and severed fingers, men falling down from the scaffolding, young children running into saws or stepping on large nails with their bare feet. She had feared the worst right from the day that Anne had knocked the first little window out of the wall.

But summer came and the house stood like an old horse that was letting itself be shoed, lifting its hooves dutifully instead of defending itself, and for the first time in many years, the thought struck Vera that this house might just be nothing more than a house. Not an avenging angel that sent old women up to the attic with a clothesline if an old cupboard was moved or thrust young men down on their hands and knees into the shards of a punch bowl just because an old side door was replaced.

It was a ridiculous childish belief. She knew that and was ashamed of it by day.

But she firmly believed in it again at night. As soon as it got quiet and dark, and the forgotten ones shuffled through the hallway, and the old voices whispered to her from the walls, she believed the house capable of anything.

The following summer, when the thatched roof was finished, they would start on the inside—the walls, the floors, and the ceilings—and perhaps after that there would finally be peace, even in the night.

It seemed to Vera that in addition to the house, they had also refurbished Heinrich.

He played skat with them long into the night and didn't set his alarm for the morning. He was suddenly breaking his own rules. Maybe Heinrich Luehrs sensed that he had been a slave to rather than the master of his life, and that his strict rules weren't much use.

Vera had never done the right thing and yet everything seemed to be turning out well for her. She had a little boy who sat in the kitchen in the mornings drawing, and a niece who resembled her and dared to ride her horses. And her house was now being put in order for her, even though she had never done anything to it.

He, on the other hand, was all alone in his house, took care of his yard for nothing and no one, and his grandchildren trampled his flower beds and pelted him with chocolate chicks.

On Easter Sunday, Heinrich Luehrs must have decided to become a different person, *the stupid kid no more.*

He'd told Steffi there would be no more Easter egg hunts in his yard, nor any birthday or Christmas visits. He didn't even find it difficult. Only Jochen should come, on his own, for three or four days in September. That was enough for him.

It was possible to say things like that. You could decide to no longer invite your grandchildren and daughter-in-law over and nothing bad happened, life just carried on.

Heinrich built a big pen for Leon's pygmy rabbit behind Vera's shed. Willy was no longer alone because Theis zum Felde had taken the matter into his own hands.

He had *lent* Leon a rabbit and put it in the hutch with Willy, and now they had six little ones.

Heinrich picked dandelions every morning because Leon couldn't manage it on his own yet.

And also because he liked sitting on an overturned pail next to the rabbits, as he had done as a boy, breeding German Giants. Back then, the rabbits couldn't be big enough, and today everyone wanted dwarves. Heinrich Luehrs didn't understand it, but he liked the little ones too.

Vera saw him sitting on his pail with two rabbits on his lap. Heinrich Luehrs, the best.

He had taught Anne how to dance in the hallway. Put his cards down and rolled up his sleeves, then shook his head at her socks with the large holes in them.

"What can you young women actually do? You can't mend socks and you can't dance!"

Carsten fiddled around with the kitchen radio until he found the Hits Station.

"May I have the pleasure?"

Heinrich was a good dancer, always had been.

And it only had to be good enough for the party at the Cherry Orchard Dance Bar, the volunteer fire department's ball. Anne had received a written invitation from a blond man with dimples, and sure enough, she wanted to go.

"Nothing serious, Vera," she said with a grin. "Just a bit of fun."

Dirk and Britta went every year. The local fire department turned out in force, its members in formal uniform. It was an important event in the village, even bigger than the hunters' ball.

People would have something to look at this year: a woman with dark curls in a dress that wasn't all that long.

Vera hadn't ever been to a ball. Who would have danced with her anyway? She had given most of the men her age a pounding behind the school or out on the street at some time or other when she was young, because they had called her names.

On one occasion, Vera had danced with Heinrich, a Viennese waltz in the hallway. Karl had had to play it three, four, five times over, before she started to get the hang of it.

And before she had worked it out completely, Hinni's father had arrived and drunk the strawberry punch from the bowl.

Vera Eckhoff couldn't waltz to this day.

Watching Heinrich Luehrs dance with Anne, she wished she were young again, but properly this time.

At the beginning of September, the days became bright and cool, the sky turned a serious shade of blue, and there was a rasp in the air, as if someone were about to make a farewell speech.

The apples turned red, and in the mornings, the first plums started falling onto the damp grass. Only the swallows and bumblebees were acting as though they didn't yet sense that it was autumn.

It was very quiet in the house. All of the journeymen had left, and Anne hadn't hired any new ones yet, because Vera needed to listen to the walls again for a few days.

Only Carsten was allowed to come, on the weekends as usual, since he never disturbed anyone during his rounds of the house.

Toward evening, Vera and Anne would fetch the horses from the paddock and ride to the Elbe. They'd encounter Heino Gerdes on his folding bike. He never raised his eyes when he saw them, just looked at the road, but he always tipped his cap with one finger by way of greeting.

They saw Hedwig Levens with her skinny dog. Both of them looked as though they were afraid of being beaten, as if they were running away to avoid being punished.

Gradually Anne was starting to remember everyone's names. Vera always repeated them for her, including the names of all the birds they met along the way. She explained their forms and characteristics to Anne. She classified people in the same way as animals. She didn't differentiate between them.

When they got to the sandy shore, they would let the horses gallop.

Anne played requests on the weekends, when the others were playing skat in the kitchen. "Für Elise" over and over, although Heinrich also liked Chopin, but not the wild pieces. Carsten wanted to hear boogie, while Vera made no requests. She liked hearing everything except the "Turkish March."

One time when Anne played the opening bars, Vera jumped up, ran out into the hallway, and slammed the piano lid shut. "NOT THAT!"

Anne had just managed to get her hands out of the way. For a couple of seconds everything seemed to stop. Carsten and Heinrich sat rigid at the kitchen table, and Anne's hands hung in the air.

"Not that," said Vera.

"Are there any other pieces that are banned?" Anne asked once she had pulled herself together. "If so, tell me now!"

"No," Vera said, "just that one."

During the week, Anne played lullabies for Leon. She would leave his door ajar and play until he fell asleep.

And she continued playing if she saw Vera sitting in the

kitchen, flipping through some sort of travel magazine with her blue hands. Anne played until Vera sank back in her chair, took off her reading glasses, placed her hands in her lap, and fell asleep, as only Vera Eckhoff was capable of sleeping, sitting up, with her back perfectly straight. Only her eyes closed.

She often had to play for a long time, and some nights only Satie helped, in halting three-four time, *lent et douloureux*. Anne would almost fall asleep herself while playing it.

It was a while before she finally dared to send Vera off to bed. "Vera, go lie down. I'll hold the fort."

Vera just laughed at first and shook her head, as though Anne were joking. She had to repeat it the next day, and the day after that. It wasn't until the winter, in fact, that Vera Eckhoff finally got up the nerve to go to bed.

Two doors were left open in her house, two people slept—an old woman, a little boy. Someone stayed awake and watched over their dreams.

The house stood still.

Acknowledgments

Thanks!

Barbara Dobrick (Eight till twelve and not in the summer!)

Alexandra Kuitkowski (I'm meeting up with Anja anyhow.)

Sabine Langohr (Let's just keep our cool for a bit.)

Claudio Vidoni (It's not the house's fault.)